"Take it off," Lauren whispered.

Maris released the remaining buttons, spread open the nightshirt and kicked the sheet and blanket off the end of the bed. "It's getting warm in here," she said. The sight of Lauren's breasts, the gentle curves, the passion in her eyes sent a surge of desire through Maris. Lauren lifted her shoulders, and Maris helped her out of the nightshirt, dropping it on the floor. Maris's hands roamed over Lauren, trying to touch her everywhere at once. She stroked her stomach, thighs, and breasts. Her lover moved with her, her cool fingertips seeking and finding places of heightened sensitivity. Maris urgently parted Lauren's thighs and her fingers danced as Lauren's grip tightened on her shoulder.

LOOKING FOR NAIAD?

Buy our books at
www.naiadpress.com

or call our toll-free number
1-800-533-1973

or by fax (24 hours a day)
1-850-539-9731

SHATTERED ILLUSIONS

THE 4TH MARIS MIDDLETON MYSTERY

BY KAYE DAVIS

THE NAIAD PRESS, INC.
1999

Printed in the United States of America on acid-free paper
First Edition

Editor: Christine Cassidy
Cover designer: Bonnie Liss (Phoenix Graphics)
Typesetter: Sandi Stancil

Library of Congress Cataloging-in-Publication Data

Davis, Kaye, 1956 –
    Shattered illusions : a Maris Middleton mystery / by Kaye Davis.
        p.   cm.
    ISBN 1-56280-252-6   (alk. paper)
    I. Title.
PS3554.A934925S48   1999
813'.54—dc21   98-48238
                                                                    CIP

To Lynda

Acknowledgments

A special thanks to my sister, Karolyn Davis, a perinatal educator and LVN, and Vicki Patsdauter, a certified professional midwife, for their valuable information about pregnancy, labor and delivery. And to Emily J. Will, a certified document examiner, for taking time from her busy practice in North Carolina to provide expert advise on forensic handwriting comparisons.

About the Author

Kaye Davis is a criminalist in a Texas Department of Public Safety regional crime laboratory with twenty-one years of experience. Her areas of expertise include the analysis of drugs, the examination of paint samples and the comparison of shoe print and tire track evidence. She has testified in court about four hundred times and has participated in numerous crime scene investigations.

Kaye lives in the Dallas area with her partner of nineteen years and two dogs, Trooper and Dispatcher. Her first novel, *Devil's Leg Crossing* (the first Maris Middleton Mystery), was published in 1997 by Naiad Press, followed by *Possessions* and *Until the End* in 1998.

PART I

Chapter 1

The frigid wind roared across the railroad tracks on the
north side of Starr's Pet Salon, whipped the loose material
on Maris Middleton's protective white Tyvek coveralls as
she stood, hands on hips, at the threshold of the small shop.
Blinking from the eye-stinging cold, she longed for a double
shot of Jack Daniel's over ice, no water, and for her lover,
Lauren. She tightened her collar and tried to look past the
nude remains of the young woman sprawled less than two
yards from the door. Perfume permeated the salon at a
nauseating level; two bottles had shattered in the bathroom
beside the third victim. Seven caged dogs, the only witnesses, barked and whined, with a basset hound's mournful
bay sounding above the others.

Maris studied the blood spatters, the location of the torn clothing and the mishmash of bloody shoe prints on the linoleum while she waited for the wizened investigator from the medical examiner's office to finish writing his notes and authorize the removal of the bodies. Her gaze wandered to the toppled Christmas tree, a white-flocked pine, with blue lights, red-dyed tennis balls and other ornaments made from dog and cat treats and toys. Scattered holiday greetings and bulletins announcing lost pets and animals for sale littered the floor.

Anxious to start processing the crime scene, Maris glanced at the clock above the entrance to the grooming room and hoped the death investigator would complete his paperwork soon. By Texas law, she had no choice but to wait. It was illegal, except in emergencies, for a police officer or anyone else to move the body or take evidence from the place of death without authorization from the medical examiner's office or a justice of the peace. She noticed the uniformed officers guarding the police line were getting antsy and couldn't blame them. A blue norther had hit about three that Wednesday afternoon, plunging the temperature thirty-five degrees in two hours. Since nightfall, it had continued to drop. So far the streets were clear, but if the temperature dropped much lower and the rain continued, they'd be treacherous by daybreak. The luckier officers came and went as they searched the side of the building and the alley behind it. The only businesses nearby were Lucky's Stop and Go just over the railroad tracks and Parmer's Automotive Service two blocks south on the corner of Main and the old Lewisville Highway.

After the death investigator, a gentleman well into his sixties, arrived, Maris had assisted him as he performed a cursory check of the bodies, taking temperatures to get an estimate on the time of death. He'd been tender with his touch and murmured sympathetically under his breath while he worked. Then, he'd folded his gloved hands, the latex stretched tight over arthritic joints, and prayed quietly over each woman before attaching a tag.

Maris looked over her shoulder at the death investigator. He sat in the front seat of a ten-year-old Chevrolet and

4

bent over a clipboard propped on the steering wheel. Occasionally, in the flash of rotating police lights, she saw him grimace and stretch his hand and realized it'd be cruel to rush him. She sighed, resigned to waiting. At least she'd already videotaped and photographed the three bodies and the chaos surrounding them. It'd been impossible to avoid stepping in blood, although she skirted the larger pools, tacky on the edges and syrupy in the center. More than once she'd almost slipped despite the plastic protectors covering her boots. She turned her attention to the scrawl in blood on the far wall: MERRY FUCKING XMAS. WELCOME TO MY HELL. Below, in mixed-case, smaller letters were the words, *Satin Lives. Kill the Whores.* The misspelling of *Satan* could be important, and she hoped no one leaked it to the press.

Behind her, a mother sobbed and begged to see her daughters. Not wanting to witness her agony but unable to stop herself, Maris shifted her stance. A Bass Cove police officer, only a few years older than the victims, quietly told the mother that she couldn't, didn't want to see them. Despite her husband's pleas, she refused to leave. Maris frowned and rubbed her brow with the back of her wrist. The red and blue flashing lights from four Bass Cove police cars combined with the constant peal of a nearby church bell and the overpowering odor of perfume made her temples throb.

From the gathering crowd in the field across the street, a stream of young women clad in brown dresses carried Bibles to the police line and knelt on the damp asphalt. Each prayed silently, crossed her chest and left so another could take her place. A group of young men, in brown tunics and loose-fitting trousers, stood at the edge of the onlookers and watched. As it began to sleet, a Channel Five news van from Dallas pulled up behind the patrol cars. Flashlight beams sliced through the air as Chief Deputy Sally Trent and the Bass Cove chief of police, Troy Dan Kenedy, searched the girls' cars, a white Trans Am and black Honda Accord. Other than that only Maris's two-tone-blue Ford pickup with a camper shell and a green Ford Expedition were parked inside the police perimeter. The

5

latter belonged to the worried father, Charles Kerr. He'd discovered the bodies about seven-thirty after the girls didn't come home at the expected time and failed to answer the phone when he called. His oldest daughter, Jennifer, eighteen, worked at the salon, and her sixteen-year-old sister, Jill, had borrowed her car, the Trans Am, to go shopping on the condition that she return in time to take her home. Jill had, at the cost of her life. The third victim was presumed to be the other store employee, Lynette Donley, also eighteen.

Blood smeared the door of the Expedition where Mr. Kerr had frantically sought his cell phone to call 911. Although the phone lines to the pet salon were intact and functional, the wall phone near the cash register had been ripped free and flung across the room, landing near the Christmas tree. The base for a portable, located on the other counter, was disconnected and heavily damaged. So far she and the other investigators hadn't found the phone.

The first Bass Cove officer on the scene searched the building and called the paramedics, who could do nothing for the girls. After that, every officer with the tiny Bass Cove police department had traipsed through the scene. But what was done was done, and she couldn't be angry. The little town wasn't prepared to handle anything like this. Named after Sam Bass, the famous outlaw, and not the fish, as commonly believed, Bass Cove was located in Denton county, west of Prosper and north of Frisco and The Colony. On the northern edge of Lake Lewisville, the little town had been discovered by developers looking for cheap land with easy access to the cities of Denton, Lewisville, Plano and North Dallas. Almost overnight, gated developments sprang up, attracting doctors, lawyers, managers from JCPenney and Electronic Data Systems in Plano and other high-income professionals looking for good schools, low crime, easy lake access and good golf courses. The growth overwhelmed city services as Bass Cove tried to evolve from an isolated farming community into a mid-sized city. The police department struggled to catch up.

Luckily, Sally Trent, the chief deputy with the Bass County Sheriff's Office, secured the scene before any further damage was done, then called Middleton Forensic Services to request Maris's assistance as a crime scene specialist and forensic chemist. It wasn't the first time they'd collaborated on a case. For six years, Sally had been a detective for Tyler P.D. and routinely submitted sexual assault and murder cases to the Texas Department of Public Safety in Garland, the lab where Maris worked before opening her own. In April, Sally went to work for the Denton County Sheriff's Office but quit to take the Bass County job when she was offered the position of chief deputy. Last January, while she was still in Tyler, she'd been assigned to the task force along with Maris, Texas Ranger Wayne Coffey and Lauren O'Conner, Maris's lover, to investigate a series of rape-murders. A sadistic killer had targeted lesbians, and although they'd never discussed it, Maris suspected that the case had made Sally reevaluate her deeply closeted existence in Tyler and was a factor in her decision to move to Denton.

It took Maris only forty-five minutes to get to Bass Cove from her forensic lab in Allen. She'd arrived in time to walk through the crime scene with Sally and the chief while the principal of Bass Cove High School, a former Marine, tentatively identified the bodies as tears rolled down his cheeks.

She jumped when the investigator from the M.E.'s office touched her elbow. "I have granddaughters about this age." He shook his head sadly and ran his fingers through his thin gray hair. "Thanks for your help. I gave the deputy the papers. I estimated the time of death at five-thirty p.m."

That could explain why a customer hadn't found the bodies. According to Sally, Starr's closed at five on Wednesdays so the Kerr girls could go to church. Checking the time, Maris noted that they had been dead about four and a half hours.

He squeezed her shoulder. "Every time I think I've seen the worst, something more horrible comes along. I hope I never see anything worse than this."

Watching him shuffle across the wet concrete, she silently agreed. Shucking off her gloves, she tossed them in a biohazards box in the back of the truck and gathered the plastic multi-drawered tackle boxes that held her investigation supplies. Sally Trent trotted over, rubbing her arms to stay warm. "They found some threatening letters from Lynnette Donley's ex-boyfriend in her Honda. A guy named Reed Wilson. He doesn't spell much better than our perp." Sally shivered. She stood five feet, eight inches tall, two inches shorter than Maris, with sandy hair and a slim build. A swimmer in college, she'd qualified for the 1980 Olympics as a freshman, the year the U.S. Boycotted them. Injuries kept her from having another shot. "I've sent a deputy to nab Reed for a little talk. You got another one of those protective suits? I swear I've never seen so much blood."

Maris flipped her a new suit, still wrapped in plastic. "The Edwards case that Wayne and I worked last summer was bad, but nothing like this. You know, the one where the whole family was killed." God, she'd never forget the sight of the strangled and violated little girl on a blood-soaked pink bedspread.

Crawling into the back of the truck, Maris grabbed a case of cotton swabs in clear plastic tubes. They were perfect for collecting blood samples on site. Their best feature was a holder in the cap designed to fit the stem of the swab and keep it upright while it air-dried, better preserving the biological specimens.

Sally zipped up the coveralls and took the box from her. "I asked the news guys to tape the crowd for us and give us the tape."

"Good idea," Maris said. It was always possible the murderer was standing there, watching them. "As long as the vultures are here, you might as well use them. Say, who are these weirdos dressed in brown?"

Sally rolled her eyes. "They're from the Trinity Outreach Church of Redemption. It's a religious organization that helps kids with drug problems. Seems cultlike to me, but the preacher running it has a good reputation. The kids rarely cause any problems."

The Bass County fingerprint specialist, Shirley Grimes, place her heavy fingerprint satchel on the tailgate. She nodded a greeting to Maris and Sally. Short and dumpy, with mouse-gray hair down to her shoulders, Shirley looked like a lost flower child from the sixties, especially in her faded jeans and light-blue cotton shirt with small yellow and orange sunflowers. She draped a dingy rubber apron, stained with fingerprint powder and amido black, over her neck.

Maris handed Sally a box of plastic shoe covers. "Have everyone put these on. I'd prefer just the three of us go inside . . . and the chief, if he wants —"

"He wants," Chief Kenedy said in his northeastern accent. He snapped and unsnapped the safety strap holding his Colt .45 in the holster. Bass Cove had employed only two full-time officers when the city council recruited Kenedy from out of state. He'd promptly fired them and hired six more of his own choosing.

She'd never met him, although one of his men, Rick Robertson, called "Little Ricky" by the guys for his youthful appearance, routinely brought Bass Cove P.D. evidence to her lab and joked about his chief.

"If you want to make him mad," Rick had said, his blue eyes flashing playfully. "Call him Troy Dan. He's swears he'll fire any officer he hears use both his names."

Chief Kenedy ran a finger across his black, pencil-thin mustache. "I don't want to seem ungrateful for the assistance, but this is my town and my case." He looked from Sally to Maris. "I'm in charge of this investigation. Is that understood?" He hooked his thumb in his gun belt.

Sally's face clouded, but Maris spoke before she could. "Sally said you wanted my help. If you don't, say so. Once I start processing this scene, I'm responsible for maintaining the integrity of the evidence, and I'll not tolerate any inter-ference from you or anyone else. Your officers did enough damage before this scene was properly secured." His face reddened, and Maris added, "What's done is done. We'll work with what we have."

"You know damned well that you need all the help you can get in a case like this." Sally drew herself up to her full height and glared at the police chief. "We all do. This is too important to fuck up."

"Of course," the chief said. He unsnapped and snapped the safety strap.

9

"Then let's get started," Maris said.

The chief took a step back. "I never meant to imply —"

Sally hoisted the box on her shoulder and picked up one of Maris's investigation kits. She glared at Kenedy. "Don't worry. We'll make sure you get your fair share of the publicity." To Maris, she said, "He and the sheriff have a running feud over jurisdiction." Facing Kenedy, she added, "We're not going to have any petty political bullshit. We'll all work together on this, including the FBI. I've contacted Special Agent Lauren O'Conner, the offender-profile co-ordinator for this area, and requested her assistance. She was in Oklahoma today for federal court but will be here as soon as possible, weather permitting."

Chief Kenedy squared his shoulders and snapped the flap on his holster closed one last time. He seemed about to speak but shrugged his shoulders instead.

To break the tension, Maris handed him a pair of protective booties. "Then let's go to work," she said. Taking the second tackle box, she felt her neck stiffen and the tautness between her shoulder blades increase as if some giant hand had reached down and ratcheted up the pressure a couple of notches. The last thing she needed was a stacked deck due to early mistakes and internal bickering. Justice, always elusive, if not an illusion, escaped easily enough under the best circumstances.

Chapter 2

Shouted curses and the sounds of a foot chase caught
Maris's attention before she entered the salon. Sally
dropped the cardboard box and Maris's investigative kit on
the sidewalk and raced on Chief Kenedy's heels toward the
commotion. Bass Cove Officer Rick Robertson tackled a
young man in black behind Mr. Kerr's Ford Expedition. The
chief yanked the man up by the collar of his black Marilyn
Manson T-shirt while Sally helped the angry officer to his
feet. Kenedy slammed the guy against the side of the truck
and searched him, handing Sally a wallet. Turning him
around, the chief cuffed his wrists in front so he could hold
a handkerchief to staunch the flow of blood from his bloody

nose. Kenedy guided him to better lit area next to a patrol car, and Maris saw him gesture to one of the guy's hands.

Sally returned to the sidewalk. "That's Reed Wilson, Lynnette Donley's ex-boyfriend." She pointed over her shoulder. "He claims he just heard about the murders and came to see if Lynette was one of the victims. Says he'd been at work all day, but one of my deputies has already talked to his boss and he never came back after lunch. He has stitches in a fresh cut on the web between his thumb and forefinger. Looks like blood on his T-shirt and trousers."

Maris glanced his way. Sandy-haired with a scraggly goatee, Reed stared at her. She estimated his height at a little under six feet. Slim but muscular, he could easily overcome three teenage girls. "The blood could be from the cut on his hand," she said.

Sally nodded. "Kenedy is taking him to the station while I stay to help. He's going to talk to the doctor who sewed Reed up and get a warrant for his clothing and to search his car and apartment. Then we may let the little bastard stew in a holding cell for a few hours until we see what we have here."

Maris sighed. "Well, we're going to be here a while." And it was past time to get started.

Maris began with the nearest body, Jennifer Kerr. She lay in the customer-greeting area of the salon, between the overturned artificial Christmas tree and scattered papers and pictures from the bulletin board. Trying to ignore the incessant barking from the back room and the stifling odor of perfume, Maris looked with dismay at the crisscross of muddy shoe prints and made a mental note to examine the loose flyers and cards for any potentially useful impressions. She glanced around the room. On her left was Patrick Starr's tiny office with the entrance protected by a red-topped counter with the cash register. A second counter stood at a right angle to the first, separated by a three-foot-tall swinging door. Together, they formed a barrier between the customers and the rest of the shop. A closed door near a supply closet in the far left corner opened to the kennel area with the rest room and dog pens. A cinder-block wall separated the kennel from the grooming room on the right. Through an open door, Maris saw a lifeless cocker spaniel on the grooming table. His head hung at an awkward angle, and blood smeared his golden coat.

Maris, Sally and Shirley ignored the noisy wall phone near the cash register. Since Sally had found it near the Christmas tree and plugged it in to determine if the lines were intact, it hadn't stopped ringing. The shrill clamor added to her headache. Maris squatted near Jennifer. Eighteen and the oldest of the Kerr girls, she was beautiful despite a bruised cheek, a cut chin, the pallor of death and the pronounced rigor mortis in the skeletal muscles around her jaw. She rested on her back, nude, with one leg straight and the other spread wide and bent at the knee. In a bizarre ritual, the killer had shaved Jennifer's pubic hair using a pair of electric dog clippers, and the loose cuttings stuck to her thighs and the bloodstained floor. Multiple stab wounds covered her torso. Brown paper sacks, placed on her hands by Maris and the death investigator, protected possible trace evidence on her hands, which were damaged by deep defensive cuts. She still wore her jewelry, consisting of a Seiko gold-toned watch, her senior-class ring and a heart-shaped diamond necklace. Maris collected the cut pubic hairs and puzzled over the significance. The act of shaving her had been careful and deliberate. It didn't fit the frenzied, blitzkrieg attack. She watched Shirley Grimes dust the gray electrical plug on the dog clippers with black fingerprint powder before pulling it from the outlet.

"Too smudged." Shirley dropped it. Holding the clippers by the cord, she carefully brushed the plastic case. "But we got 'em all over this thing." She used clear tape to lift the prints and placed them on white cards that she labeled. Shirley raised her voice to be heard over the dogs. "Why would he shave her?"

"Maybe to shock whoever found her — and us." Maris wrote the date, December 10, on the envelope with the hairs, initialed it and tossed it into her cardboard box that she'd set nearby to hold evidence. "Or he wanted her to look younger — prepubescent."

"He must have killed the one behind the counter first."

"Lynette Donley. Yes." Maris pointed to some blood spatters on the counter and floor near the swinging door. "Jennifer was probably grooming the cocker when she heard the ruckus and came to see what was happening. He stabbed her the first time over there, near the counter. But she put up a hell of a fight." Maris went over to the tree. "I think she shoved him into the tree and made a break for the front door. She was already bleeding profusely and left this blood trail. He caught up with her and slammed her into the wall, knocking the bulletin board down. He stabbed her at least twice more. Somehow she fought him off..." Maris paused. If only Jennifer had made it out the door. Would it have made any difference? And where was her little sister during the attack? Wouldn't she have heard the struggle? Another blood trail led through the waist-high swinging door between the counters in to the kennel area. Did the murderer cut himself? That was always possible in frenzied attacks such as this. Or maybe Jill did try to assist her sister but was injured and forced to retreat. Maris turned to Shirley. "The initial incapacitation of the victims came swiftly. Then he returned to each one and, if they were still alive, killed them. The sexual activities took place after the girls were dead."

Shirley shook her head sadly. "Such a tragedy, such a waste." She bent and closed her equipment case. "Since there doesn't seem to be any blood in the office, I'm going to print it next while you finish here."

"Good idea," Sally said. "I'll need to get in there later to check Starr's lists of customers and suppliers."

Maris smiled at Shirley. "I'm afraid you're going to spend most of the night waiting for me to collect the blood samples so you can fingerprint." Coordinating the retrieval of blood and other trace evidence with the search for finger-prints could be a challenge. Sometimes the investigators had to decide which evidence was the most important, blood for serologic examinations or potential fingerprints, because unfortunately the techniques to discover one could ruin the other.

"Before you go to the office, would you print the damned phone?" Sally pointed to the phone near the cash register. "I might as well answer it." She crossed her arms over her chest. "I can't figure out why Jill Kerr ran into the bathroom. Why run into a dead end? Why not run out the back door into the alley and go for help?"

"I don't know," Maris said. "It's bothering me too. Maybe she didn't think she could outrun him. Maybe she didn't realize how quickly he could get into the bathroom. Or her escape route was cut off somehow."

Sally jotted a note in her leather-bound spiral notebook. "I want to think about that."

Maris turned her attention to the crumpled blue towel resting near Jennifer's right shoulder. She wanted to know if the killer left it where it was or if someone had moved it or even brought it from somewhere else in the salon. Sally left to ask the first people on the scene while Maris picked it up and placed it in a brown paper sack. Several dark brown hairs, the length of Jennifer's, clung to it, and Maris wondered if it had been left covering her face by the man who killed her. This seemingly trivial detail could be important to interpreting the killer's behavior.

She picked up a bloodstained blue sweatshirt with the image on the front of the Bass Cove High School mascot, a Yosemite Sam look-alike with dual six-shooters and a handlebar mustache. Puncture marks nearly severed Sam's head, his hand and a boot with a dangling spur. Maris counted roughly ten more holes as she folded the shirt carefully to avoid losing any important trace evidence. She placed the shirt in a brown paper sack, sealed and initialed the sack, then added it to the list of recovered items.

"Here," Sally said, returning. "You dictate and I'll

write." She took the pen and pad from Maris. "God, it's a circus out there. Some fool started a rumor that half of the dogs are dead and the rest injured. Little Ricky's got his hands full trying to keep the pet owners from storming the building." She shook her head and sighed. "I found out nothing specific about the towel, except no one admits bringing it here from another location. The first officer to arrive swears it was on the floor next to her. Mr. Kerr doesn't remember if it was covering her face or not. We'll probably never know for sure." She shrugged. "You know, we haven't located Lynette Donley's parents yet. They're divorced. Her mother sells real estate, and her father is a plastic surgeon in Dallas. A neighbor told one of my guys that he might be in the Bahamas."

Maris gathered up Jennifer's Levi's. Wrong-side out, they were less bloody than the sweatshirt and had no readily apparent cuts or tears. She checked the pockets and handed Sally a gold key chain with *Jennifer* stamped on it, a five-dollar bill and two ones. "He emptied the cash register and rifled their purses but missed this."

"And he didn't take the jewelry." Sally seemed deep in thought as she dropped the items into an envelope. "I'm taking one of your boxes for the things that don't need to go to the lab."

Collecting the evidence went faster with Sally's help. Under the jeans, Maris found Jennifer's bra, with three slits on the left cup. Her crumpled panties lay between her legs near her right knee. Maris dropped them into a small sack and said, "Make a note that a stain, possibly semen, was observed in the crotch of the panties."

"Fucker jerked off on them," Sally said, and Maris grunted an agreement.

The last item of Jennifer's was a pair of Doc Marten boots, each with a rolled-up sock inside, placed neatly against the wall. After they were labeled and secured, Maris said, "I guess she's ready to go."

Sally sighed. "I'll get the body bag."

"There's a box with clean white sheets in my truck that we can use to line it. You might as well get three." Since the police seldom carried sheets, she'd added them to her

16

supplies. She'd read too many cases about murder victims being carried in used body bags, tainting any hairs, fibers or other trace evidence that might be recovered during autopsy. Although these bags were unused, they'd wrap the bodies as a precaution.

When Sally returned, they lined the slick plastic with a sheet. Maris took a piece of chalk from her investigation kit and roughly outlined the body. Maris lifted Jennifer's stiff upper body, Sally the feet and legs.

Sally said, "I didn't expect her to be so stiff so soon."

Maris shrugged. Blood leaked from stab wounds as they lowered the girl onto the sheet. "Rigor mortis varies so much. Starting from two to four hours after death, it's usually complete in six to ten. She put up a fight and that can cause it to form quicker."

She fastened the sheet with safety pins. Grasping the bag at the corners, they struggled to keep a grip. Two Bass Cove patrol officers met them at the door and carried the bag to the waiting hearse.

The phone rang and Sally grabbed it off the receiver.

After changing into clean gloves, Maris dropped to her knees and examined the linoleum. Cut pubic hairs littered the area, and she used a small vacuum cleaner designed to recover trace evidence to pick them up. A fabric impression pressed into a dried bloodstain caught her eye. She'd hoped to find shoe prints under the body where they'd have been protected from the first officers on the scene, but none were visible.

Maris set the tripod over the fabric impression, focused the camera and snapped a picture. She framed the impression with a black-and-white photography ruler to provide a scale and clicked off a couple more photos. In the magnification provided by the camera lens, Maris observed a crisscross of the threads from the material and the outline of a ragged circular tear.

Sally leaned over her shoulder. "This is where he knelt to shave her?"

"Or where he tried to mount her. Who was on the phone?"

Sally said, "Patrick Starr, the owner of this place. He's

another one we had trouble contacting. Kenedy tried calling him when we first arrived, but he wasn't home. We sent an officer to his house, and a neighbor told him that Starr bowls every Wednesday at an alley in Lewisville. The officer went there and told him what happened. Starr was extremely upset and gave us permission to check his records and to do whatever we needed in the salon. I guess the shock is wearing off. He wants to come check on the dogs and get the names and numbers for the owners so he can call them, especially the owner of the deceased cocker. He also wants to know when we'll release the building for him to clean up and reopen. I told him we'd get the numbers for him, if he can tell us where to find them. Otherwise the shop is off limits until you're finished."

"That won't be until sometime tomorrow morning," Maris said.

Sally squatted next to the tripod. "Am I interpreting this right? That whoever left this has a hole in the knee of his pants."

"Yes."

"Reed Wilson's trousers were ripped," Sally said. "I figured it was from the fall after Rick nailed him. Maybe not."

Maris set the camera and tripod aside. "Let's take the tile. I'd rather work with it in the lab and — who knows — photographs have been known to fail or film to get lost."

"No sweat. I'll handle it."

"My toolbox is in the back of the truck," Maris said. She changed gloves again, adding the soiled ones to her rapidly growing pile. Shirley waited for her patiently at the swinging door. "Sorry it's taking so long."

Shirley smiled. "Don't worry about it, honey. It all has to be done." She held up a stack of cards with lifted fingerprints. "I found umpteen on this door. Some could be our guy. Some look like leather-glove prints."

"Probably the patrol officers." Maris pushed through the gate, carefully stepping over a series of blood droplets. "This is the one I dread."

Lynette Donley barely looked human. She lay spread-eagle on her back with only her lower legs and feet undamaged. He'd penetrated her vaginally with a broom handle, and from the amount of broom visible, Maris knew he'd pierced her abdominal cavity. Her simple emerald-green ribbed sweater and white bra had been sliced in the center and peeled open. Stab wounds covered her breasts and stomach. She still wore her thick-soled platform shoes, although her crumpled khaki cargo pants and pink panties had been carelessly tossed aside.

Sally broke into her thoughts. "I'm also curious about some of these bloody marks." She indicated some dried smears and streaks near Lynette's head and shoulders.

"I noticed those earlier when I was taking the photographs and helping the death investigator." Maris cocked her head. "I think they're crawl marks. I don't think she died instantly, but she was barely conscious. He left her to attend to the other girls. When he returned to her, he rolled her on her back, making these swipelike marks near her side." She pointed to them and then to the outer edge of the deeper pool of blood between her legs. Four trails led from a crusty brown outer ring and thinned, becoming lighter in color and thickness. "This is where he dipped his fingers to write the messages on the wall. DNA should confirm it, but notice how the blood was disturbed after skeletonization occurred."

"What does that mean?" Shirley asked.

"When blood is spilled, it usually dries from the outside to the center of the stain. The outer ring that forms a hard crust takes no longer than fifty seconds after bloodshed. It can't be easily removed, even if someone tries to clean it up. When he dipped his fingers in this pool of blood, skeletonization had already occurred, but the deeper portion of the pool was still liquid."

Sally nodded. "You know, I thought he used that bloody Taco Bell paper cup — the one in the trash — to hold the blood while he dipped his fingers into it and wrote his messages."

"Maybe the blood was drying too quickly and he switched to the cup." Maris was puzzled. How could he, in an emotionally charged, adrenaline-rushed state, calmly hunt for a paper cup, dip it in blood, scrawl his messages of hate and then casually deposit the cup in the trash?

Chapter 3

After collecting Lynette's khakis and bikini panties, Maris fished the Taco Bell cup from the trash can, took a sample of the blood and handed it to Shirley for fingerprints. Sally had pulled up the tile with the fabric impression, and Maris was ready to move Lynette Donley. They had positioned the body bag and sheet when Little Ricky called to them from the front door.

A smallish man, Patrick Starr, Maris presumed, stood in the open doorway next to the Bass Cove officer and nervously shifted from foot to foot. He stuck a bony finger under his wire-rimmed glasses and dug at the corners of his blurry eyes. Sniffing, he ran a shaking hand through dark hair that appeared dyed when compared to his silver-streaked beard and mustache. "This is the worst thing that's ever happened in this little town," he said.

"Yes. It's terrible." Sally nodded. "I know you've already talked to the P.D., but I'd appreciate it if you'd run through your day again for me?"

"I bowl in a league every Wednesday. So I left today at three-thirty and went home to get my bowling things and change clothes. I picked up a friend, a coach at the middle school, about four-thirty, and we went to the bowling alley. Sat in the bar until league started at six." He twisted his hands. "I don't know what I'm going to do. Everyone is blaming me for leaving them here alone. My phone is ringing off the wall with dog owners wanting to check on their pets. Even the out-of-towners are calling already." He stretched to peer past Maris and Sally. "Poor Mrs. Travis will be devastated about her cocker. I need my files so I can call her and the others and tell them what's going on." He told Sally where to find the gray card file with the names and other information for the pet owners who had dogs in the kennel.

She found it and gave it to Little Ricky. "Take it and Mr. Starr to the P.D. and copy all the records for us. Then he can have the index box and cards." To Mr. Starr, she added, "As soon as we're through processing the crime scene, I'll get with you about the missing cash and so forth."

"What about the dogs? They'll —"

"Be fine until tomorrow morning. Then you can take care of them."

"I've got to contact my insurance agent and —"

"Tomorrow. It'll have to wait until tomorrow." She thanked him and nodded to Rick, who took Starr by the elbow. Before the pet salon owner could protest, he was out the door. "Where were we?" Sally asked.

"Ready to move Lynette's body," Maris said.

The cramped quarters behind the counter made the task difficult and they struggled getting her into the body bag. They carried her to the door and handed the bag to the waiting officers. Back inside, Sally picked up Lynette's over-turned purse, scooping up two tubes of lipstick, some mascara, loose quarters and a Bic cigarette lighter. She laid them on the counter and emptied the imitation-leather bag of its contents. She handed the purse to Shirley.

"No cash in the pocketbook." Sally snapped the clasp shut on a red billfold. She flipped up the lid on a pack of Marlboro Lights and held up a plastic sandwich-size bag of marijuana and a piece of foil paper. "Here's something for you," she said to Maris.

Maris poured the marijuana into an evidence bag and handed the plastic bag to Shirley for prints. Taking the piece of foil, she peeled back the corner. "Two heroin capsules," she said. "Guess I ought to do an official analysis."

"Yeah," Sally said. "Here's an address book. I'll have to go through it later."

At midnight, Maris and Sally left Shirley to dust the cash register for fingerprints and went to the third victim, Jill Kerr. Maris opened the door to the kennel area, and the dogs lapsed into silence as they waited to see who was coming before barking with renewed vigor. Before turning into the tiny bathroom on her left, Maris noticed bowls of food, mostly untouched, in each cage. She paused near the shattered door. The air, heavy with the spilled perfume, burned her nose and smothered her chest, making her stomach churn. Jill was bent over the commode with her jeans and panties pulled down to the tops of her red Western-style Justin Ropers. Multiple stab wounds covered her back. A hairbrush with blood and fecal material on the handle rested near the sink, next to a pink towel.

Maris ventured inside, watching where she stepped. Patrick Starr must have conceded the bathroom to the girls. Signs of female presence existed everywhere. A brass tray containing makeup, perfume and hair spray had toppled off the back of the commode, throwing its contents into the bathtub and across the floor. Two bottles of perfume, Calvin Klein's CK One and Fetish, as Maris noted from the labels, were shattered on the floor.

"Maybe you can open that window," Sally said between sneezes.

Maris eased past Jill's boots and stepped into the tub. The light gray bathtub tile looked like someone had splashed it with a bucket of red paint. Maris studied the tub. "Arterial spurts." Maris pointed to the vertical blood trails on the wall. The arc of the pattern indicated the rise and fall of blood pressure as the blood spurted. Leaning closer, she saw the remnants of air bubbles in the stains, showing that the arterial spurt had originated from a lung or airway injury. "Up here is a swipe mark, probably caused by her hair." She glanced at Jill and saw the back of her hair was stiff with dried blood. "She struggled in here with her attacker."

Half of the pink floral shower curtain, smudged with mud, lay crumpled in a heap on the bottom. The remainder hung on the rod by only three rings. A travel-size bottle of Pert Plus shampoo had fallen and lost its cap, adding to the mess coating the white porcelain. A mildewed plumber's helper with a wooden handle rested in the shampoo. Maris spotted the beige portable phone under a fold in the curtain. "There's the other phone," Maris said. "Guess you'd better hand me a camera. I didn't notice it when I took photos earlier." She coughed. "The window is cracked," she said, gripping the window latch. She tried to turn it. It refused to budge. "Goddamn. No wonder she couldn't open the son-of-a-bitch." Grimacing with effort, she forced the latch free, but it took a series of firm shoves before the window swung outward. The frigid night air felt good. "I can hear it sleeting," she said as Sally handed her the camera.

She clicked off a couple of shots of the phone and bottom of the tub. A shard of glass near the shampoo bottle caught her attention and she pressed it with her gloved index finger and picked it up, then dropped it into the palm of her other hand.

"What is it?" Sally asked.

"Glass from the window." She studied the cracked pane. "It fits right here . . . where a chunk is missing. She couldn't open it so she probably tried breaking it with the wooden handle of the plunger." Maris held it in place while Sally snapped a couple of photographs. When finished, she said, "Hand me an envelope, will you?"

24

Sally handed her one. "Her last few moments must have been sheer terror."

Maris agreed. "She, more than the other two, knew what was coming. At least it's easier to breathe in here with the window open."

Going to the sink, she collected the stained hairbrush and lifted the pink towel, almost missing the somewhat X-shaped dark-brown impression on the fabric. The bloody outline silhouetted the shape of a long blade and tapered to a sharp point. It originated from a quarter-size ring with a commalike extension and crossed the remnants of another blade, this one with a jagged break in the middle where the point was missing.

Maris whistled softly and held it up. "An imprint of the murder weapon . . . pet-grooming shears. He must have broken the blade in one of them."

"We haven't found any damaged or bloody scissors," Sally said. "He must have taken them with him. If we find them, can you match 'em to this towel?"

"Probably. And to the broken blade, if it's recovered at autopsy."

After she and Sally moved the last body, she went into the grooming room. Gently she cradled the cocker spaniel and slid it onto the table. Using clean cotton swabs, she took a blood sample and set it aside to dry before using her tweezers to take some of his hair from different areas of the body. Although she didn't have the resources to do it, DNA typing was possible on animals.

At one-thirty a.m., Maris walked back across the railroad tracks after taking a break at Lucky's Stop and Go about one hundred yards north of Starr's Pet Salon. The store usually closed at midnight, but the owner kept it open so that they could use the facilities and warm up with hot coffee. The cold night air and the caffeine helped clear her mind. She shivered as the fierce north wind cut through her blue coveralls with *Middleton Forensic Services* across the back and penetrated her long-sleeve thermal undershirt. Ice coated the rails of the train track, but the roads remained clear.

Nearing the salon, Maris noticed Chief Kenedy's solid blue police car parked between her truck and Sally's county car. Since it was the only Bass Cove patrol vehicle lacking the P.D.'s insignia on the bumper and the gold shield on the door, it was easy to spot. Clutching her coffee cup for warmth, she entered the pet salon and caught her lover, Lauren O'Conner, clad in a black raid coat with *FBI* across the back in white five-inch letters, engaged in a heated conversation with Kenedy. She flipped her thick red hair over her shoulder and tossed her head in a familiar gesture of anger. Sally stood near the counter with her arms folded and a scowl on her face. At the sound of the door closing, Lauren glanced over her shoulder with a look of pure exasperation. Her green eyes softened when she saw Maris.

Maris joined Sally. "Problem?"

In a loud voice, Sally said, "Chief Kenedy wants to clarify the role of the FBI in this matter — for about the tenth time."

"And that's my prerogative." He unsnapped the clasp on the safety strap on his holster. "This did happen in my jurisdiction."

His nervous habit grated on Maris's nerves. She wondered how soon he'd wear out the fastener.

"It's in all of our jurisdictions." Sally unfolded her arms and stepped forward. "Just what the hell is your problem? I thought that you and I had already agreed to bring in the FBI."

"Okay. Damn it. I'll tell you." He drew himself to his full height and ran a finger across his black mustache. "I don't believe in all this profiling hocus-pocus. When in the hell has a profile ever solved a murder or rape?"

Maris had heard enough. "About as many times as DNA," she said.

His head jerked in her direction.

Maris said, "DNA doesn't solve cases. Good police work

and investigative techniques solve cases. DNA is a tool — like offender profiling."

"At least DNA is a hard science," he said. "This profiling stuff is little more than psychic guessing disguised as art and intuition. I don't buy into that bullshit. Besides, it can get an investigative team off on the wrong track."

Maris shrugged. "So can unreliable eyewitness accounts or focusing on the wrong fingerprint from a crime scene. Yet no one suggests that we don't fingerprint or ignore eyewitnesses."

"Look," Lauren said. "I'm here to offer support services and advice only — not to take over the investigation. I'd be the field coordinator between you and the FBI's Child Abduction and Serial Killer Unit. We can help analyze the crime, develop investigative strategies and suggest interview and interrogation techniques once you have a suspect. The analysis of the behavioral characteristics of the unknown offender, the profiling, is only part of the package. Let me deploy Rapid Start."

He shook his head and fastened and unfastened the safety strap over his Colt .45 two more times. "I told you no when we talked on the phone earlier."

Maris glared at him. That explained why the Rapid Start team of special FBI agents weren't already somewhere in the area setting up the command center for their computerized major-case management support system. The goal was to provide an on-site automated system with one database where all pertinent facts could be sorted, filtered and analyzed, hopefully resulting in more effective investigative approaches. It was supposed to prevent important leads from being overlooked or buried in the deluge of information that accumulated in major cases. In the Son of Sam killings in New York in the seventies — long before Rapid Start — a traffic ticket placed on David Berkowitz's Ford Galaxy for parking near a fire hydrant provided a key piece of evidence that could have been easily lost. After one of the shootings, a woman recalled seeing a man race to one of four vehicles that had been ticketed. Police traced the registration on all four vehicles, including one that belonged to Berkowitz. Theoretically, Rapid Start pinpointed such information, prevented it from being lost in the shuffle and brought it to the attention of lead investigators much sooner than in the past.

Maris glared at Kenedy. Failing to use all available resources in a case like this verged on negligence. She wondered what the parents, friends and family of the victims would think.

Sally threw up her hands. "Jesus, Troy Dan. Why did you refuse Rapid Start?"

"It's Troy or Chief Kenedy." His face turned red in fury. "I don't have to explain a goddamn thing to you. We don't need it. We've already got a good suspect."

Lauren thoughtfully placed a finger to her lips. "Tell me about this suspect," she said.

Maris smiled. Lauren had obviously caught Kenedy off guard with the question. He sputtered before answering.

"His name is Reed Wilson. He sent threatening letters to Lynnette Donley after they broke up. And he showed up here tonight with blood on his clothing and a cut on his hand."

Sally nodded. "He told us he'd cut his hand at work, but his boss knew nothing about it. And Reed only worked until noon today. He'd also been drinking when he showed up here."

"Well, maybe you do have a good suspect."

Maris saw Lauren glance questioningly in her direction, but she remained noncommittal.

Lauren paced. "Let's do this. Let me work with you as the field coordinator and help you complete the VICAP crime analysis report."

That's good, Maris thought, hoping Kenedy would agree. The crime report was a detailed account of time and place, victim status, identification, physical description and the style of clothing. Any information known about the offender was included, such as modus operandi, location of events, initial offender-victim contact and details regarding his or her activities at the scene. Did the offender write or carve on the body or leave other writings and drawings at the crime scene? What was the condition of victim when found and the location of victim's clothing? What was the cause of death? Was there evidence of sexual assault or other pertinent forensic information? The completed report went to the National Center for the Analysis of Violent Crime, where agents determined if the crime was similar to any other cases in the VICAP system. Even if this was a first offense for this particular perpetrator, the event could be compared to similar crimes in an attempt to learn something about the offender that could help in his apprehension, interrogation and prosecution.

"We're going to do the report anyway," Sally said. "We might as well have help."

"Fine." Kenedy threw up his hands. "Whatever. I'm going to take a look at Reed Wilson's apartment." He patted the warrant sticking out of his uniform pocket. "Maris, I'll get his clothing to you later and let you know if you need to process anything in the apartment. And we'll set up a time for you to check the car."

Maris nodded. "I've got a lot of work left here. I still have to road-map the blood spatters." She pointed to the bloody epitaphs on the wall behind her. "And cut out that part of the wall."

"No hard feelings." Kenedy smiled and extended his hand to Lauren. "I just want what's best for this case so we can put away the bastard that did this."

"Then we have at least one thing in common." Lauren shook his hand.

"Prick," Maris said as soon as he left. She touched Lauren's shoulder. "I'm glad you're here. I missed you." She sipped the lukewarm cup of coffee she'd almost forgotten.

Lauren squeezed her hand. "I thought about you today when I was sitting on the hot seat with three defense attorneys going after me on that fraud case." She laughed softly. "I wondered why in the world you like going to court. I was a nervous wreck."

"Listen to that, Sally." Maris smiled. "Her good looks and she's nervous."

Lauren pulled her hand away and walked to the end of

the counter where she could see the bloody writing on the wall. "God, this is horrible." She turned, slowly scanning the room.

"Wait until you see the photos of the bodies," Sally said.

"I wish I didn't have to," Lauren said, and Maris knew she meant it.

A commotion out front caught their attention. The door opened a crack and Little Ricky said, "I'm sorry, ma'am, but you can't go in there. I'll get an investigator to come out and talk to you."

In a shrill voice, a woman said, "I've got to see her. I've got to see her."

Rick stumbled backward, shoving open the door as he struggled to stop a platinum blonde in a shimmering red strapless dress. She froze and her eyes widened as she spied the overturned Christmas tree, scattered cards and bloodstains. She shrieked, and her hands flew to her face. Maris and Sally rushed forward at the same time, but Maris arrived first. She caught one elbow and Rick the other just before the woman's knees gave way. She was short, about five feet, four inches, and slightly dumpy with breasts that appeared too large for her slight frame. She smelled strongly of alcohol, and her arm felt cold. Sally sent Lauren to Starr's office to find a chair. They lowered the distraught woman to the seat.

Maris glanced out the door as Rick closed it and saw an eight- to ten-year-old silver Mercedes sitting partly in the street only inches from the bumper of a squad car. Rick stripped off his coat and wrapped it around the woman's shoulders. She rocked forward, elbows on her knees and moaned. "I can't believe my baby's gone." She looked up, tears streaming down her face. "Where's Patrick Starr? Did he do this? I told her, warned her to quit." The sobs grew louder, and she grabbed Lauren's hand. "She was going to, you know. She'd promised. Lynette was going to quit this job."

Chapter 4

Over the next forty-five minutes, Lauren knelt in front of the hysterical woman and patiently drew out her story while Sally took notes and occasionally interjected a question. In the meantime, Maris watched the clock creep toward three a.m. And was unable to finish her work until they were out of the way. The woman said she was Lynette Donley's mother, Allison Donley. She'd left home about three to check into her room at the Dallas Anatole at Market Center and Stemmons where she attended a Christmas party. She'd not taken her phone or pager to the party and was unaware that anyone was trying to contact her until she returned to her room. Before she could check any messages, her ex-husband called from the Bahamas where he was vacationing with his new young wife. Bitterly, Allison described his telling her that their daughter was dead and that he'd return as soon as possible. She'd rushed — foolishly, she guessed now — to Bass Cove, leaving her things in the hotel room. In response to questions, Allison added that she was forty-five, a real estate agent, and had been divorced for about five years.

When she appeared to regain most of her composure, Sally asked, "Why did you want Lynette to quit?"

"That awful man, the owner, Patrick Starr. Lynette told me that he often made lewd comments and told off-color jokes intended to embarrass the girls. She said that he'd press up against her or brush against her breasts. Not overtly, but very subtly in a way that made it hard for her to confront him. If she did, he'd play innocent."

"Was she afraid of him?" Lauren asked. She stood stiffly and brushed the knee of her pleated trousers.

Allison laughed with a trace of irony. "Lynette wasn't afraid of anything. She thought it was some kind of game." She wiped her eyes with the cuff of Rick's coat.

"Why didn't you do something — make her quit?" Lauren asked.

"Honey, you don't make Lynette do anything she doesn't want to do." Grief overcame her again and she doubled over. "I tried," she said, between sobs. "She said that he was no different from any other boss and that she'd rather work in the kennel than sling hamburgers or sell shoes."

A little after three, Lauren drove Allison home in the Mercedes, and Sally followed to bring her back. Maris recruited Little Ricky to help her road-map and sample the blood spatters. They were hard at it when Sally and Lauren returned. Reluctantly, at Maris's urging, they left to get some rest so they could resume interviewing witnesses and potential suspects in the morning.

Rick turned out to be a good assistant. He listened attentively, made labels and helped her take measurements. They started at the front door and worked their way back. She added labels, "road maps," with an exhibit number and scale to each major stain group. Then she took overall surface photographs and zoomed in on the individual patterns or spatters. It was a painstaking process, requiring her to analyze the motion and directionality of each spatter, occasionally marking the direction of travel with a sticky-backed red arrow before taking additional pictures. Each stain offered a clue to the sequence of events in the pet salon. The cast-off patterns, sometimes covering the floor, opposing walls and ceiling, allowed her to estimate the minimum number of times the scissors struck each victim. The numbers were staggering. As she worked, she explained what she did and why to Rick and took additional blood samples for DNA-typing. The identity of the source of certain patterns and trails would help sequence the events and reconstruct the crime.

When they finished at six, Maris's joints ached with fatigue and her stomach growled with hunger. Rick insisted on helping her pack her investigation kit and double-check the evidence to make sure it was properly packaged for transport to the lab. Taking care to avoid cracking the Sheetrock and damaging the bloody epitaphs, they cut out a section of the wall. About nine, Thursday morning, another Bass Cove patrol officer backed his patrol car into the parking lot next to Maris's truck and relieved Rick. Maris left a few minutes later to find bright sunshine, icy roads and slow-moving traffic. Her usual forty-five-minute drive from Bass Cove turned into a two-and-a-half hour journey. Lauren's government-issue Taurus was gone when she passed the front of the house and backed into the separate drive for the lab. Catching a second wind, she unloaded the evidence and checked her voice mail with dread. Relieved to find nothing urgent, she opened the sliding door separating her lab from the living quarters and was greeted by her border collie, Earnhardt. He barked boisterously, danced around her feet and made a game of darting away when she tried to pet him.

"Damn it, boy. Is that fucking TV loud enough?" She caught him and ruffled his head. She almost slipped on the metro section of Thursday's *Dallas Morning News* that littered the floor and coffee table. Stale cigarette smoke stung her nasal passages, and her irritation grew when she saw the overflowing ashtray and empty Miller Lite can on the floor beside her recliner. She grabbed the remote control and lowered the volume on the television. Jesus, hadn't Lauren seen this mess when she came home?

As part of the conditions for staying there since her release from prison, Lauren's sister, Irene Beauchamp, was not supposed to smoke in the house. It appalled Maris that Irene had managed to get out after only one year. She'd thought for sure that she'd have to serve at least three after admitting to running over her only daughter with a three-quarter-ton Dodge Ram and conspiring to hide the body. Maris supposed it helped Irene to have an FBI-agent sister vouch for her and agree to help supervise her first six months of probation. She also figured that the two million dollars Irene received for the sale of her husband's trucking business hadn't hurt either. She picked up the front section of the newspaper and folded it in disgust, trying to avoid the headline about the Starr's Pet Salon murders. She heard Irene moving around in the guest bedroom and the sound of running water. Disgruntled, trying to control her temper, she wandered into the kitchen. Her stomach burned from bad coffee and the lack of food. A note with Maris's name across the front in Lauren's neat handwriting caught her attention. She picked it up and caught a whiff of perfume. It almost made her smile. She unfolded the note and read, "Patience, darling. Please. I'll talk to her when I get home. Love, Lauren. P. S. Be nice." That did make her smile as she wadded up the paper and shot it into the kitchen trash.

"Two points," Irene said from behind her. Maris jerked her head in surprise and saw Irene, wearing faded blue jeans and an unbuttoned red-and-black plaid flannel shirt, with rolled-up sleeves, over a white T-shirt. At thirty-nine, she was eight years older than Lauren and similar in stature, with heavier, fuller breasts, more freckles and dark brown somber eyes instead of Lauren's green. Faint streaks of red and bands of silver highlighted her brunette hair. Lines etched around the corners of her eyes and tight, thin lips lent an air of world-weariness, making her seem mysterious, vulnerable and surprisingly attractive.

"You're back," Irene said in a whiskey voice, raspier

than Lauren's from years of smoking and heavy drinking. "Don't worry about this mess. I'll clean it up later." She waved her hand and, without waiting for Maris to answer, added, "I promise not to smoke in the house anymore. It was just so damned cold last night."

"You should have been working in it." Maris pulled a Big Red out of the fridge. Irene didn't like them so there were plenty left.

"I'm having a club sandwich and vegetable soup. Want some?" Irene leaned on the cabinet and smiled at her.

"Sounds good." She slid onto a stool at the kitchen bar and popped the top on her drink.

"You look exhausted. So did Lauren when she left this morning. She only slept about three hours. She said it was horrible." She opened a can of soup and poured it into a saucepan. "She dreaded talking to the parents today."

Maris nodded. It would be hard to question the grieving parents about their children's habits and quirks. And their friends, lovers and enemies. A murder victim has no privacy.

Irene started the bacon frying for their sandwiches and got out a tomato. "Parents should cherish their children, indulge them and spend time with them every day. You never know when they'll be snatched away."

Maris stared at her. Was this the same woman who knowingly allowed her husband to sexually abuse her daughter, Karin, and did nothing? All for financial security, or so she said. After building a successful trucking company, her husband developed a damaged, weak heart and wasn't a good candidate for a transplant. Irene knew she'd be his only beneficiary when the fatal heart attack finally came, and convinced herself the money would make up for all the pain and humiliation her daughter suffered. Later, she blamed her muddled thinking on too much booze and speed.

"You're a fine one to give parenting advice," Maris said, unable to hold back her disgust.

Irene faced her. "Whatever you think of me is no worse than I think of myself. I know what I've lost, and I feel for the parents of those girls."

At Thanksgiving when she bitched about Irene, her mother and Lauren had ganged up on her. "Where's your compassion?" her mother asked. "It's not your place to judge."

And Lauren added, "What would you have Irene do? Kill herself?"

Instinctively, Maris touched the scar on her cheek, struck by the irony. Irene would be dead if Maris hadn't stopped Brian Blake, Karin's boyfriend, from plunging a knife into Irene's chest and sacrificing her to demons that only he could see. She dropped her hand from the scar. "What I said was out of line and I'm sorry." Her mother and Lauren thought Irene deserved a chance at redemption. Well, maybe so, but she couldn't help but think once a fuckup always a fuckup. "Just don't smoke in the house again, okay?" She hated the smell of stale smoke.

"You know . . ." Irene flipped the sizzling bacon. "It blew me away when Lauren divorced Robert and told us she was a lesbian." She put a hand on her hip. "Well, actually Robert told."

Maris said nothing, wondering where the conversation was going.

Irene sliced a tomato for the sandwiches. "Poor David. I'd known about him for years. He was no surprise to anyone but Mom and Dad."

Maris laughed, thinking of Lauren's and Irene's brother, with his clean good looks, gentle manner and wicked sense of humor.

"I was eight when Lauren was born. My mother had two miscarriages between us, and she and my father thought they wouldn't be able to have more children. Then two years after Lauren, David was born. They were always so close. I blamed it on the difference in our ages, but it didn't stop me from being a little jealous." She paused to wash the lettuce and smiled. "I was the rebellious one, always in trouble. Lauren was the smart one, a teachers' pet who helped grade papers and ran errands to the office. David was the athlete in the family and a real charmer. You should have seen how the teachers and the old ladies at church doted on him." Irene poured the steaming soup into two bowls and carried one to Maris along with a club sandwich.

"Looks good," Maris said.

Irene pulled out the other barstool and sat down her own soup and sandwich. "Lauren is the one who's changed."

"What makes you say that?"

"She's lost something." Irene paused with her spoon halfway to her mouth. "Her innocence, maybe. A part of whatever it was that made her personality brighter, fresher than mine . . . or David's." She tasted her soup.

"Lauren's had a hard time the last couple of years."

"I know. Some of it's my fault and some is yours."

"My fault?" Maris set down her sandwich.

Irene held up her hand. "Hear me out. She loved Karin. I should have given her up and sent her to live with Lauren years ago. She'd be a wonderful mother. What I did hurt her very much, but you're the one who got her into what she's doing now." Irene played with the crust on her sandwich.

"She's an FBI agent doing her job. She likes it, and she's good at it."

"She was working white-collar crime doing accounting work before she met you."

"She might have never met me if you hadn't dumped your daughter's body in a well." She glared at Irene. She was too tired to get into this conversation.

Irene flushed, and the hand holding the spoon trembled. "Maybe. But you're the one who exposed her to the monster who attacked her in this very house and almost got her killed. You're the one who drew her into this *profiling* thing. Into the mind of those who do things like kill three girls, shave the pussy hair off one and —"

Maris slammed down her sandwich, sending a tomato slice sliding across the counter. "You don't know what the fuck you're talking about, and it's none of your goddamn business."

"I'm sorry. I wasn't trying to make you mad."

She sounded sincere, but Maris saw a gleam of satisfaction in her eyes at hitting a nerve.

"I'm just worried about her," Irene said. "I've never seen her so thin."

Acknowledging the truth in Irene's words, Maris took a

deep breath and tried to swallow her anger. "What happened when Donnie Wade Baker assaulted her, taking her gun and . . . all." She sighed. "It's taken a while for her to get over it. Going away to school for ten months so soon afterward was hard on both of us, especially with me tied up all summer in Apache County on the investigation into Sherf's murder." Maris retrieved the tomato slice and put it back on her sandwich. She missed the tough old woman. Descended from pioneer ranch stock, Sherf had been a west Texas sheriff for over forty years. Lauren's infrequent visits often came at Sherf's Saddlehorn Canyon Ranch. And God, she'd been so thin, distant, still struggling with the nightmares. At least the resolution of Sherf's case and her role in it had renewed her confidence. Yet she wondered how cases like this would affect her. "Your sister can handle it. She'll be okay," Maris said. She'd paint her butt white and run with the antelopes before she'd admit her worries to Irene. Maris's neck and shoulders ached with exhaustion. Irritated that her soup was cold, she ate it anyway and had almost finished the sandwich when she remembered what Irene had said. Looking up, she asked, "How did you know he'd shaved the pubic hair on one of the girls?"

Irene blinked in surprise. "It was in the newspaper."

Maris groaned. Damn it, that detail should never have been released. A leak so soon was a bad sign.

Chapter 5

After a shower, Maris stretched across the carpet with the *Dallas Morning News* and leaned against the hearth of the fireplace. The warmth spread across her back, and she felt some of the tension began to slip away. She and Irene had managed to restore their uneasy truce, and Irene had retired to her room to read the latest Stephen King novel and watch a trashy talk show. Occasionally, a phrase or two reverberated down the hallway.

Earnhardt flopped on the carpet next to her. Sticking his nose under her elbow, he begged to be stroked. Shaking the front page to smooth out the crease, Maris stared at a photograph depicting the front of Starr's Pet Salon. In it, Sally and Chief Kenedy searched Lynette Donley's car while

Maris stood in the doorway in a white Tyvek suit, hands on her hips. Smaller pictures of the three victims appeared above a companion story about the reaction of family, friends and school officials. On page five, the story continued with a Kerr family portrait taken in front of an old tin barn. Jennifer and Jill rode matching sorrel quarter horses. Charles and Elizabeth, the parents, embraced between them. A gray, white and black Australian shepherd sat at their feet. Jill held two barrel-racing trophies, and a ribbon hung from her horse's bridle. Jennifer carried a Texas flag, the shaft stuck in her stirrup for support.

According to the article, Lynnette Donley's divorced parents couldn't be reached for an interview, but there was a shot of her mother, Allison Donley, that Maris recognized as one she'd seen on numerous flyers and billboards advertising a real estate agency. Funny, she'd failed to make the connection between the heavyset realtor, with Dolly Parton-like hair and tits, and the woman in the red party dress at the pet salon. There was also a stock photograph of Lynette's father, Dr. Lance Donley, a prominent Dallas plastic surgeon. After reading the secondary story, she returned to the front page for the account of the brutal murders and, dismayed, read a vivid description of how the murderer shaved Jennifer Kerr. Thankfully the bloody writings weren't mentioned.

Thinking of the macabre messages, she brushed the paper aside and rose to her knees. Earnhardt licked her cheek. Playfully pushing him aside, she walked on her knees until she could reach the cord and pull the phone to her. Earnhardt nipped at her heels as she backed to the fireplace and settled against the warm brick. Grabbing his tennis ball from his toy box in the corner of the room, he flipped it in the air and chased it across the carpet. Mouthing the ball, he rolled over on his back near her.

"Leave me alone, big guy. I've got to call Shannon," she said. She glanced at the clock on the VCR. Four p.m. The pretty blonde should be at the office. The phone rang in Maris's hand, startling her, and she almost dropped it.

When she brought it to her ear, she heard a familiar voice but couldn't quite identify the female caller.

"You there? Maris?" the woman asked. "This is Robin Fisher."

"Robin?" Maris said, surprised to hear from Shannon Stockwell's partner. Robin had certainly never called her before. Her next thought went to Shannon's pregnancy. "Is the baby here? Is Shannon all right?"

"No. Not yet." Robin groaned. "Her due date is not until December thirtieth, but Shannon keeps threatening to have the doctor induce labor." She laughed. "But I may beat her to it. One moment she's crying and the next she's laughing. Then, to keep me on my toes, she's mad about something. Take my advice. If Lauren decides to do this, tell her every morning how pretty and sexy she is, even if she's throwing up or crying because something doesn't fit." She let out a breath. "Don't listen to me. It's been . . . I can't even describe it. Wonderful, fantastic. Sometimes I lay my head on her stomach and just listen. I can actually hear the little thing moving around, feel it kicking."

"I'm glad she's doing okay. Funny, I was going to call her office when the phone rang. Then I've got to go to bed. I've been up over twenty-four hours."

Robin cleared her throat. "Because of the murders, I assume."

"Yes."

"That's why I was calling. I know this is irregular, but I need to ask you something. The paper said that the killer shaved the pubic hair on one of the victims. Is it true?" Maris hesitated and Robin added, "I wouldn't ask if it weren't important. Did I tell you that I used to be a prosecutor in Tarrant County? Specialized in sex crimes."

"You never said, but other people have mentioned it. Why are you asking?" Maris heard a tapping noise in the background, like Robin was bouncing a pen on her desk. "Where are you?"

"Work. Look, it seems that I remember a similar incident in a rape case a few years ago. The behavior is unusual enough that I thought, if the paper is accurate, I'd get in touch with the investigators. Long shot, I realize."

"Actually it may not be. The story is accurate. He used some electric grooming shears to shave her. When was this other case?"

"In 'ninety-one."

"Was there a suspect identified? A conviction?"

"Hmm." Maris heard paper shuffling in the background. "Let me look into it. Talk to the D.A. Who's lead investigator?"

"Chief Troy Dan Kenedy of Bass Cove P.D., but you'd probably rather talk to Sally Trent with the S.O. or to Lauren."

"Thanks. Why were you calling Shannon?"

"I've got something I'd like her to look at. Tell us if she can do anything with it."

"Not related to this case, I hope."

"Yes."

"Don't!" Robin said, her intensity suprising. "Think about what happened the last time you involved her. Leave her out of it."

Maris winced. For the second time that day, someone was reminding her of how she led Donnie Wade Baker to the two women she cared the most about. Thankfully, he hadn't hurt Shannon physically, but he'd killed Buster, a horse she'd had since she was a teenager. It could as easily have been Shannon. "I haven't talked to her yet. It's possible that she can't help us. And this case is different. She won't be in any danger."

"Don't be so sure."

The voice faded, and Maris knew she was getting ready to hang up the phone. "Wait," she said. "Why did —"

"Just don't be so sure, that's all."

There was a click and Robin was gone before Maris could ask her why she left the D.A.'s office. Punching in the numbers, she called Shannon. "Is this the beautiful and world-famous Shannon Stockwell?"

"No. This is a tired, fat, very pregnant and furious Shannon."

"Well, you still have a sexy phone voice. Who or what has you riled up?"

"My lover, who else?" Shannon laughed. "It's really nothing. She was supposed to escort me to a Christmas dinner party tonight and she has to work. She's trying to stay ahead so she can take off when the baby comes. I don't really want to go tonight, but the host is an important client. I probably wouldn't be aggravated with her if it wasn't for my mixed-up hormones. But that's okay. I have a very handsome gentleman who'll take me."

"Timothy?" Maris guessed, thinking about Shannon's good-looking gay receptionist.

"I swear you and Robin think alike. You both assume he's the only one I can get." Shannon sounded indignant.

"I figured he's the only one you'd ask. So who is it?"

"Timothy — but I didn't ask anyone else."

"The two of you will be the envy of the party." Amused, Maris shook her head, beginning to empathize with Robin. She could imagine Shannon jauntily tilting her head and tossing her blonde hair. "I've got something I'd like you to see." She described the words drawn on the wall in blood. "What do you think you can do with it?"

"Probably nothing until you have a suspect and I can get exemplars from him. The problem is that we have a limited amount of writing to work with. Four phrases, I think you said. That may not be enough for identifying characteristics to appear. I'll search the literature for similar cases. Might get some ideas there."

Maris heard her tapping on computer keys and waited.

"Think I should bring it over or wait until we have a strong suspect? The blood is dry, but I don't know how much, if any, it will fade or otherwise change with time."

"Hmm. I don't know either. I assume you have good photos."

"Yes." Maris hesitated. There was a thought that'd been nagging her since she first arrived at the crime scene. "There's another reason I'd like you to see it now. Two actually."

"What?"

43

"I want to know if the bloody graffiti was written by one person or two, and if you can tell whether the person, or persons, is right- or left-handed."

"There are three things that cannot be reliably ascertained from handwriting — handedness, age and gender. I may be able to tell you if it was written by one or two people, depending on the uniqueness of the handwriting. But it's iffy with a limited sample, using an unusual medium. Bring it on over. If I can't do it, no one can."

"That's the Shannon I know and love," Maris said.

"Will I get paid this time?"

"You always get paid, darling. Don't I always take you out to eat at your favorite restaurant? Sometimes I even get you cash."

"Then Joe T. Garcia's it is. Make it tomorrow afternoon and bring Lauren. Robin and I still haven't met her. Someone has to order a margarita — just so I can smell it. If I'm ever able to drink again, I swear I'll never take tequila for granted. It's the elixir of life."

Maris went to bed still chuckling. She was almost asleep when she realized that she'd forgotten to tell her that Robin had called.

Enticing aromas from the kitchen drifted into the partially opened bedroom door followed by snippets of conversation, music and laughter. Maris glanced at the alarm clock and saw it was almost eight p.m. She ought to get up until ten and try to return to a normal schedule, but she snuggled deeper under the covers. More laughter. Lauren was clearly enjoying her sister's company. Maybe having Irene around for a while wasn't such a bad thing. She rolled over on her back to listen, catching the end of Eric Clapton's "Lay Down Sally.". Earlier she thought she'd heard disco. What were they doing? She rose up on one elbow and sniffed the air. Making cookies? Queen's "We Will Rock You" shook the hallway. The phone rang twice and stopped.

Light from the hall brightened the room as Lauren

pushed open the door. She wore a Christmas apron decorated with colorful elves baking in Santa's kitchen. Maris recognized it as Mary Ann's favorite. No one had worn it since she'd died.

"You're awake," Lauren said. In three bounds, she was on the bed in Maris's arms.

Maris kissed her and brushed a stray hair from her forehead. "You smell like cookies." She fingered the apron. "Where'd you find this?"

"In the kitchen . . . with the hot pads and cup towels."

"Mary Ann always wore this whenever she baked, no matter what time of year it was."

"You don't mind if I wear it?" A worried frown crossed her face.

"Of course not." She nibbled Lauren's neck and whispered, "Sometimes she'd wear it with nothing on underneath."

"That's an idea."

Maris pulled the tie on the apron and reached for the buttons on Lauren's shirt.

Lauren caught her wrist. "Not now." She laughed. "Irene's waiting."

"She won't care."

"You know I feel funny about it when she's around." Lauren rolled away. "Don't be angry."

"I'm not." Maris rose to one elbow and kissed her cheek.

"I got an interesting message from a Fort Worth detective. He left it on my voice mail this afternoon. When I called him back, he told me that in 'ninety or 'ninety-one there was a series of rapes around TCU. All of the victims were college students, and in each case the attacker shaved her pubic hair. He's going to pull the files for me and make copies."

Maris sat on the side of the bed and wrapped her arms around Lauren. "Robin Fisher, Shannon's lover, called me today and told me the same thing." Maris frowned. "Except she indicated it was only one. She used to be a prosecutor in Tarrant County." She nibbled Lauren's neck. "Sure I can't interest you in an early-evening romp?"

45

"No." Lauren laughed and pushed her away. "You almost made me forget that Sally called to see if you could meet her at the S.O. about seven tomorrow morning to look at Wilson's car. I told her you'd call her back if it wasn't good."

"Fine. Hope you told her to have the coffee ready."

Lauren started to the door. "We've got stew and cornbread for dinner."

"The perfect weather for it." Maris slipped out of bed. "What's with the music?"

Lauren laughed. "Irene dug out her old record albums while she was home at Thanksgiving." Over her shoulder, she added, "It's been kind of fun listening to them."

"I'm surprised my turntable still works." Maris slipped on a pair of sweats and a T-shirt and padded after Lauren.

Earnhardt met her in the living room and danced around her, barking. Nosing the back of her calves, he ushered her toward the kitchen.

"Damn it, quit herding me. And how'd you get flour on your head?" She caught Lauren at the cabinet and threw an arm around her waist. "Smells good in here."

Lauren saw her eyeing a plate of decorated and iced sugar cookies in the shape of Santas, snowmen and Christmas trees. "Not those. They're for Irene's therapy group, and I'm taking some to the office tomorrow. But we saved these for us."

Irene slid another platter of cookies closer to her. "They came out a little odd."

Maris studied the deformed cookies and selected a Santa with head trauma. Taking a bite, she gazed at the mixing bowls, measuring cups and other dishes piled in the sink. Flour and cornmeal covered the cabinet. Stew had bubbled out of the pot and splashed the stovetop. Her kitchen looked like a home, for the first time in a long time.

Chapter 6

Inside the garage at the Bass County Sheriff's Office at seven-thirty Friday morning, Maris completed the initial photographs of Reed Wilson's beat-up, red '85 Mustang, convinced it hadn't been cleaned since the Cowboys won their last Super Bowl. Empty Budweiser cans, French-fry boxes and hamburger wrappers from Jack in the Box littered the front and back floorboards. Dirty shirts, jeans, underwear and towels covered the back seat. Loose compact discs by Metallica and the Beastie Boys were stacked on the console with loose change, two packs of Kool — one with three marijuana joints — a cigarette lighter and a balled-up mechanic's grease rag. Cigarette butts and roaches spilled out of the ashtray. The car smelled like stale smoke and ashes — and decaying food.

Sally loitered nearby. "So when I called, Lauren and Irene were making cookies and listening to disco?" She chuckled. "And they were sober?"

"Yeah. And they made some damned good stew and cornbread." Maris placed the camera on top of the car and squatted next to the open door and shone a flashlight on the floorboard, across the seat and on the door panel. She'd already photographed and sampled bloodstains on the steering wheel and stick shift. With a gloved hand, she picked up a Budweiser can and handed it to Sally, followed by a crumpled hamburger wrapper. "Looks like bloodstains on both of them."

Sally set them aside near Maris's investigation kit and camera. "Sounds like Lauren and her sister are trying to heal old wounds."

"I suppose." Maris rocked back on her heels. "The blood that's here is consistent with the cut on his hand, but there's not as much as I'd expect if he killed those girls and drove this car away from the salon. He should have had blood on his shoes, jeans, his shirt . . . hell, all over." She stood and leaned over the bucket seat. The rag on the console caught her attention. She picked it up and stepped away from the car. It was stiff with dried blood. "I'll photograph it later with anything else we find. Let's go through that crap in the back seat and then I'll Luminol the front." Although she didn't expect to find any invisible bloodstains with the Luminol, she wanted to be thorough.

"Okay. You take this side, and I'll go around." Sally slid the seat forward on the passenger side and began rummaging through the trash. "This may be the notebook he used to write the threatening notes to Lynette." She flipped through a yellow legal pad. "Looks like he started another letter and didn't finish it." She tossed it on the roof of the car.

"There's nothing but trash and dirty clothes here," Maris said. She stood up, stretched her back and retrieved the camera. "Let's check the trunk."

"And get done with this." Sally dug the keys out of her

pocket and fumbled with the lock on the trunk. "I already feel like I need a shower."

The trunk lid squealed open on rusty hinges. Full and empty plastic containers of oil and brake fluid mixed with loose wrenches, screwdrivers, a hammer, a crowbar and more clothing.

"Doesn't this guy have a closet?" Maris clicked the camera.

"According to Kenedy, his apartment is as trashed at his car, but nothing there linked him to the murders." Sally stepped aside. "The bartender at Charlie's Bar and Grill in Denton, Reed's favorite hangout, said he came in about seven the night of the murders. He'd been drinking and had stitches in his hand."

One by one, Maris examined and dropped the soiled items on the concrete floor. "He'd have been hard pressed to kill the girls, get cleaned up, see a doctor about his hand and get to the bar by seven." A pair of brown cloth gloves caught her eye. When she retrieved them, she saw one blood-soaked glove was slashed between the thumb and forefinger. Slowly, she eased her latex-protected hand into the glove. "I don't see how he could cut his hand like this with a scissorslike murder weapon." She put on the other glove. "The bloodstains on this glove are consistent with grabbing his cut hand to staunch the blood flow." She demonstrated. Holding the damaged glove closer, she peered at the torn threads. "There're glass particles adhering to it."

"Don't forget he installs vehicle glass for a living."

"This doesn't look like automotive glass." She frowned. "Does Reed have a record for burglary?"

"Juvie breaking and entering. No adult convictions." She pursed her lips. "I'd better find out if any break-ins were reported on Wednesday where the burglar cut himself."

"If there is, I hope someone saved a blood sample." Maris removed the brown gloves and replaced her own with fresh.

"He'd sure make things easier if he'd talk to us." Sally leaned against the car. "Whether he did it or not."

"At this point, he has nothing to lose by keeping his mouth shut." Maris knelt next to her investigation kit and labeled a round metal container. Using tweezers, she collected as many glass particles as she could from Wilson's brown gloves. "Why don't you go ahead and start your phone calls. I'll finish. I doubt if we find anything else of interest."

After cataloging and securing all of the recovered items, Maris entered the data in her laptop and locked all of the evidence in the back of her truck. She finished by ten and went to Sally's office. There she found a haggard-looking Aubrey police officer squeezed into a chair near Sally's desk. Sipping coffee from a ridiculously small plastic foam cup, he smoothed his wrinkled blue uniform and shifted uncomfortably in the chair. When he saw her, he grabbed a brown sack with a sheet of paper attached and stood.

Although he looked familiar, she introduced herself and shook his hand.

"We met a couple of years ago when you testified for us in a rape case." She must have given him a blank look because he added, "The pregnant schoolteacher."

"I remember."

Maris nodded. "She wasn't feeling well and left school early. Walked into a burglary in progress. The attack was so vicious, she lost the baby." During the trial, the defense kept Maris on the stand most of the day, answering DNA questions. The nineteen-year-old defendant's parents had refused to believe their dope-fiend son was capable of anything so awful and blew most of their retirement savings trying to save the little bastard. As the trial progressed, their transformation from doting parents to deceived patsies was painful to watch. "How is she ... the teacher?" Maris had admired her bravery and perseverance during the trial.

"She and her husband divorced shortly afterward. She resigned at midterm to move back home. Somewhere in Illinois, I think." He shrugged and handed her the sack. "I hurried over as soon as Sally called. It's from a residential burglary I worked Wednesday afternoon. The owner came home about five that afternoon and found the glass broken from one of the windows near his back door. Blood everywhere. We found some glass cutters and a suction cup. I think he planned to cut the glass out and remove it with a

50

suction cup so he could reach inside and unlock the dead-bolt. Something went wrong, and the glass or the cutter slipped. He fled after he cut himself. Here's some of the glass with blood on it."

Maris tore a sheet of paper from a pad on Sally's desk and made a note of the time and date. She had the officer sign it and initialed it herself so she'd have a record of the chain of custody. "Thanks," she said. "I'm glad you brought it right away."

He finished the coffee and tossed his cup into the trash. As he was leaving, Sally returned carrying an inch-thick stack of papers. She clapped him on the shoulder and thanked him. To Maris, she said, "He sent notices to all of the agencies in the area and the hospitals to be on the look-out for a burglary suspect with a cut hand. As soon as I started asking about recent burglaries, one of our guys told me about it."

The officer smiled proudly. "If it matches your suspect, let us know. We'll charge him with this attempted break-in and talk to him about a whole rash of recent burglaries."

"If it works out, maybe we can all clear some cases," Sally said.

When he was gone, Sally gingerly stepped around three cardboard boxes piled against the wall and slipped behind her desk. She held up the stack of papers. "Telephone logs. These represent less than a third of the calls we've received since the bodies were found Wednesday night. And it doesn't include the forty million calls we've gotten from the press. It's causing problems with our nine-one-one system. The sheriff has pulled in all able bodies to help man the phones. God knows when we'll get time to check these tips." She slammed the papers on the desk. "All because Kenedy made the Texas Rangers so mad when he first arrived in Bass Cove that they won't work with him, and now the idiot wants to refuse help from the feds. " She shook her head.

"I don't understand why." Maris lowered herself to the chair. "I knew we had problems when Lauren couldn't persuade him."

"At least she got him to compromise . . . somewhat."

Sally leaned forward and lowered her voice. "Shirley thinks he's heard rumors about you and Lauren, and that's part of the problem."

"I hope not." She sighed. "Not that I care what the little fucker thinks, but it won't help Lauren if he complains." She shifted in the chair. "Maybe I should pull out. Turn all the evidence over to the state."

"If we need specialized investigative support on scene, we call you. The other cases we send to DPS to help defray costs. It almost always takes three to six months to get the results back." She picked up a pen and tapped it thoughtfully. "You'll have the results a lot faster."

"Just because I'm putting everything else on hold. They can't do that." Maris picked at a callus on the palm of her hand. She got them lifting weights, but the moisture from wearing the latex gloves caused them to soften and peel. "I figured Kenedy's problem was little man's syndrome." She looked up at Sally and grinned. "Maybe I should just beat the shit out of him and solve all our troubles."

"It may be a race to see who decks him first." She reached for the phone. "I asked the sheriff to request additional FBI assistance, but he wouldn't because . . ." She looked uneasily at the open door. "You know why."

"Too political. And this way he can blame Kenedy if we can't solve this case."

"Not *just* solve it, but solve it in a *timely* manner." Sally bit her lip and frowned. "Wait till I tell Kenedy we've just about eliminated our only suspect. Especially after the way he keeps shooting his mouth off about a quick resolution."

"We can't completely discount Reed Wilson until I get the DNA-typing done. So I suppose I'd better get out of here and go to work." Maris rose to go. "What's the next step?"

"I'm going to retrace Jill Kerr's day. She'd borrowed her sister's car to go shopping. Maybe she encountered some weirdo who followed her back to the shop. I've got a deputy interviewing the victims' friends. I've got another man checking into registered sex offenders in the county." She thumped the stack of telephone logs. "And I'm going to get someone to start checking these."

Maris paused at the doorway. "By the way, did Robin Fisher call you?"

Sally looked puzzled. "Robin?"

"Shannon Stockwell's lover."

Sally shook her head. "Not that I know of."

Maris crossed her arms and leaned against the doorjamb. "She called me yesterday ..." She stopped to think. "Before I went to bed. She wanted to know if the account in the paper about Jennifer's pubic hair being shaved was true. Said it reminded her of a rape case that she handled when she was with the Tarrant County D.A.'s office. She didn't recall the outcome but was going to find out if the suspect could have been recently paroled or something. She referred to one case. Fort Worth P.D. called Lauren about a series of similar assaults. I told her to call you."

Sally jotted a note in her investigation log. "I'll get with Lauren on this."

Maris waved and ducked out the door as Sally punched out the numbers for Bass Cove P.D. She wondered what Chief Kenedy had done in the last twenty-four hours to bring about a quick resolution.

Chapter 7

The forty-five-minute drive home from Bass Cove gave Maris a chance to wolf down two Taco Bueno burritos and prioritize the examinations, starting with those items most likely to tell her something about the killer and to either include or exclude Reed Wilson as a suspect. She'd examine the clothing that he was wearing when arrested and the flannel shirt, mechanic's rag, Bud can and hamburger wrapper from his car. Eager to start work, she glanced at the clock on the truck radio. Eleven-thirty. If there weren't too many interruptions, she could do a lot before she had to leave for Fort Worth. She hoped Lauren still planned to go.

As she passed the duplex, she noted Irene's white Grand

Cherokee parked out front already and wondered if it was a bad sign. After an appointment with her probation officer at nine-thirty, she was supposed to have a job interview scheduled across town. Maris wheeled into the drive for the lab half of the duplex and carried the evidence from Reed Wilson's Mustang inside. She checked her messages and returned two calls, one to an officer needing an interpretation of some lab results and the other to a prosecutor wanting to set court in January. After deactivating the alarm on her evidence vault, she found the paper sack with Reed Wilson's clothes. Before donning gloves and lab coat, she decided to make a quick trip inside to grab a drink of water and to check on Earnhardt and Irene.

The smell of cigarette smoke and whiskey hit her as soon as she cracked the sliding door. Irene hunkered on the floor between the sofa and the coffee table. With a cigarette dangling carelessly from one hand, she rocked back and forth, shaking her head over a picture album and the photos scattered around it. She swatted a crumpled piece of notebook paper and sent it skittering across the table in a cloud of ashes.

"Goddamn it." Maris stepped inside. "I thought that we'd agreed that you wouldn't —"

As Irene jumped and twisted to face her, she dropped her cigarette and knocked over the ice-and-whiskey-filled tumbler at her elbow in her haste to find it. Out of reflex, Maris rushed forward to upright the glass. She was taken aback when Irene scooted away from her.

Eyes wide with fear, she slurred, "Don't hurt me." She feverishly wiped the tears from her eyes, using her shirt sleeves, and continued to slide away until she collided with the brick hearth. "I swear I won't do it again."

"Don't worry about it." Maris bent, scooped the ice into the glass and stubbed out the burning cigarette. "I'll forgive you, honey, even if you are wasting good whiskey." Shaking her head, she hastened to the kitchen to grab a towel and found a half-empty fifth of Wild Turkey on the cabinet, top off. She screwed on the lid and returned to the living room.

Irene shakily rose to her feet and warily watched as

Maris soaked up the mess. She carried the towel to the kitchen sink, rinsed it out and grabbed a spray bottle with carpet cleaner. Until she finished scrubbing the damp spot and looked up, she didn't realize Irene had gone. Dropping to the edge of the sofa, she perused the picture albums and loose photos. Most of them were of Irene's daughter, Karin. The jingle of car keys caught her attention. She glanced up to see Irene, shoulders hunched, attempting to sneak down the hallway, keys in one hand, purse in the other. Maris moved to intercept her, catching her in the entryway.

"Where you going?" Maris grabbed her elbow.

"Don't hurt me." Irene's eyes darted nervously and she shrugged out of Maris's grasp.

"Quit saying that, damn it. I'm not going to hurt you. But you can't drive like this." Maris blocked her and crossed her arms. "Where do you need to go?"

Irene squared her shoulders belligerently but held the pose only a second before dissolving into tears. "I want to visit my baby."

"You mean visit the cemetery?"

Irene nodded and dabbed at her eyes.

Gently, Maris put an arm around her and reached for the keys in her hand. "Let's wait until the weekend, when Lauren can go with us."

"No!" She tried to pull away. "You don't understand."

"I understand that you're not in any condition to drive. Now give me those keys." She wrenched them out of Irene's hand and stuck them in her jeans pocket.

"Damn you." Irene lashed out at her, swinging wildly.

Maris ducked, stepped away and waited for the storm to dissipate. Suddenly, Irene froze and her hand flew to her mouth. She retched as she turned and stumbled, falling to one knee. Using the wall for balance, she righted herself and awkwardly make her way toward the bathroom. From the sound and the odor, Maris knew she didn't make it. Oh, God, she thought as her own stomach threatened rebellion. She closed her eyes and steeled herself to help Irene. The front door opened abruptly. She whirled and felt a surge of relief when she saw Lauren.

Her smile fading, Lauren wrinkled her nose. "Lord, Maris, what's going on?"

Irene gasped, and Lauren followed the sound.

Maris cleared her throat and called from the foyer, "Apparently Wild Turkey doesn't sit well with your sister this early in the day."

"Why? You were doing so well," Lauren said, talking to Irene. "Why this? Why now?"

Maris raised the window on the storm door and inhaled the fresh air. "When I found her, she was looking at Karin's pictures."

"Let's get you cleaned up and in bed." Maris heard Lauren say. In a louder voice, she called, "Come help me get her into the bathroom."

"I don't think I can right now."

"Don't tell me this makes you sick."

Maris stuck her head around the corner. "Okay. I won't." She returned to the fresh air.

"Oh, forevermore," Lauren said.

Between sobs, Irene said, "Don't be mad at me for fucking up."

"We'll talk about that later. Let's just get you cleaned up and in bed."

Irene's voice rose in anger, and Maris heard her bump against the wall. "Stay away from me. I don't need or want your help. What do you know anyway? Lauren, the perfect one." Yelling, she added, "Things were different for you. Everything was always better for you."

"Calm down. You're making a bigger mess," Lauren said. "You need a shower and change of clothes."

Maris shook her head. She didn't have time for this. Reluctantly, she turned from the window.

"Fuck you," Irene said, slurring her speech. "Poor little Lauren. Always having to clean up after her big sister. Who the fuck asked you?"

Maris rounded the corner in time to see Irene, her blouse and jeans saturated in foul liquid, shove Lauren. "All right, damn it, that's it." She grabbed Irene by the shirt collar and the belt loop of her jeans. She kicked and screamed as Maris dragged her through the entryway and into the front yard. Tossing her on the dead winter grass, Maris angrily connected the water hose to the faucet and turned the handle. Finding the open end, she stuck her finger in the flow of water. It was ice cold. " 'At'll do," she said.

Lauren came to her side. "What are you doing?"

Using her thumb, she directed the stream on Irene. "Stay out of this, Lauren."

Screaming obscenities, Irene struggled to rise. Balancing on one leg, Maris hooked the toe of her boot behind Irene's knee and tripped her. "Not until you're clean." When the water flowing from Irene's clothing and arms ran clear, Maris tossed the hose aside and shut off the water.

Lauren, her green eyes glinting with amusement, stood aside as Maris stomped by her and said to her sputtering sister, still prone on the grass. "I'll get you a towel."

As Maris wiped her boots on the welcome mat, Lauren rushed inside for a towel. She returning with a blue bath towel, and Maris took it from her. Pitching it to Irene, she said, "You're on your own there, bud. Do as you damned well please."

"You have her keys?" Lauren asked.

Maris grabbed her elbow and directed her to the house. "Yes. She's not going anywhere. But I don't have time to baby-sit a fucking drunk. She can, by God, take care of herself."

Lauren laughed as they entered the house and she pressed against Maris. "She certainly looks contrite after her cold shower." She kissed her cheek.

Maris glanced at her watch. "I've got to get some work done before we go to Fort Worth." She cocked her head. "Do you still want to go by the P.D. first?"

"Yes. I'd like to pick up the records on the rapes in 'ninety-one." Maris followed her into the kitchen, trying to ignore the odor from the living room. Lauren continued, "I talked to the Fort Worth detective this morning. Robin was more involved in that case than she let on when she called you." She bent under the sink to get the cleaning supplies. "She was the lead prosecutor and very outspoken to the press. Even if those assaults aren't related to the Bass Cove murders, I may reopen the investigation. See if I can do anything." She shrugged.

Trailing water, Irene ran through the living room and fled down the hall.

"I was supposed to work with Sally this afternoon." Lauren sighed. "But I'll call her, tell her what happened and take the rest of the afternoon off to clean up this mess." She smiled. "And yes, I still want to go to Fort Worth with you."

"Good." They heard water running in Irene's shower. Maris grinned. "I'm going back to the lab. Don't be babying her. Make her take care of herself."

Lauren tilted her head and frowned. "What do you think she meant . . . 'things were always better for me?' "

"Don't put stock in a drunk's bullshit." Maris held her breath and adverted her eyes as she crossed to the lab.

Maris's anger gradually disappeared as she examined Reed Wilson's black Marilyn Manson T-shirt and trousers. Since the dark color of the cloth made finding the bloodstains difficult, she turned off the lights and sprayed the back of the shirt and the jeans with the Luminol reagent. No blood was detected on the back of the shirt, but an area on the back of the right trouser leg glowed. She quickly photographed it since the chemical reaction was short-lived and circled it with chalk. The stain did not appear to be a spatter but a wipe mark. Large areas of blood covered the stomach area of the T-shirt, and some spatters were on the front of the trousers. After taking more pictures and circling the bloodstains, she turned on the lights and drew up a stool to record her observations. The stains were all consistent with Wilson's injuries. When he cut his hand, he wiped it across the back of his leg. When he realized how serious it was, he held it tight against his stomach until he could find something to bind it, probably the red mechanic's rag that she'd found in the Mustang. Even the spatters on the front of the trousers were consistent with blood dripping from the wound. She cut out samples for further analysis but suspected all of the blood was Reed's.

She processed the rag, the Budweiser can and hamburger wrapper from the Mustang and then opened the sack from Aubrey P.D. Carefully, she drew out a plastic evidence bag with a triangular piece of jagged glass about five inches long at the base. Luckily the blood adhering to the glass was dry, or it might have ruined in the plastic evidence bag.

The lab doorbell announced Chief Kenedy's arrival with the items taken from the bodies of the three girls during autopsy. Looking around the lab, he stroked his mustache while she filled out the paperwork.

Maris scanned the submission form. "Good. You brought blood from the victims."

He nodded. "And the broken tip from the murder weapon. They found it buried in Lynette's sternum."

"If we find the shears, I can fit the pieces back together. Makes damned good evidence."

"We'll get 'em." He paced the floor between her desk and the table she used to receive evidence and watched as she finished the submission forms. On his way out, he asked, "How can you stand it in here without windows? I'm too claustrophobic. I couldn't take it."

After he left, she returned to the blood samples. Thanks to Irene, she had only enough time to start the anti-humans on the stains from Reed's car to determine if the blood was human in origin. Although it seemed a given in most instances, she had to prove it. Then she'd start her extractions for DNA-typing and let them set overnight. She heard a knock and saw Lauren smiling at the glass sliding door. She held up a glass of red liquid over ice. Maris let her in.

"Thought you might be thirsty for a Big Red."

Stripping off her gloves, Maris noticed she held a piece of crumpled paper. She washed her hands and took the glass. "A beer would be better, but I can wait."

As Lauren pulled up a lab stool, Maris dropped into her desk chair and sipped the drink. "What's that?" She pointed to Lauren's hand.

"I think it's what sent Irene on a drinking spree." Lauren gave the paper to Maris.

"I'm not sure it takes much." Maris leaned back. "How is she anyway?"

"Fine. She's sleeping it off. The cold water out of the hose may not have changed her blood alcohol level, but it sure altered her attitude."

"Good." She chuckled. "I hope she doesn't get pneumonia." She absently smoothed the wrinkles out of the notebook paper as she scanned it. The note was handwritten in sharply slanted cursive letters using a bold-tipped red marker. The blood-red ink matched the venom in the words written with a religious fervor that vacillated from a plea for redemption to a promise of damnation. She groaned when she reached the signature. "Brian Blake," she said. "I should have recognized his style."

She remembered the tattooed teenager in a hospital bed, spewing forth his own version of Revelation. It was his references to the 'blood of the goat' and 'the hand of Satan in the form of the Ram' and ramblings about 'the mother of the harlot' washing the altar 'free of her daughter's sin' that alerted her to what really happened to Lauren's niece, Karin, and to the threat against Irene. She touched the scar on her cheek, a souvenir from Brian.

"I should have killed that bastard when I had the chance." Maris handed the note back to Lauren. "How'd he get this to her?"

"I called her probation officer. Brian mailed the note to the prison, and they forwarded it after some discussion. Do you think it's a threat?"

"I think you can read anything you want into that

garbage." Maris took a drink. "It could be interpreted as a threat or as Brian's brand of forgiveness. Is he still in the loony bin?"

"I don't know yet." Lauren folded the paper. "But I plan to find out."

She looked at the far wall, and Maris saw concern in her expression.

Lauren cleared her throat. "I asked her what she meant . . . about my having it easier. She said to forget it. It didn't mean anything. Only it's not the first time she's told me that."

"Older children always think the younger ones have it easier."

"I don't know if that's all it is."

Maris drained her glass and stood. "I've got to get busy if we're going to Cowtown." She kissed Lauren's neck, and Lauren embraced her. Maris lifted her chin. "Think I can interest you in some Mexican food and a margarita or two."

"I wouldn't miss it for the world." Lauren twirled the end of her hair and smiled mischievously. "I thought you might be nervous about introducing me to Shannon . . . finally."

"And why would I be nervous about that?" Maris cocked her head.

"Most women are when they introduce their lover to their other girlfriend," Lauren said.

"Not nearly as nervous as introducing a girlfriend to the other lover."

"You have experience with this?" Lauren nuzzled her neck.

"Nope. Just speculating." Maris kissed her. "Besides that's not nearly as nerve-racking as introducing my lover to a friend who is almost full term into her pregnancy."

"It's not catching."

"No." Maris looked into her eyes. "But maternal instinct is."

Lauren had hinted that she wanted to have a baby before she left for her ten-month internship in offender-psychological profiling with the FBI and the University of Virginia. Maris held her breath, not quite believing that she'd brought up the subject she'd been dreading since Lauren's return.

After a moment, Lauren patted Maris's chest. "I'm only thirty-one," she said. "I don't have to decide today." She pecked Maris on the cheek and, with a wave, slipped away.

Maris stood, unsure if she should be relieved or worried.

Chapter 8

"Damn it, Lauren." Maris, dressed in starched and creased black Wranglers, a pink oxford shirt and a charcoal Western-style jacket, slammed the refrigerator door harder than she'd intended. "She drank my last fucking beer again. You'd think if she could buy herself a fifth of Wild Turkey, she could at least buy me a six-pack." All afternoon she'd looked forward to a beer.

Lauren stepped in front of her. "I wish you wouldn't slam the door." She opened the refrigerator and pulled out a lower drawer. "Here." She twisted the cap off of the bottle and handed Maris a Miller Lite. "I hid you a couple in the vegetable bin. Now quit your whining."

After taking a sip of her beer, Maris grinned. "I'm not whining."

"Yes, you are." Lauren put her hands on her hips.

She pulled Lauren closer. "Butches don't whine; they bitch."

"I'll have to think about that." Lauren kissed her and darted away. "I'm almost ready. All I have to do is finish my makeup."

"Good thing there were two beers in that drawer." For Lauren, finishing her makeup usually meant brushing her hair, changing her blouse two or three times while agonizing over which of her nine hundred pairs of shoes to wear. It was a wonder Irene found a place to put her clothes. She hoped Lauren didn't change again. She liked the deep V-neck on the beige sweater and the soft, crumpled material, especially with her tight jeans and new black suede boots with silver buckles and two-inch heels.

"Come talk to me while I get ready." Lauren took Maris's arm. "After Irene's stunt this afternoon, I've been thinking that we need to make some changes." She led her down the hallway into the bathroom and began applying her eyeliner. "As long as she's not working, she needs to do more around the house. Maybe take over the grocery shopping." She paused. In her reflection in the mirror, Maris saw her cock an eyebrow. "Especially since you won't do it."

"I do when I have time." She squared her shoulders defensively.

"I think the groceries are like the laundry..." Lauren resumed applying her eye makeup.

"And how's that?" Maris leaned against the wall and flashed a grin.

"When I'm here, you forget how to do it."

Maris laughed. She'd argue, if it wasn't true.

"Now don't get angry, but —"

"I hate it when you start out that way." Maris shifted her stance restlessly.

"I haven't even told you yet." Lauren put the finishing touches on her hair and picked up the can of hair spray.

Maris retreated to the hallway as the can hissed. Lauren hastily put on her lipstick. "I'm ready," she said. She caught Maris's hand. "I'm going to ask Irene to start looking for a bigger house for us."

"I can't afford a bigger house. And I didn't think Irene was going to be with us that long."

"You and I can afford a bigger house if we buy it together. And you've said yourself that the lab is getting cramped with all the new automated equipment you've added. You don't really have the space to add an evidence tech or another chemist when you do decide to hire one."

Maris rubbed her chin thoughtfully. After she lost Mary Ann to cancer, she'd bought the duplex and converted one half of it into the lab. It'd been perfect for her and Earnhardt, close quarters when Lauren moved in and damned near crowded with Irene. "If we bought another house, I could expand the lab into the living room and guest bedroom and still keep the kitchen, a bathroom and bedroom."

"It'd give you a place to clean up and rest when you've had to work all night."

"I'd hoped to put it off a little longer, but what the hell —" Maris shrugged. She went into the kitchen to get the second beer while Lauren put on her gun and grabbed her purse.

From the living room, Lauren called out, "We can put together a list of requirements, and Irene can help us look. After all, she has more time than either of us."

Maris caught up with her and slipped an arm around her waist. "Some people say it's bad luck to buy a house together."

"Some people say it's bad luck to have your picture taken together —" She glanced down at the pager stuck in her waistband. "Oh, damn. I better answer that."

Feeling vaguely uneasy yet unable to define a reason, Maris stepped out on the front porch. Although it was almost four-thirty and nearly dark, it was warm for December, and she found it difficult to believe it had been so miserable Wednesday, only two nights ago. She heard laughter and walked to the end of the porch to watch the kids across the street. Two girls, about thirteen or so, practiced cheerleading drills while a younger one mocked them and brandished a water pistol.

"Let's go." Lauren kissed her on the cheek.

Grinning, Maris pointed across the street. "Watch this. We're fixing to see family violence break out before our very eyes."

The little one blasted the cheerleaders with a couple of short bursts of water, and the race was on. She eluded the enraged older girls by climbing a mimosa tree.

Lauren hooked her arm through Maris's. "I didn't think you liked kids."

"Well, I like this one." She chuckled. "She reminds me of me at that age."

Lauren said nothing, but Maris saw a slight smile playing on the corner of her lips. Her pager went off again, and she threw up her hands. "Now what?"

Maris continued to watch the kids until Lauren called her inside. "We may have a break in the case." Her green eyes flashed with excitement. "Sally found a receipt in Jill's purse for gas and a Dr. Pepper from Parmer's, the gas station just south of the pet salon. The date and time on the receipt puts Jill there on Wednesday afternoon, shortly before she was due back to pick up her sister. A former employee of Starr's Pet Salon told Sally that Kyle Parmer, the station owner's son, used to sneak in the back door while they cleaned the kennels and watered the animals. She was afraid of him, but Jennifer Kerr sometimes let him help with the dogs. Sally says he's about twenty-one, but seems younger due to brain damage he suffered in a bike accident as a kid. He can drive, and he works for his dad, pumping gas and doing some mechanical work. When she and Kenedy went to the station to interview him this afternoon, they learned that he hasn't been to work since the murders. He told his dad he was sick."

"Sounds like someone to talk to." Maris tore the label on her half-full beer.

"When they picked him up for questioning, he had what

looks like bloodstains on his shoes." She touched Maris's arm. "Little Ricky is bringing them here to the lab. If they test positive for human blood, we're going to get a search warrant for his apartment."

Maris nodded. "I'll call Shannon and tell her we'll have to see her another day."

Lauren frowned. "Sally is concerned. She likes Kyle and finds it hard to believe that he could hurt anyone, much less do something like this."

About nine-thirty Friday night, a steady rain fell as Maris drove into the potholed parking lot of Parmer Auto Parts. Owned by Kyle's uncle, it was located two blocks east of Parmer's Automotive Service. A rusted metal sign, showing a can of Pennzoil and a seventies vintage racecar, swung precariously, attached to the post by one stubborn bolt. Making a wide arc, she whipped the truck around the yellow-and-black wrecker and backed between Sally Trent's beige Chevy Caprice and Chief Kenedy's blue Bass Cove police car. Sally and Kenedy waited under the awning of the closed auto parts store next to two men that Maris didn't recognize. She assumed one was Wylie Parmer, Kyle's dad. The chief, in a heavy coat, puffed on a cigarette and paced. Sally pointed to the set of rickety wooden stairs leading to the small second-story apartment over the parts store. Maris lowered the tailgate and gathered her investigation kits. Once Rick had arrived with Parmer's bloodstained odorous shoes, it'd taken her only an hour and a half to confirm the presence of human blood, giving Sally and Kenedy the basis for a search warrant.

Lauren parked her Taurus nearby. Dodging mud puddles, she ran to help Maris, wearing black five-pocket trousers and a black windbreaker with *Federal Agent* across the back. The downpour continued as Maris handed equipment to her and Sally and tried to protect her 35 millimeter camera with the electronic flash attached. She closed the tailgate, and they raced up the fragile staircase. The small overhang on the tiny wooden porch offered little protection from the rain.

"Thanks for coming," Sally said. "Both of you."

"I was surprised Kenedy wanted me here." Lauren shifted Maris's investigation kit to her other hand.

"He's coming around." Sally smiled. "I convinced him that having the FBI more involved would take some of the heat from the press off us."

"Gee, thanks. That explains all the calls I've been getting." She shivered.

"I also told him that as the profile coordinator you needed to be present for the search and to see Kyle's living quarters. So you could complete the VICAP report and help us figure out the best approach for questioning him."

"True enough," Lauren said.

"Who are the other guys?" Maris asked.

"Wylie Parmer, the dad, and Kyle's uncle. The uncle owns the parts store and lets Kyle live in this apartment." Sally shook her head. "Wylie's a pretty good guy. The S.O. uses his wrecker service. He's cooperating with the investigation and asked to be here. We agreed as a courtesy."

"Where's Kyle?" Lauren asked.

"Holding cell at the S.O."

The porch shook as Kenedy and Wylie climbed the stairs. Sally joked that the tiny wooden porch might not hold them all as Kenedy fished a key out of his pocket. "Kyle's," he said, showing it to Wylie. Over his shoulder, he hastily introduced Maris and Lauren to Wylie and added, "I ordered Rick to wait in his car and watch the front."

A barrel-chested man with a bull-like neck, Wylie shook first Lauren's hand and then Maris's. She read worry and concern in his eyes as his callused grip swallowed hers.

The odor of a dirty cat box, rotting food and trash hit as soon as the chief opened the door and stood aside, letting them enter first. Maris, Lauren and Sally set the investigation kits, camera and other equipment inside the doorway of the tiny loft apartment. Maris kicked an aluminum pail aside while searching for the light switch and felt water hit her cheek. A cat squeezed between her legs, and she heard the mewing of kittens.

"The roof leaks," she said. She flipped on all the light switches she could find.

Sally checked the apartment for other occupants. "It's empty, if you don't count roaches and cats and . . . bacteria."

"God," Lauren said. "I don't care if it is raining. We're leaving the door open."

Maris righted the pail under the drip and, hands on her hips, scanned the room. One large open area contained the living area, kitchen and dining room. An opening between an ancient Kenmore refrigerator and a yellow Formica-topped table led to a short hallway with a tiny bathroom on one side and the only bedroom on the other. Light fixtures were nonexistent, and the glare from the naked bulbs fell harshly on a dilapidated green armchair and matching sofa. The sofa sagged and leaned perceptibly on one end. An RCA nineteen-inch color television, Sony videocassette recorder and stereo rested against the far wall on shelves made of black spray-painted boards stacked on cinder blocks. Empty Dr Pepper cans, McDonald's and Taco Bell wrappers littered rusty TV trays alongside crumpled Camel cigarette packs and ashtrays made of old vegetable cans. Dirty dishes and glasses of every color and style overflowed the sink. *Superman* and *Batman* comic books, catalogs, *Playboy* and *Penthouse*, and other raunchier pornographic magazines spilled from the sofa onto the floor and were stacked four-feet high in the corner. Scantily clad, big-titted women smiled at them from faded auto-parts calendars thumb-tacked to the wall.

Standing in the threshold, Wylie twisted his cap between his beefy hands and shook his head. "I had no idea this place had gotten so bad." His voice quivered. "When his mother was well, she helped him clean. Did his laundry. She's too sick and . . ." He looked down. "I don't have the time. He told me he was doing okay. Taking care of things. I believed him. You know, we tried to respect his privacy."

Kenedy strode through the apartment, hands stuck deep in his pockets. He paused near the magazines and began flipping through them.

"I haven't photographed anything yet," Maris said.

He shot her a dirty look and dropped the magazine. "Why don't we wait outside?" He nodded to Wylie. "They can handle the search."

"I didn't even know he had a cat," Wylie said as he waited in the doorway for Kenedy. "Why didn't he tell us about the leaks? My brother and I would have fixed the roof."

To Sally, Kenedy said. "If you find anything, let us know."

"Sure," Sally said.

"I'm glad the bastard thinks we can handle a search," Maris mumbled to Lauren.

"Behave," she said. The yellow-striped mother cat rubbed against her leg. "She acts hungry."

"They care more about Kyle than to let him live like this," Sally said, "if they knew."

Maris squatted and opened her investigation kit. "Hope everyone's tetanus shots are up to date." She handed out latex gloves. "I'd double-glove. Tyvek suits and booties are in that box."

"Good idea," Sally said. "Let me have your camera, and I'll start taking pics."

Maris slipped the camera from her neck and handed it to Sally. Opening a notebook, she jotted down the time, address and some initial observations.

Sally returned. "Need more film," she said.

"What's it look like back there?" Maris handed her some film and slipped into a Tyvek suit and pulled on booties. She gloved up and waited as Lauren did the same.

Sally loaded the camera and set it aside to pull on a suit and gloves. "Nasty," she said. "Don't even ask about the bedsheets or the bathroom."

Using the corner, Maris peeled back the centerfold of a magazine on the sofa. A well-endowed blonde, on her hands

71

and knees, peeked over her shoulder as she spread her cheeks. Despite her disgust, Maris found something sad about a brain-damaged kid masturbating on a worn-out, filthy couch and dreaming about a woman like that. "We better get a photo of this."

"Yeah," Sally said. "I imagine we need to catalog his taste in porno."

"And take any that depict rape or other violence," Lauren added. "I'll search through these nasty things, and I guess I'd better check the videotapes." She dropped to her knees near the stack of magazines.

Sally and Maris decided to start in the back and work their way forward. They stripped the crusty, dirty sheets from the bed. Maris raised the mattress so Sally could search between it and box springs.

"His dad and uncle ought to burn everything in here, except the stereo and television, and start over." Sally reached for something under a corner of the mattress. "What's this?" She pulled out a colorful tin Christmas box that originally contained a Mary-of-Puddin-Hill fruitcake and popped the lid.

Maris looked inside. "Marijuana, assorted paraphernalia and..." She lifted a piece of foil paper and struggled to open it with her gloves on. She worked a flap loose. "Heroin capsules."

Sally's voice dripped in sarcasm. "As if this kid's not brain-damaged enough."

Lauren walked into the bedroom holding a magazine. "Look at this." She pointed to a series of black-and-white photographs depicting a nude, flat-chested woman, clean-shaven in the pubic area, legs spread.

"Where he got the idea?" Sally asked.

"Could be," Lauren said. "I'll bag it for evidence."

Maris dropped to her knees and searched under the bed with a flashlight, but found nothing except more trashy magazines, comic books and empty fast-food containers.

Lauren returned and helped sort a pile of grease-stained T-shirts, yellowed underwear and stiff towels, tossing them on the bed. "So far, despite his criminal housekeeping and taste in porno, I've seen nothing to link him to the murders."

"Yeah," Maris said. "No pants with a tear or other clothes with blood. No broken shears."

"Guys, in here," Sally called from the bathroom.

Maris heard excitement in her voice. She and Lauren found her standing near the dirty-clothes hamper built into the wall under the linen closet. Using her ink pen, she held up a bloodstained pair of shears with a broken tip. "Bingo," she said. "Found them here with the kittens." She squatted.

Maris dropped to one knee. The mother cat cut between her, and Sally and stood over five kittens, about ten days old, as they crawled through some soiled clothing. Maris reached for the kittens, and the cat hissed. "She doesn't want us messing with her babies."

Sally spoke into the radio clipped to her belt and requested a cage from animal control. "Maybe Kyle's dad will take them, so we don't have to send them to the pound."

Rick answered and said that Kenedy was going after the cage.

An earsplitting report shook the tiny apartment, rattling the window. Rain pounded the roof, and a leak sprang in the hallway over Lauren's head. She jumped and shrieked when the cold water dripped on her cheek. "That was eerie." She handed Maris a box, lined with a towel. "For the kittens."

Maris kept the mother at bay while Sally caught the kittens and placed them in the box. They tried to catch the mother, but she bolted and fled. They decided to try again later, and Lauren carried the box and kittens out of the way. Sally lifted a bloodstained towel from the bottom of the bin and handed it to Maris. The towel appeared to have cut pubic hairs and animal hair stuck to it. She looked at the label. "Same brand and style as the towels from Starr's."

Sally sat on the floor. "Hand me the camera. There're some jeans and a shirt in there."

Lauren brought her the camera. After taking a couple of

photographs, Sally handed Maris a stiff pair of jeans. Twisting the leg, she saw a jagged tear in the right knee. Dark stains soaked the ragged fibers. Fingerlike streaks ran up the front of both thighs.

"Two days," Sally said. "We got him in two days." She groaned. "But I never thought it'd be Kyle Parmer."

Maris bent and spread the legs of the jeans against her side. She held the beam of the flashlight on the jeans and her heart pounded. The jeans lacked the cast-off blood spatters consistent with swinging a pair of bloody shears. She straightened the blue T-shirt that Sally handed her. *Property of Dallas Cowboys* was on the front in cracked white letters. Heavy blood smears and wipe marks covered the front. She turned it to look at the back. No blood. Kyle Parmer could not have been swinging the bloody shears, not if he was wearing that shirt or pair of jeans. "Maybe he had an overcoat," she mumbled.

"What?" Sally struggled to her feet. "Damn, my leg went to sleep." She stomped her foot to restore the circulation. "That's all that's in here."

Maris explained the blood spatters to Sally and Lauren. "These stains could be from kneeling in the blood, wiping his hand or brushing up against something, but they are not cast-off patterns from wielding the shears."

Sally frowned and Lauren said. "We better start looking for an overcoat or something."

Lauren and Sally searched every drawer, cabinet, closet, cardboard box and other likely hiding place in the apartment while Maris secured and tagged the evidence they'd already discovered.

"Nothing," Sally said. Hands on her hips, she surveyed the apartment.

"I need some air." Lauren walked to the door. "What now?" she asked.

Sally peeled off her gloves. "We need to search the alleys between here and the pet salon again for a coat or some other garment."

"I'll ask the father if Kyle has a coat missing." Lauren jotted in her notebook. She sighed. "He fits the profile for a disorganized killer. He's a loner. Socially immature, probably due to his childhood head injury. Likely sexually incompetent —" She rolled her eyes. "At least with real women. He lives or works near the crime scene . . ." Her eyes brightened. "When we question him, maybe we should confront him with the shears. Before you take them back to the lab." Lauren put her fingers to her chin thoughtfully. "Could we put them in a plastic bag?"

"Sure. A little while won't hurt it. The blood is dry anyway." She rummaged through her investigation kit. "Here's a good Kapak bag." Maris put the shears inside after all three of them had inscribed their initials in the metal using one of Maris's tools.

Still wearing the white Tyvek suits and the slippery booties, Maris and Sally risked running down the hazardous staircase to keep her equipment and the evidence as dry as possible.

When Maris returned, Lauren asked, "Would you mind hanging around the S.O. while we show Kyle the shears? That way you can maintain official custody and keep the chain simpler."

"To be near you, my dear, I'd do anything." Maris bent and swept her hand gallantly.

"You're so full of shit," Lauren said, but her green eyes sparkled.

"I assume the search warrant covers biological samples from Kyle," Maris asked.

Sally appeared in the door. "Guess that's the last of it. Let's take one more look around before we go." She stomped her wet feet. "About Kyle's blood sample. It's part of the warrant the judge signed."

"Is there a way to get it tonight?" Maris asked.

"Sure. There's a staff nurse on duty at the jail on Friday and Saturday nights. She can draw the blood. She does for DWI cases."

After they walked the apartment one more time to make sure they missed nothing, Maris picked up the plastic bag that she'd set aside for any trash they generated and their worn Tyvek suits and booties. "Strip, ladies, and I'll take your suits," Maris said as she stepped out of hers.

"She always this romantic?" Sally asked. She leaned against the doorjamb to peel off the protective gear.

Lauren laughed. "Usually she says please."

"No. Usually I'm on my knees begging." Maris grinned and winked at Sally. After collecting the used gloves and suits, she tied the bag, and they waited for Kenedy to bring the cage. When he arrived they showed him the shears and told him about the clothing they'd discovered. By then, the mother cat had calmed enough for Lauren to catch her and put her and the kittens in the cage. Sally gathered all of the cat food that Kyle had in the apartment, placed it in a plastic grocery bag and tied it to the top of the cage. Kenedy carried it down the stairs to Wylie Parmer, who agreed to take care of his son's pets. Maris waited in the truck for Sally to secure the apartment and to string police tape. Rick and some of the other boys were going to spend a long night keeping the curious and the press away once word got out about Kyle Parmer's arrest.

Chapter 9

Clutching a plastic foam cup in one hand and the bag
with the bloody shears in the other, Maris sipped her hot
coffee and leaned against the pale green cinder-block wall
that framed the smoky, one-way mirror of the Bass County
S.O. interrogation room. An institutional-style clock, a stark
pine table, three folding chairs and a mirror mounted in the
corner, pointing at Kyle Parmer's back and the door,
provided the only decor in the bunkerlike room with ashen
walls. Kyle, clad in a white jail jumpsuit with his hands
cuffed in front, sat bolt upright when Sally Trent and Chief
Kenedy strode into the room. Sally nodded to him and
pulled out a chair. She pushed aside the notebook and pen
on the table and clasped her hands, resting them in front of

her, and spoke earnestly. Her words were wasted. Kyle, mouth agape, never took his eyes from Chief Kenedy who paced from one end of the room to another, popping his gum and snapping the safety catch on his holster.

Maris cursed under her breath. Lauren should be handling the interrogation with Sally, not Kenedy, but she'd spent the last hour and a half talking to Wylie Parmer while they officially arrested Kyle and booked him into jail.

Lauren ducked into the observation room. "How's it going?"

"Just started. You need to get Kenedy out of there," Maris said. "The kid is too distracted by his theatrics to state his name." She glanced at her watch, noting it was almost one a.m.

"The sheriff is going to make a news release shortly." Lauren observed for a moment. "I called the girls' parents and told them we made an arrest. I wanted them to hear it from us first." She sighed. "God, it's a relief to have him in custody."

Maris pressed her shoulder against Lauren's. "I thought we'd get him . . . but not this soon."

Lauren leaned into her. She gazed at Kyle. "He looks so . . . inadequate." Shaking her head, she turned away from the window and crossed her arms. "I think I'll convince the sheriff to invite Chief Kenedy to the press conference."

"Very diplomatic."

With obvious disgust, Lauren lifted a grimy receiver from a nearby wall and punched the sheriff's extension. She spoke to him briefly and cradled the phone. "Guess I'll tell Kenedy his audience awaits. Then I can help Sally."

In a nonthreatening tone, Sally explained to Kyle the charges against him and added that their conversation was being recorded. She reiterated that Kyle didn't have to talk to them, had a right to an attorney and could stop the questioning anytime. Sipping her coffee, Maris wondered if the courts would find the kid mentally competent.

Lauren said, "They're having trouble finding a lawyer. None of the local boys want it."

"I can imagine," Maris said. "The lawyers have to live and work in this community. Their kids went to school with the victims. They'd be vilified if they did their job too well."

"The judge may have to order an attorney to take it unless the family comes up with one."

"Someone who wants the notoriety will jump on this case sooner or later." Maris drank the last of her coffee and set the cup on a nearby table. "What's Kyle's dad say?"

"I asked him if Kyle had an overcoat missing. Wylie said the only coat Kyle owned was the one he was wearing when arrested. It's a waist-length ski jacket, and Sally and Kenedy didn't notice any blood on it. About Kyle's mental capacity, Mr. Parmer says that he's good at handling his gas station duties and repairing small engines. He can drive, but his dad helps with his finances."

"From the looks of his apartment, it's questionable whether he can take care of himself."

"His father was embarrassed about that. Said he'd allowed the boy —" Lauren frowned as she stared through the one-way glass. "I keep calling him a boy, but he's twenty-one. He allowed him to read *Playboy* and *Penthouse* as a sexual outlet. Kyle had one girlfriend briefly before he dropped out of high school, but his father doubts that he's ever been intimate with a woman. He was surprised about the raunchier material. About the apartment, Mrs. Parmer used to clean it and take care of his clothes, but she hasn't been able to since September, due to complications from her diabetes." Lauren sighed. "I think Mr. and Mrs. Parmer have done the best they could with him." She pushed away from the window. "The D.A. says to expect a mental competency hearing to determine if he can knowingly understand and waive his constitutional rights and if he's capable of assisting in his own defense. All we can do is Mirandize him, keep accurate records of all that is said to or by him and proceed with the questioning until he refuses to talk or demands an attorney. If he confesses, we'll have to provide evidence of his condition and demeanor at that time." She gestured, palms up. "Then it'll be up to the courts whether to accept the confession. We'll have done all we can do."

Maris watched as Sally, proceeding slowly and trying to establish a rapport, assured Kyle that his parents had agreed to take care of the cat and kittens.

"Does it ever make you feel strange to hold a murder weapon?" Lauren touched the bag Maris was holding with the shears.

"No." When Lauren looked at her quizzically, she added, "Not anymore."

Lauren frowned thoughtfully as she moved to the door. "Now that they've covered the legal necessities, I'm going to get Troy Dan out of there. Then Sally or I will motion for you when it's time to bring the shears in."

Maris smiled. It was the first time she'd heard Lauren call him that. Maris moved over until she could see Lauren's reflection in the mirror as she entered the room. Her image expanded and contracted wildly in the mirror as she approached the table. Without a word to Sally, she motioned for Kenedy to follow her outside. Kyle's gaze chased them out of the room.

Sally maintained her earnest yet calm posture. "You have many girlfriends, Kyle?"

He averted his eyes. "No."

"Maybe you get lonely sometimes." Sally placed her hands flat on the table.

He squirmed in the chair and shrugged.

"I think you were more than lonely. Lynette, Jennifer and Jill were all good-looking women. Which one was your favorite?"

"Jennifer." Kyle's eyes flashed. "She liked me."

"What about Lynette? Did you like her?"

"Sometimes."

"Only sometimes. Were you angry with her, Kyle?"

Maris heard a knock on the interrogation room door in confusing stereo from outside the observation area and through the speaker system. Glancing up at the mirror, Maris saw the deformed reflection of a nurse enter the room. A silver-haired woman in faded jeans and a nurse's smock with colorful balloons and Teddy bears came into sight. Wearing ordinary, white athletic shoes, she strode

80

purposely to the table and plopped down a purple plastic tray with blood-taking supplies.

Kyle squared his shoulders and straightened in the chair; his eyes widened as the nurse snapped on a pair of gloves. When she grabbed a rubber tourniquet and Vacu-tainer, he screamed and bolted, knocking over his chair. Slamming against the back wall, he felt his way across, touching each brick as if searching for a hidden door. When he hit a deadend, he pressed his nose into the corner and slumped to his knees. Sally raced around the table.

"Shit," Maris said. She rushed the short distance to the interrogation room. Sally and the nurse stood uncertainly a couple yards away from Kyle. "Wait," Maris said. "It's okay. We can get my samples another way."

Kyle curled his body and burrowed deeper against the wall.

Maris pitched the plastic bag with the shears on the table and rummaged through the nurse's tray, taking a tongue depressor and a clean urine specimen bottle. She pushed the tray into the nurse's arms and shooed her out of the room. Trying to appear casual, she slipped into the chair next to Sally's. "Both of you, come back," she said. "We don't have to take blood. Kyle, the nurse is gone."

"It's okay." Sally lifted him by the elbow.

"Come sit down," Maris said. "I know another way."

Kyle shook, rattling his handcuffs, and stared at her.

"Relax," Maris said. "This is easy." She handed him the tongue depressor. "Too bad it doesn't taste like a Tootsie Roll Pop."

"I like Tootsie Roll Pops." He wiped a tear from his eye and took the stick.

"Gently scrap the inside of your mouth. Not hard. You don't need to draw blood."

His handcuffs clinked as he rubbed the inside of his jaw with the stick.

"A little more. That's it." She took the stick from him, broke off the used half and dropped it into the specimen bottle.

Then he saw the shears and froze.

"Yes. We know about those. We found them in your apartment." Sally pointed a finger at him. "It's time we talked seriously."

Maris started to rise, but Sally nodded for her to stay. "Do you know who she is?"

Kyle shook his head.

"She's a scientist. By analyzing the blood on those shears, she's going to tell us where it came from. We also have other evidence. In fact, Kyle, from the results of our investigation, it's clear that you're responsible for killing those three girls."

"No." His eyes cut to his lower left, and he blinked rapidly.

"Can you think of any other reason why your fingerprints were found inside Starr's Pet Salon?" Sally, her palms flat, leaned on the table.

Although it could have been a bluff, Maris suspected that Sally told the truth. Shirley Grimes, the Bass County ID tech, had found dozens of prints that she couldn't identify. They must have sent Kyle's to her as soon as he was booked at the jail.

His eyelids drooped, and he stared at his cuffed hands. "I didn't do it."

Maris could barely hear him.

"You only liked Lynette sometimes. Was it because she wouldn't be your girlfriend?"

He didn't answer.

"You wanted her for a girlfriend, didn't you?" Sally drew circles on the table with her finger. "You wanted to be with her. To have sex with her. Only she wouldn't have anything to do with you. You were angry." She leaned forward. "I know what it's like to be lonely."

Kyle's face reddened. "I didn't like Lynette. She was mean to me." He stared at the wall. "Not like the others."

"The others?" Sally leaned back in her chair and stretched out her legs. "Jennifer and Jill?" she asked softly.

"Jennifer. She didn't laugh at me." His eyes brightened and the corner of his mouth twitched. "I went with her once to change a flat on Jill's horse trailer. We brought it back to the shop, and I fixed it good. When we took it back, she was hungry so we stopped to eat, and she bought me a hamburger. She treated me real good."

Quietly, Lauren came into the room and sat at the end of the table to Sally's right. Kyle gawked at her until Sally cleared her throat. "But you were angry at Lynette?" Sally asked.

"She wouldn't let me fuck her." His chest caved, and he slumped dejectedly.

"Kyle," Lauren said. She introduced herself to him and clarified her presence for the tape recording. "I have a theory."

Maris knew what was coming. Lauren intended to provide Kyle with a rationalization of the crime to lessen his guilt and provide an excuse he could embrace, making it easier for him to confess.

"You know, I think you only wanted to be accepted . . . to be friends with the girls. But it was so hard, the way they sometimes laughed at you. Made fun of you."

Kyle's attention never left Lauren. His eyes softened and moistened.

She continued, "But Lynette was worse. She teased you. Made you think she wanted you but then pushed you away. Is that what happened?"

"She was mean to me." He wiggled, opening his legs wider.

Maris interpreted this to mean he was warming to Lauren's line of questioning.

"You had to be very frustrated, so you went to see her at the pet salon — just to talk to Lynette. But something happened. Did this happen on the spur of the moment?"

He trembled. Shaking his head slowly at first and then more vigorously, he said, "I didn't kill them."

Sally tapped the table. "Just a minute, Kyle. There is no question from our investigation that you were in that pet salon."

Kyle's eyes narrowed.

"Why don't you tell us what happened?" Lauren asked.

He tensed, and a vein in the side of his neck throbbed visibly. Yet when he finally answered, his voice was soft. "Satan did it," he said.

"You mean Satan made you do it?" Sally said.

"No. Satan did it."

"Can you read and write?" Lauren asked.

"Yes."

She took the notebook and pencil on the table and walked to his side. "Do you remember Deputy Trent telling you that you don't have to talk to us?"

"Yes." He squared his shoulders and looked up at her.

"If we take off the cuffs, would you write something for us?"

He nodded. "Can I have a Coke?"

Sally said, "Sure."

Maris jumped up. "I'll get it."

When she returned with the drink in a plastic cup, his cuffs were off and he held the pen. She handed him the soft drink, and he gulped it noisily.

"Can you write your name and the date?" Lauren asked. He nodded and complied after asking the date. "You don't have to do this if you don't want to," she added.

"I don't mind." He took a sip of Coke.

"You said that 'Satan did it.' Can you write that?"

Sticking his tongue between his lips in concentration, he printed *Satin did it.*

Lauren smiled. "Very good. Now write out these words in a sentence as I call them out to you." Slowly, with a pause between each word, she said, "Satan lives and kill the whores." Smiling at him, she added, "Very good. Now try 'Merry fucking Christmas and welcome to my hell.' "

When he finished, she took the pen and pad. "We have to put the cuffs back on, okay?"

He shrugged and finished the Coke.

After he was handcuffed, Lauren returned to her seat. "Are you ready to tell me what happened when you went to the pet salon Wednesday evening?"

A sharp knock echoed in the sparsely furnished interrogation room. Maris whirled in her chair to see a lanky lawyer step inside. Achingly slim, he wore a gray, Western-cut jacket over a powder blue shirt with a bolo tie sporting a large turquoise stone. She recognized him immediately. Hal Childress, defense, Dallas. He'd almost been disbarred for using and selling cocaine but managed to wiggle out of it. Rumor held that having an uncle on the federal bench hadn't hurt. How Wylie Parmer had managed to snag him, she couldn't imagine. It must have been the lure of a high-profile murder case and the resulting publicity.

"Fuck," Sally muttered under her breath.

Maris picked up the bag with the shears and stood aside. She knew it was finished.

"This party's over." Hal smirked. "My client wishes to remain silent. Direct any other questions to me." He stuck his hand out to his new client. Kyle drew back. Childress put his hand in his pocket. "I want my client moved to another room so I can talk to him. One without any recording equipment."

"Fifteen more minutes," Lauren said once they were out of earshot of the attorney. "Fifteen more minutes, and he'd have told us everything." She held up the notebook. "Look how he spelled Satan. Like the cloth, satin."

Maris brushed her hand discreetly and tried to reconcile the image of a man who panicked and fled at the sight of a nurse's needle with a cold-blooded killer who brutally stabbed three young women to death.

Chapter 10

Maris made it home about four Saturday morning, and Lauren was even later. Yet the pretty redhead beat her out of bed by at least an hour. When she finally rose at one, she found Lauren and Irene locked in a deep conversation. They sat on the sofa, half facing each other with knees nearly touching. Sensing an emotional discussion, Maris froze, unsure whether to continue to the kitchen. Although in the small duplex, she had few places to go.

"It's okay," Lauren said. She wiped a tear from her cheek. "Come on in." She patted Irene's knee. "Make the appointment for next week, and I'll go with you."

"Thanks," Irene said. "I think it will help."

Lauren nodded. To Maris, she said, "I'm going to counseling with her next week to discuss some family problems."

"That's nice." She stretched. "Still want to go to Shannon's today, if it works for her?"

"Sure. I still need to pick up the files on the Fort Worth sexual assaults, even though we now know they're not related to the murders." Lauren rose. "I'll get you some coffee."

Maris followed her into the kitchen. "What's that all about?" she asked.

"Irene has something important to tell me about our childhood, but she wants to do it with her therapist present."

"Must be some story." Maris poured some Cheerios into a bowl and added milk.

"By the way," Lauren said. "My office Christmas party is next Friday. We've combined parties this year with DEA and the U.S. Attorney's office. It's at the Adam's Mark Hotel downtown."

Maris whistled. "Expensive."

"Open bar before dinner, dancing afterward." Lauren cocked her head and smiled seductively. "Want to be my date?"

"I'd love to, if you're sure you want to be that open." She grinned. "And you're sure they won't transfer you to some God-awful place afterward."

"Yes, I'm sure." She twisted her hair. "But I may not be brave enough to dance with you."

"You just don't want to make the others look bad." Maris finished her cereal and sipped her coffee, wondering why Lauren had decided to make a statement at the Christmas party.

By Saturday afternoon, the sky had cleared and the temperature climbed into the low sixties. The Fort Worth skyline came into view as Lauren said, "I think Irene's going to tell me she was sexually abused as a child."

Looking beautiful in a cream-colored blouse with a low-cut V neck, black jeans and a floral vest, she turned sideways and leaned against the pickup door.

Maris glanced at her. "What makes you say that?"

Lauren shrugged. "A feeling."

"Well, maybe it'll do her good to talk about it."

"Maybe." She frowned. "I checked on Brian Blake. He was released from Wichita Falls on October fifteenth to live with his sister in Pierce. Supposedly he's on medication and has gotten religion." She rolled her eyes. "They told me that he wants to become a minister."

"To preach hellfire but not the damnation, I'd bet." Maris laughed. She passed Shannon's office, a handsome red brick building on the corner of Jones Street and East Belknap, and drove to the Fort Worth P.D., only a few blocks away. She waited in front while Lauren ran inside to get the files on the rape cases. The detective working with her was off on Saturdays, but he'd arranged for her to retrieve the records. Within a few minutes, she returned with a young officer pushing a stack of boxes on a dolly. Maris unlocked the back of the truck and helped him transfer the files.

Five minutes later they parked in front of Shannon's office where they'd agreed to meet. Shannon frequently worked a few hours on Saturdays. Lauren flipped down the sun visor and checked her hair in the small mirror. "Are you sure she's here?" she asked. "I don't see any other cars."

"She usually parks in back." Maris rang the doorbell and waited a long moment before ringing it a second time. Shannon seldom kept her waiting, especially when she called ahead. "She's probably busy." Trying to hide her uneasiness, Maris stepped back and peered in the window. Between the miniblinds and sheer curtains, she could see little except for the dim glow from the floor lamp in the reception area where Timothy, Shannon's gay secretary, greeted clients, answered the phone, typed reports and maintained the records on a state-of-the-art computer system. She'd often heard Shannon complain that Timothy insisted on having the latest bells and whistles on his computer and would go into a blue funk if she refused. She'd once let him choose between a new computer and a raise, and he took the computer. If anyone was in the front office, Maris couldn't tell. She tried the door.

"Maybe she forgot," Lauren suggested.

"I just talked to her a couple of hours ago."

"Maybe she's having the baby," Lauren said.

"I'm going around back to see if her car —"

Just then, Shannon opened the door and waved them inside. She held a telephone receiver with its long cord stretched tight. Maris knew immediately from her lack of color and the tension in her tightly pressed lips that something was wrong. She became more concerned when Shannon avoided her eyes. Maris's first concern was the baby, and her attention riveted to Shannon's swollen stomach. But she looked healthy, wearing loose-fitting indigo denim maternity jeans and an oversize white long-sleeve blouse with a navy yolk. And although she held her back as she waddled to Timothy's desk, she displayed no other signs of discomfort. They followed her inside.

Maris glanced at Lauren and saw her studying Shannon. Catching Shannon's attention, she said, "We're going to go get the evidence."

When they were back outside, Lauren leaned close and whispered, "Why didn't you tell me she was so pretty?"

"Girl, this ain't my first rodeo." Maris tucked a manila envelope with photographs under her arm and lifted the frame that she'd made to stabilize the Sheetrock before loading it in the truck. She tried to avoid tearing the butcher paper stapled to the front. "Watch out for splinters." She slid out the frame until Lauren could grab an end.

When they entered the office, Maris heard a catch in Shannon's voice as she concluded her conversation. "Yes,

I'm sure everything is okay. Thanks for returning my call."
She hurried to open the door to the lab. "In here. Put it on
the cabinet near the sink."

They slid the frame onto the cabinet, and Maris set the
envelope next to it.

Shannon smiled warmly and hugged Lauren. "It's nice
to finally meet you."

"Thank you." Lauren smiled. "But the pleasure is
mine."

Maris wrapped an arm around Shannon and pecked her
cheek. "How's the baby? Robin told me she could feel it
kicking."

Shannon frowned. "When did you talk to her?"

"She called after the murders to tell me about a series
of rapes over here in Fort Worth."

"Oh." Shannon took Maris's hand and placed it on her
lower abdomen. "Feel it?"

"I can." Maris grinned at Lauren. "I feel him kicking."

Shannon reached for Lauren's hand. Lauren hesitated
before letting Shannon guide it to the right spot. "Her
kicking," Shannon corrected. "It's a girl." Her blue eyes
sparkled. "I didn't want to know at first, but it does make
it easier to plan."

"She'll be beautiful like her mother," Maris said.

"Thank you." Shannon flipped her blonde hair away
from her face. "Want to unwrap it?" She pointed to the
section of wall.

Maris used her Case pocketknife, a long-ago gift from
Mary Ann, to cut away the paper.

"I saw on the news that you made an arrest last night."
Shannon looked at Lauren.

"Yes, thank God. It's a relief to have him off the street
so soon."

Maris felt Shannon gently squeeze her shoulder as she
bent to look at the Sheetrock. She gasped when she saw the
messages in blood. As if thinking aloud, she read, " 'Merry
fucking Christmas' — with an X and in all caps. Interesting.
And 'Welcome to my hell' — also in all caps." She shook her
head. "Damn, I wish he hadn't used all caps. There'd be
more individual characteristics revealed. 'Satin lives' . . . I

see your perp can't spell. And lastly, 'Kill the whores.' " She put her hands on her hips. "Do you have exemplars of your suspect's handwriting?"

"A limited sample. We hope it's good enough for you to make a comparison," Maris said.

Lauren said, "We aren't even sure if a comparison is possible."

"You have pictures?" Shannon asked.

"Tons. And I brought copies of the negatives as well." Maris handed her a copy of the photos of the wall taken when it was still intact.

Shannon thumbed through the set. "Good quality." She set the photos on the cabinet and rubbed her forehead. "Now, for the bad news. I've never had a case like this, although I'm aware of some similar situations documented in the literature." She sighed. "People do have identifying characteristics in their handwriting. The problem is that we have a limited amount of writing here to work with — four phrases. That may not be enough for those identifying characteristics to appear. Also, if the writer is attempting to disguise his handwriting, he might be successful with this small amount of writing and the uniqueness of the situation, whereas it would be hard to maintain the disguise over the course of a whole anonymous letter, for example."

"So it might be possible to make a comparison?" Lauren asked.

"Yes. There's another problem — the piece is hand-lettered — that is, printed, instead of written in cursive. That's not altogether bad. There are some characteristics in hand-lettered writing that we can study, such as the slant of the letters and the relative size. Also, whether each letter is a continuous whole stroke or several distinct ones."

"Several repetitive strokes, wouldn't you think?" Lauren said. "Considering the medium he was using and substrate."

"Probably. But that means this may not be his normal method of hand-lettering."

Lauren handed her an envelope with the sample of Kyle's handwriting. Shannon slit the flap and slid out the notebook paper. She pursed her lips as she studied it. "I don't know how much this will help. It'd be better if I could reproduce this —" She pointed to the cut-out section of wall. "As much as possible. Have the suspect or suspects write on a wall with red paint using their fingers or whatever you think they might have used at the scene."

"That's an interesting point," Maris said. "Do you have a magnifying glass handy?"

Shannon waddled over to a drawer and returned carrying a magnifying lens and holding her back with her free hand.

Lauren said, "I think we'll have trouble getting a court order for him to write exemplars in blood."

"I expect his attorney will fight it like hell." Shannon handed Maris the magnifying lens.

Maris leaned over the wall section. "See the top lines — *MERRY FUCKING XMAS* and *WELCOME TO MY HELL*." Shannon and Lauren gathered around her. "See the tiny lines on the edge and the pattern where the end on the letter smears to a stop. I think he used gloves on the top two lines. Notice the letters are wider also. Look at the rest of the message. The letters aren't as wide, and see how they trail off . . . like a child's fingerpaints. I think he used his bare fingers to draw these."

"I've got to sit down for a minute." Shannon dropped into a stiff-backed chair near a small table with a microscope.

Lauren pulled up a lab stool. "I seriously doubt our subject would have disguised his handwriting. He'd be too agitated. Plus, he's no rocket scientist — a head injury as a child."

Shannon said. "Are you sure this crime was carried out by one person?"

"There's no reason to think —"

Maris touched Lauren's hand, interrupting her. "Why do you ask?"

"Maybe I shouldn't have said anything yet. At least until I've had time to examine the writing more carefully." Shannon struggled to rise from the low chair. "When I'm not as tired."

"Come on, little mother." Taking her hand, Maris helped her to her feet.

Shannon chewed her lower lip as she studied the bloody writing. "There are some subtle differences between the top two phrases and the lower ones." After a moment, she shook her head. "This may not be something I can put in a report." She tapped the Sheetrock. "It wouldn't surprise me to find out two people wrote these things. Of course, it could be due to different writing instruments — a gloved finger versus a bare finger — as Maris said. Hence the possibility that nothing can be concluded positively. I'll know more after I study the exemplars you brought."

The telephone rang, and Maris saw Shannon's gaze dart to the lab clock. "I better get that," she said. "I'm expecting a call. Sorry."

"Please, go ahead," Lauren said.

"If that's Robin —" Maris grinned. "Tell her that if she's late, she has to buy the first round of margaritas."

Shannon didn't reply as she hurried to the front office. She caught it on the fifth ring.

"Something's wrong," Maris said.

"Maybe she's just tired. Apprehensive about the baby coming."

Maris reached for her hand. "Something about this case bothers me. So what do you think? Could there be two?" She sat on the corner of a desk.

"Almost everything about these murders and the crime scene indicate a disorganized offender." Lauren's face clouded, and she frowned thoughtfully. "It was a spontaneous offense with a quick, brutal blitzkrieg-type attack on the victims. He did things to depersonalize them —"

"The mutilation of Lynette's face, the way Jill was bent over the commode, facedown, and possibly there was a towel over Jennifer's face."

"Yes," Lauren said. "Plus, the sexual acts were after death. All indicate to me one offender who had a passing acquaintance with the victims." She shrugged. "I agree there are some inconsistencies as well. But they may be explained by the length of time he spent in the salon. Maybe he had time to calm down." Lauren looked troubled, and Maris pulled her closer. "I have to admit the killer's calmly shaving Jennifer Kerr after such a frenzied attack bothers me."

"His taking the weapon with him bothers me," Maris said. "That usually doesn't happen in these kind of quick, brutal attacks."

Lauren played with the silver bullet on a chain around Maris's neck. "I've seen crime scenes where characteristics of both the organized and disorganized offender were present."

"Yes, I have too. Sometimes because there were two killers."

"There can be several reasons." Lauren sighed again. "Sometimes the crime starts out well-ordered but disintegrates into disorganization after something unexpected occurs. In other cases the offender tends toward organization but his behavior is altered by alcohol or drugs."

"I've always wondered, assuming multiple personalities are real —"

"That may be a big assumption." Lauren smiled. "Except for the movies."

"I know. But assuming it's possible, couldn't the killer exhibit both organized and disorganized traits? Depending on *who* manifested himself at the time in question."

"So now we have one killer with two personalities."

"I'm speaking strictly theory, my dear." She leaned closer. "I don't think Kyle is smart enough for two personalities — or to plan anything."

"Lord, Maris. I can't believe we're joking about this."

"Don't worry. It's expected of me, and you'll be forgiven."

Lauren started to reply until she glanced over Maris's shoulder. She whispered. "It's Shannon. She's been crying, but she doesn't want us to know. She just blew her nose and wiped her face."

Shannon hurried back into the room and apologized for taking so long. Even if Lauren hadn't seen her crying,

Maris would have known her cheerfulness was forced. She eased off the desk and caught both of Shannon's hands.

"Don't." Shannon looked away.

"We know you're upset. And I don't think it's *all* because you can't have a margarita."

Shannon laughed once before dissolving into tears. "It's Robin." She repeated it twice before Maris understood. "She didn't come home Thursday night, but she called early Friday morning. She said she couldn't explain but that she had to have some time alone. She loves me and the baby and asked me not to stay at the ranch alone until after the baby comes."

Maris and Lauren exchanged glances. This wouldn't be the first time that Robin has gone AWOL on Shannon. She'd been known to disappear for days at a time, often without calling, while she indulged in her latest fling. But she'd promised those days were over.

"Where is she?" Maris asked.

"She wouldn't say." Shannon took a tissue from the nearby desk. "Damn her. This is the same old shit, except this time she called."

"You think there's another woman?" Lauren asked.

"I don't know." Shannon dabbed at her eyes. "She says there's not."

"Maybe she's freaking out about the baby." Maris shrugged.

"Well, now's a fine time." Shannon paced a few feet and leaned against the cabinet. "Don't worry. I'll be fine."

Maris frowned. Although Shannon's family lived in Fort Worth, only her brother was independent enough to buck her father and maintain contact with her. Her mother and sisters refused to take her calls, convinced by her father that if Shannon were ostracized long enough, she'd come to her senses and grow out of this lesbian phase. Her brother bred, trained and showed cutting horses and traveled frequently. "Could you stay with your brother's family?" she asked.

"I could, but I don't really need to stay with anyone." Shannon smiled. "Besides, he's going to be in and out of town until the twenty-second, and his place is even further from the hospital than mine. I think I'd rather stay at the Chisholm Hotel, if I feel like I need to be closer to town."

Maris nodded. She knew Robin's absence was probably just another one of her stunts. In a day or two, she'd show up, tail between her legs, begging for Shannon's forgiveness and, as usual, Shannon would take her back. Except for being further from the hospital, she didn't understand why Robin didn't want Shannon staying at the ranch. Since Buster was killed, Shannon had hired a full-time caretaker to oversee the ranch. He and his wife lived in a house that Shannon had built on the other side of the barn about three hundred yards from her own home. They could assist Shannon if the baby decided to make a sudden appearance. Yet Maris couldn't shake or explain the uneasiness that she felt. That fucking Robin ought to have her butt kicked, she thought.

Chapter 11

Maris sat on the edge of the brown leather couch in Shannon's reception area and seethed. The more she tried to reel in her anger, the harder it became. Clenching her teeth, she rose and paced back and forth in front of Timothy's desk. That damned Robin. Her timing, as usual, was impeccable. Why couldn't she have waited until the baby was born? Of course, the baby's impending birth might be behind this. A triggering factor, the FBI called it. They ranked the birth of a child up there with the trauma of job loss and divorce. More than one murderer and rapist struck while his wife was in the hospital with his newborn. She had known men, supposedly good husbands and fathers, who inexplicably celebrated with a one-night stand.

Lauren came in from Shannon's small kitchenette and break room, drying her hands on a paper towel. She balled it up and tossed it into the trash. "I'm making some hot tea. Want some?"

"No, thanks," Maris said. "I need something a little stronger. How is she?"

"She's having contractions, but —"

"Contractions?" Fucking hell, that goddamn Robin would have to be gone. "Don't we need to think about going to the hospital instead of making hot tea?"

"Her doctor thinks it's false labor, so don't get excited. She's freshening up." She looped her arm through Maris's. "What do you think happened to Robin? Nerves over the baby?"

"I don't know." Maris peered down the hallway. "But I may join her, wherever she is, if those contractions are real."

"You wouldn't leave her to have this baby alone?" Lauren squeezed her arm. "Her first one? She has to be scared to death."

"So am I. I'm afraid she'll ask me to coach if Robin doesn't show."

"She asked me how I'd feel about that," Lauren said.

"And?"

"I said it'd be good training." Lauren kissed her and slipped away.

In less than five minutes, Lauren and Shannon returned. Carefully balancing a cup of hot tea, Shannon lowered herself into the plush leather armchair near the sofa. She leaned back and sighed, propping her feet on the coffee table. "I always loved this chair."

Lauren handed Maris a beer in a thick-glassed brown bottle. "The only beer we found. It's Jamaican."

Maris frowned and, somewhat cautiously, sipped it. The first taste had a whang to it, and she made a face.

"Probably needs a lime," Shannon said. "It's one of Timothy's leftover experiments."

"Actually this beer ain't bad." Maris dropped to the sofa on the end nearest Shannon, and Lauren sat next to her. "Any ideas where Robin would go?"

"I don't know. I've been calling our friends — and those of hers that I know." She bent forward, almost spilling her tea. Her hand trembled. "I called her law partner, Starla Glasscock. She's in Lubbock on a change of venue in the Alice Kendall case. You know, the mother who killed her two sons."

Lauren nodded. "I'm the one who suggested that Richardson P.D. set up a mike and video camera at the grave site."

Maris remembered the case well. The police had caught a tearful confession when Alice knelt by the graves two days after the funeral and begged her sons' forgiveness.

Shannon turned to Maris. "Do you know Starla?"

"The little woman with the big voice," Maris said. For Lauren's benefit, she explained, "Starla is a little thing, but she's tough as a boot." Maris sipped her beer. "Says she's straight."

"Robin says she's queer as the rest of us but won't let it happen. They've been best friends since college. They went through law school together and both worked at the D.A.'s office for a while. Starla quit first. They say it was always part of the plan for Robin to handle the personal injury cases and other civil litigations and Starla the criminal defense work, although they help each other when necessary." Shannon wiped the tears from her eyes. "Sorry. I can't seem to get hold of myself. God, I can't believe she's done this, especially now."

"What did Starla say?" Lauren asked.

"She's as shocked as I am." She blew her nose and took a deep breath. "When things were at the worst for Robin and me, Starla used to call me looking for her. Seems she forgot to go to work as often as she forgot to come home. It almost dissolved the firm and destroyed their friendship. Starla feels as betrayed as I do. We were both taken in by the new Robin." Shannon leaned forward and picked up her teacup. She grimaced.

"What's wrong?" Maris asked.

"Another Braxton-Hicks contraction." She sighed and sipped her tea. "I've been on my feet all day and haven't taken in enough fluids."

"What the fuck is Braxton-Hicks?" Maris asked. "Do we need to call the doctor again?"

Shannon touched Maris's hand. "Relax. It's false labor. Braxton-Hicks contractions are normal in the last month. They prepare the cervix for labor. Maybe I need to eat."

"What do you think you can handle?" Lauren asked.

"Why don't you two go on to Joe T.'s like you planned? I'll check into the Chisholm tonight and have room service. I stay there often when I'm too tired to drive home or have an early appointment."

"We're not leaving until we're sure you're all right. I'll pick something up and meet y'all at the hotel." Maris ran a hand through her hair. "How will we know if it's real labor?"

"If it's the real thing —" Lauren leaned against her. "The contractions will get stronger and closer together. And the cervix will start changing."

Maris arched her eyebrows. "What makes you such an expert?"

She saw Lauren cast an amused glance at Shannon. "I don't run out of the room when women starting talking about these things."

Even Shannon chuckled at Lauren's reply. Maris ducked her head. "See if I ever tell you anything again."

She'd recently told Lauren about the first and last women-only baby shower she'd attended the first year she went to work for DPS. She'd never heard any lesbian talk as disparagingly about men as those women did. After bashing their husbands and boyfriends, they discussed babies and hysterectomies, sex afterward and first-baby horror stories. Although she felt like an interloper, she hung in there pretty good, even when they talked about how painful breast-feeding was. But it was all she wrote when they pulled out a breast pump and decided to demonstrate it. She'd jumped to her feet and dug a silent pager out of her pocket. Sorry, got to go, she explained, pretending to look at a number on the blank screen as she fled.

Maris grinned sheepishly at Lauren and Shannon. "I

may not know shit about Braxton-Hicks, but just ask me about breast-feeding."

Maris left Lauren to escort Shannon to the Chisholm Hotel and went to Joe T. Garcia's Mexican food restaurant for takeout after stopping at a liquor store. Although Shannon protested when she said they'd stay, Maris knew she was relieved. When she arranged for the room, Maris heard her ask for her usual suite and had to suppress a grin. Her usual suite at the five-star Chisholm, located near Sundance Square in downtown Fort Worth, probably cost more for one night than Maris usually spent for a week. The daughter of a second-generation wildcatter who'd long ago diversified out of oil into new growth industries like silicon chips and telecommunications, Shannon was used to the best. Although the oilman had disowned his youngest daughter for loving women, he'd judiciously kept her trust fund intact. With it, plus the small fortune that she made on her own, she could indulge in the better things in life like cutting horses, fine hotels and the brand-new Lincoln Navigator that Lauren had chauffeured the few blocks to the hotel.

At six-thirty, escorted by a bellboy who carried the plastic sacks of food, Maris stuck a pint of Bushmills Irish malt whiskey under the arm holding a six-pack of Corona and knocked on the door. Lauren answered and ushered her inside. "Shannon's taking a quick shower and changing into something more comfortable," she said.

The bellboy set the food on the four-person dining-room table next to the glass door overlooking the balcony. He unloaded the containers and laid out the paper plates and plasticware as artistically as possible. Maris tipped him generously after he filled the ice buckets. Then she fixed Lauren a whiskey over ice with a splash of water and grabbed a Corona with a slice of lime for herself. They wandered around the one-bedroom suite, replete with a sofa that pulled out to make a queen-size bed, and admired the custom antique reproductions.

Shortly, Shannon came from the bedroom. Dressed in purple maternity sweats with a pink T-shirt, she said, "I thought I heard your voice." She smiled at Maris and pulled out a chair at the table.

"Then let's eat before the food gets cold." Lauren began opening containers containing tacos, enchiladas, tostadas covered in *queso*, refried beans and rice.

Maris squeezed Shannon's shoulder as she circled behind her to another chair. Shannon picked at a taco and barely sampled a cheese enchilada. Lauren ate what amounted to less than a taste of everything, by Maris's standards, while Maris scarfed a good portion of what remained.

When Shannon pushed away from the table, Maris said, "You didn't eat much."

Shannon smiled tiredly. "Maybe I need a glass of milk."

"I'll call room service." Maris rose from the table. "How about some ice cream? That'll make you feel better."

"Talked me into it," Shannon said.

Maris made the phone call while Lauren picked up the leftovers and stuck them in the small refrigerator. The phone rang. Picking it up, Shannon moved to a comfortable armchair. Cupping the receiver, she said, "It's Starla. She's at the office."

Maris answered the knock at the door and let room service put the tray on the table. After tipping the young lady, she caught Shannon's attention and held up the milk. Shannon waved her away, so Maris put the milk and ice cream in the refrigerator. She freshened Lauren's drink and popped the cap on another Corona.

Shannon thanked Starla and hung up the telephone. She ran a hand tiredly over her forehead. "Starla practically searched Robin's office. She found a yellow Post-it on her desk with details for a flight to Denver. Flight seven-fifty-seven, leaving at two-thirteen today."

"Why Denver?" Maris asked.

"Starla says the firm has no business there." Twisting

in her chair, Shannon held her stomach and winced. "Contraction," she said. After a moment, she added, "I know her ex, Gwen, lives in Denver. Gwen has a little girl, and Robin has kept in touch. They'd been broken up for nearly two years when we met."

"Do you mind if we call Gwen?" Maris asked.

"No. But don't pressure Robin, if she's there. I want her back on her own or not at all." She struggled to her feet. "I think I'll get my milk and ice cream."

"I'd have done that," Maris said.

"No need." She opened the fridge and poured the milk from the pint carton into a glass. Carrying the bowl of vanilla ice cream, she returned. "Starla called the firm's secretary at home and talked to her. She said Robin got flowers after lunch on Thursday. They didn't look like flowers from a regular florist, but like the kind you buy on the street corner. A kid about thirteen delivered them with a handwritten note. It said, 'It wasn't me.' "

"I don't understand," Lauren said.

"Neither do I." Shannon sipped her milk and ate her ice cream slowly.

"Do you have Gwen's number?" Maris asked.

"No. Not here," Shannon said. She set the bowl and the milk on the coffee table with more than half remaining. "I think I'd better lie down. Why don't you go home? I know you're tired."

"We want to stay," Lauren said. "Unless we're making you uncomfortable."

"No. Don't ruin your evening on account of me. I know you were out late last night."

"Don't worry about us," Maris said. "We'll be fine."

"The sofa makes down into a bed," Lauren said. "We'll call housekeeping to bring us what we need. And it's early enough for me to look at the files from Fort Worth P.D."

Maris put Shannon's milk and ice cream in the fridge and hurried back to help her up. "What do you think is going on with Robin?"

She smoothed back her blonde hair and tiredly rubbed her neck. "I can't believe she'd just leave. She's as excited about this baby as I am." She shook her head. "Her phone call this morning was strange. She seemed . . . frightened, worried."

"We'll see if we can talk to her," Maris said. "Make sure she's safe."

"You've been a good friend to me — and to Robin — for a long time, and I appreciate it."

"You don't have to say anything." Maris smiled.

Shannon reached for Lauren's hand and squeezed it. "And thank you for letting her be a good friend. Some women —"

"Go lie down before you collapse." Lauren cupped Shannon's hand between hers.

Maris felt a wave of affection for both women. Embracing Lauren after Shannon left, she whispered, "Thank you."

Chapter 12

Pleased to see that housekeeping had made down the queen-size sleeper sofa, Maris told the bellboy pushing the dolly with the Fort Worth case files to put them near the table. She dropped the duffel bag with extra clothes, which she kept in her truck, on the bed and looked around for her lover. She saw her outside on the balcony. Lauren leaned over the iron rail and stared at the thirty-three-story Chase Texas Tower across from the hotel. The wind stirred her hair, and Maris felt a surge of desire as she watched her absently sweep a stray strand from her cheek.

She filled Lauren's tumbler with ice and added a generous splash of Bushmills and water. She grabbed another Corona, fished a slice of lime from the plastic container and pushed it into the neck of the bottle. Opening the sliding door with her elbow, she carried the drinks to the balcony. The breeze was cold, she guessed in the low fifties, yet refreshing.

"Thank you," Lauren said. There was enough light to see her smile.

Maris propped a foot on the protective railing and said, "Hell's Half Acre." She indicated the downtown area with a sweep of her hand. "It's what they called Cowtown in the late eighteen hundreds when the Chisholm Trail attracted outlaws and gamblers along with the cowboys and cattlemen. Sundance Square is named after the Sundance Kid."

"Oh." Lauren sipped her drink.

"So it's always been with us — the robbing and killing." Maris put an arm around her. "I see housekeeping made down our bed."

"Yes. While they were here I called Irene."

"How's she doing?"

"She's fine." Lauren smiled. "And don't worry. She's taking good care of your dog."

"Yeah, she's feeding him too much junk and letting him sleep on the couch."

Lauren was silent for a moment, then she faced Maris. "Do you love me?"

"No. But I sure like you a lot." It was out before she realized Lauren wasn't joking. Worse, she seemed close to tears. "Of course I love you," Maris hastily added. God, she hated it when women did that. Mary Ann used to ask her the same damned thing, out of the clear blue. It usually meant Maris had fucked up in some real or imagined way that she wasn't aware of. She lifted Lauren's chin and kissed her. "What the hell kind of question is that?"

"Don't be that way."

"You know I love you."

"I need some reassurance. I need to hear you tell me."

"That I love you?" Then it hit her. Shannon. She should have seen this coming. Maris took the drink from Lauren's hand and set it and her beer on a nearby table, then she wrapped her arms around Lauren and kissed her deeply.

106

Breaking away, Maris said, "I love you so much I don't know what I'd do without you."

Lauren ran a finger down the scar on Maris's right cheek.

"When you do that, it makes getting that scar almost worthwhile." Maris reached under Lauren's sweater and stroked her bare skin.

Lauren jumped. "God, your hands are cold."

Maris felt her shiver and placed a hand in the small of her back to draw her nearer. "They'll warm up."

"Before or after my heart attack?" She clasped her hands behind Maris's neck.

Maris cupped Lauren's breast and felt an aroused nipple through the thin material of her bra. "Look what I found." She nibbled her neck, enjoying the fragrance of her perfume.

"Don't you dare give me a hickey," Lauren whispered huskily.

"It'll be a reminder of my love. So you don't have to ask."

"Don't tease me."

"Never." She fumbled with the top button on Lauren's new black jeans. As she reached for the zipper, Lauren grabbed her hand.

"Omigod. My gun." She reached behind her and unclipped the leather pancake-style holster with the Sig Sauer P228 from her waistband. "I can see the headlines now: 'Half-naked FBI Agent Loses Gun rom Balcony of Exclusive Five-star Fort Worth Hotel.'"

"While engaged in torrid lesbian sex." Maris laughed. Although the FBI had recently upgraded to the .40 caliber, double-action-only Glock, Lauren preferred the Sig for her off-duty weapon. Maris took the pistol from her and set it on the table near the drinks. She started for the zipper again and changed her mind. She glanced around the dimly lit balcony and spied a plastic-strapped lounge chair. "Here." She grabbed Lauren's Bushmills and handed it to her. "Excuse me a minute."

"What are you up to?" Lauren asked, a smile playing on the corner of her lips.

"You'll see." Maris paused at the table and downed half of her Corona.

"Hmmm." Lauren cocked her head. "Do I really want to find out?"

Maris slid open the door. "How many times have I told you that you're supposed to —"

"Trust your lover. I know. And I say there's a reason you have to keep reminding me."

Maris waved at her and hustled for the blanket on the queen-size sofa bed. She glanced at the door to Shannon's room to make sure the light was still off. Hopping on first one foot and then the other, she jerked off her boots and dropped them on the floor. In less than a minute, she was naked except for a Miller Lite Racing T-shirt and her socks. She wrapped the blanket around her and carried the bedspread to the balcony. Stopping at the table, she guzzled the last half of the beer and hastened to the lounge chair. Pushing it out of the wind, she adjusted the back to a semi-upright position, folded the bedspread in half and draped it over the plastic straps. Steeling herself against the cold, she reluctantly peeled off the blanket and positioned it inside the bedspread. Holding back the top half, she crawled between the layers and held it open invitingly.

Almost before she was ready, Lauren landed on top of her. To Maris's surprise, she had already stripped out of her jeans and suede boots.

"How'd you get undressed so fast?" Maris tucked the blanket around them and pulled it up over their heads. Lauren squirmed against her.

"Like you always say, 'This ain't my first rodeo, cowboy.' "

Maris hugged her and let her hands wander under Lauren's sweater. "But you forgot a couple of things. "Like . . . this." She unhooked her bra and helped Lauren slip first one arm and then the other from her sweater. She slipped off the bra strap and started to tug the sweater over her lover's head.

Lauren stopped her. "Not on the balcony. Besides, it's cold out here." She put her arms back in the sleeves.

"At least this is out of the way." Maris balled up the bra and tossed it toward Lauren's jeans and boots piled a few feet away. It went too far, hung on the lower rail for a moment before the wind swept it over the edge. "Shit." Maris rose to her elbows.

"What? What's wrong?" Lauren twisted to look over her shoulder.

"Not a thing, darling. Not a thing."

"I swear, Maris, if you ever cheat on me, I'll know it. I'll know it the minute you come home. The only time you ever call me 'darling' is when you're trying to hide something." She started to rise, and Maris held her down.

"I'd never cheat on you, darling."

"See, there you go again." She pulled back the blanket and glanced around the balcony. "You threw my bra over the side!"

"Don't worry. I'll go get it," Maris said in her most dejected voice. She pretended to crawl out of the makeshift bed.

"Not now you won't." Lauren planted a hand in her chest and pushed her back down.

"In that case, let's get rid of these too." Maris slipped a hand under the waistband of Lauren's panties.

When they were off, she took the panties from Maris. "I'll take care of these." She dropped them next to the chair and laid her head on Maris's shoulder. "Make love to me."

Maris ran a hand under her sweater and caressed her breast. "I love you," she whispered in Lauren's ear. She couldn't resist adding, "Darling."

Lauren laughed and rubbed Maris's chest through her T-shirt.

Shifting her weight to make more room on the narrow lounge chair, Maris stroked Lauren's inner thigh. When Maris touched her, she groaned and rose to her knees, straddling her. Maris found her warmth and pushed deep inside. The plastic straps gave under her as they rocked back and forth. The blanket rose and fell, allowing cold air to swirl around them. Lauren leaned over her and raised her sweater, offering a breast. Maris took it as Lauren's knees tightened against her. She felt Lauren's muscles clench, and Maris wondered if the wind drowned her lover's cries or carried them to the street below.

Lauren collapsed against her, and Maris pulled the blankets around them. She smoothed her hair and kissed her. "I'd do anything for you," Maris whispered. Lauren stirred on top of her and mumbled something unintelligible. Maris stroked her shoulder, letting her relax.

She stretched and kissed Maris's cheek. "What about you? How are you doing?"

"I was thinking we should move inside. My back is getting a little stiff lying on this damned thing. And it's getting colder."

"Not yet. There's something I want to do for you." Lauren gave Maris's breast a quick squeeze and began to crawl down her body.

"How are you going to do that in this chair?" Maris grinned. "You'll suffocate."

"I'll manage. Like . . . this."

Maris involuntarily sucked in her breath at the almost over-powering flood of sensations. Lauren's hair tickled her thighs; her hands gripped her hips. She peeled back the blanket, allowing the cold air to engulf them. She tracked the lights of a plane far overhead and then saw another. One was incoming, probably to DFW, the other outgoing to God knows where. Then the stimulation was too much. She felt herself breaking over, and it was her turn to try not to notify the neighbors.

As soon as it was over, they were cold again and burrowed deep into the blankets. Lauren rested her head on Maris's thumping chest and traced the scar on her cheek to the corner of her mouth. Maris kissed the tips of her fingers.

"That puts meaning to gettin' lucky," Maris said.

"Why don't you want me to have a baby?" Lauren asked.

"Jesus, where did that come from?" Maris's racing heart skipped a beat and her stomach flipflopped. She cleared her throat. "You really want one, don't you?"

Lauren rose to her elbow. "Yes."

"And that's the real reason you want a bigger house."
She didn't say anything, and the fear of loss clutched Maris.

Lauren's tone was serious, her voice solemn. "I'm only thirty-one. We don't have to decide right this minute, today."

"That's the second time you've told me that recently." Maris drew her close. "I don't think it's going away." She swallowed hard. "This could break us up, couldn't it?"

"I don't know." Lauren sighed and kissed Maris's cheek. "I wish I understood why you're so dead set against it."

"A hundred reasons," Maris said. "And none."

"Tell me." She brushed a strand of hair from Maris's forehead.

"There's so much to think about. Where do we get the sperm? How do we *really* know he's not a schizophrenic, mass-murdering alcoholic with a crack habit? Is it better for two women to raise a boy or a girl? Where's the male influence going to come from? Both boys and girls need male role models." She ran a finger down Lauren's jaw line. "And what if it's a boy? Their psyches are so delicate that a bad potty-training experience can produce anything from a grown-up misogynist son-of-a-bitch to a serial sexual killer. And none of this begins to address the issues of keeping the kid safe, healthy and happy." She sighed. "And how could we make love on the balcony with a little kid running around?"

Lauren patted her chest but said nothing.

And Maris didn't tell her about the image that flashed through her mind of a little girl sprawled on a pink bedspread in a pool of blood. And of the three mutilated teenagers in a pet salon. They lay silently for several moments until Maris said, "We should go inside. I've got to fetch a wayward bra."

Chapter 13

A dark-haired cowboy in stiffly starched jeans, a colorful Western shirt and handsome gray felt hat flashed Maris a grin as she pulled Lauren's bra off the antenna of a police car where someone had hooked it. She balled it up and stuffed it in the waistband of her sweats. "Accidents happen," she said.

"That they do, ma'am." He tipped his hat and chuckled as he strode away.

After the cold drove them inside a little after nine that evening, Lauren said nothing else about the baby thing, but Maris knew it wasn't settled. She saw it in her eyes. Restless, she paced the vast hotel lobby. Before she realized it, she'd been gone almost an hour and hurried to the room, surprised Lauren hadn't sent out a search party.

She heard laughter when she entered the suite and understood they hadn't come looking for her because she hadn't been missed. Lauren, wearing Maris's faded T-shirt, with *DPS Crime Lab* across the front, sat cross-legged on the queen-size sofa bed, sharing a slice of chocolate cheese-cake with Shannon, who was propped against three pillows and wearing a pink T-shirt with a stork on the front. They glanced at her, and she felt the stab of insecurity that comes from walking into a noisy room that suddenly falls silent. The television played softly, and Maris recognized the scene from *Romancing the Stone* where Kathleen Turner and Michael Douglas sought shelter inside a crashed plane loaded with marijuana.

"Didn't mean to be gone so long," Maris said.

"That's okay." Lauren returned to her cheesecake.

Maris filled a hotel glass with ice water and carried it to the bed. Pulling the bra from her waistband, she tossed it to Lauren.

Leaning into each other, Lauren and Shannon burst into laughter. Somewhat confused, Maris looked from one to the other. Despite their gaiety at her expense, both had red-rimmed eyes and looked as if they'd been crying. "Why do I get the feeling that y'all have been talking about me?" she asked.

Lauren tousled Maris's hair. "Shannon wants to ask you something."

"Yes?" Maris asked, eyeing the cheesecake.

Shannon stared at her hands and twisted the ring on her finger, the one Robin gave her after they decided to have the baby. "It appears that I can't count on Robin to be here when I have the baby. So . . ." She took a deep breath and smiled at Maris. "I wondered if you and Lauren would be my backup labor partners."

Maris's stomach clenched with dread. Damn, she didn't want to see Shannon's pain, and she hated hospitals, with their nauseous odors and sick people. Yet how could she tell Shannon no? "Shannon, honey . . ." She squeezed her hand.

"I'm honored that you asked. I don't know how much help I'll be, but I promise I'll damned well do my best."

Shannon smiled. "I know you will."

"But you have to promise that if I fucking pass out, you won't tell anyone."

"Oh, Maris," Shannon said. "It won't be that bad."

"Hey, I've heard stories. Wayne Coffey hyperventilated, trying to help his wife breathe, and she threw him out of the room, saying he was making her crazy. I know a narc who passed smooth out and had to have stitches in his head after the doctor finished sewing up his wife."

"You'll be fine." Lauren kissed her cheek and whispered in her ear, "I knew you'd do the right thing."

Maris's back ached when she tumbled from the sofa bed Sunday morning. Whether it was from the activities in the lounge chair or the ridge in the fold of the bed, she wasn't sure. Fort Worth P.D. case folders were strewn across the table next to Lauren's laptop, but she was nowhere in sight. Stumbling to the sliding door, she saw her, coffee cup in hand, leaning on the balcony rail. Maris could tell that she'd already showered and dressed for the day in the clothes that she had worn the evening before.

A blast of cool air hit Maris. "If I didn't know better, I'd say you'd taken up smoking."

Lauren smiled and came to her. "Good morning, sleepy-head."

"Is that it? Are you smoking? Or developing a balcony fetish? Maybe I need to provide a little more reassurance." She kissed her and held her tightly. "You must have gotten up early."

"Couldn't sleep any longer. I've been studying the Fort Worth rape cases. Grab a cup of coffee. I want to show you something." Lauren followed her inside.

Maris was grateful to find a full-size coffee maker in the kitchenette of the hotel suite. "Where's Shannon?" she asked as she pulled a chair away from the table.

"Oh, she's been up and gone for two hours." Lauren

shuffled through the reports. "Her doctor agreed to meet her at the office at seven-thirty to see if she'd dilated any. She had contractions all night."

"Jesus, what time is it?"

"About nine. I figured you might as well sleep. I think we should find out what the doctor says before we leave."

"Should she be driving herself?" Maris sipped her coffee.

"She insisted." Lauren pulled a page out of the stack. "Here's what I was looking for." She handed it to Maris. "Robin was the D.A.'s representative on the task force formed after the third rape."

Maris set down her cup and took the page. She didn't know any of the police officers, but the name of the Tarrant County assistant district attorney, Robin Fisher, leapt off the page. "I can't believe I'm not familiar with these rapes. Give me a rundown."

"Where were you in 'ninety-one?"

"Working in Garland for DPS. Living with Mary Ann."

"Well, the first rape was in February of 'ninety-one. Then there was one in March, April and May. They formed the task force after the third one. He went two months without striking, that they know of, and resumed in August. The last reported rape was that December. All told there were eight rapes reported."

"But how many weren't?" Maris shook her head. "What was his M.O?"

"It appears he was on a twenty-five-day cycle, if you assume there were unreported attacks during the gaps. His victims were students at either the University of Texas in Arlington or Texas Christian." Lauren paused for a sip of coffee. "He normally entered through an unlocked door or window, but later, as the women became more careful, he'd break in. He always wore a black ski mask and gloves . . . used a knife to control them. His victims never saw him and couldn't say for sure what race he is. He'd keep them blindfolded throughout the ordeal."

Maris grimaced. "Elements of forethought and planning."

"He planned all right. He always wore condoms and re-membered to take them with him when he left. The attacks were brutal, consisting of multiple assaults — vaginal, anal and oral. In every case, he calmly shaved her pubic area after blindfolding and securing her."

"He brought the razor with him?"

"In all except for one case. Victim stated he went into a rage until he found a disposable razor in her bathroom. She was the most injured of all the women."

Maris took her cup and Lauren's to the kitchenette and refilled them. Returning, she asked, "What type of injuries?"

"Multiple bruises and contusions. Some were badly beaten around the face and had broken ribs. Vaginal and anal tearing." She gazed out the glass door. "They were so young. The oldest was twenty-two and the youngest eighteen."

Maris walked around behind her and rubbed her shoulders.

"The last thing he'd do before he left is make them shower and clean up."

Maris's hand stopped. "Even though he wore a condom?"

"Yes." She touched Maris's hand. "What do you think?"

She resumed massaging her shoulders. "Did he talk to them during the assaults?"

"Degrading, vulgar comments. Lots of profanity. He also made them comment positively on his masculinity. He used duct tape to blindfold them. Directly on their skin and eyelids." She held up a finger before thumbing through the reports. "Something else odd. Some of the women reported hearing something that sounded like a video camera and possibly the click and flash of a still camera during the assault."

"So he took souvenir photos." Maris kissed her neck and took a sip of coffee. "I think this bastard is a neat freak. He has a cleanliness thing. He's not shaving them and wearing condoms just to avoid leaving physical evidence. He's doing it in order to — at least in his mind — make them cleaner and to keep himself uncontaminated. Making them shower afterward is to avoid leaving evidence. Makes me suspect a prior conviction or familiarity with police work."

"I think you're right. The investigators then didn't see it." Lauren ran her finger around the rim of her coffee cup. "They arrested a burglar in the bedroom of a TCU coed. Her roommate came home late and saw him crawling in a window. She called the police. He was attempting to rape her when captured. He had no knife, no razor and no blindfold but was wearing a ski mask. He denied the rapes but copped to a string of burglaries. Before police caught the burglar, they questioned a twenty-year-old TCU student, a white male." She picked up a report. "The son of a woman who worked as a secretary in the theft division of the police department. His father, a police officer, was killed in an automobile accident when he was two. His mother never remarried. He was a student at TCU and worked part-time as a janitor at the P.D. He knew the investigating officers."

"Damn," Maris said.

Lauren put down the reports. "From the reports, I'd classify the rapist as sadistic with elements of a power-assertive type. This TCU kid fit the profile."

"But the rapes stopped after the burglar was arrested?" Maris frowned thoughtfully.

"So it seems." Lauren turned her laptop to get a better view of the screen. "The *Fort Worth Star Telegram* isn't archived, but the *Dallas Morning News* on-line library goes back to 'eighty-four. They covered the story, and detectives included some of the newspaper articles in their files. Robin made some very bold public statements before they caught the burglar, condemning the rapist and challenging his masculinity. It was a strategy agreed upon by the task force and documented in the reports. They hoped that he'd be enraged enough to communicate with the police or her. Maybe become bolder and make a mistake."

Maris let out a low whistle. "Wonder some young college woman didn't get the brunt of that strategy and end up dead."

"Or that Robin didn't." Lauren pushed some keys on the computer. "From the newspaper reports, Robin never believed the burglar committed the rapes. Shortly after the task force folded, she resigned from the D.A's office." Lauren peered at the computer monitor. "I ran checks on the burglar and the TCU student. The burglar is out of the pen now. The TCU kid, Al Anderson, is working for Fort Worth P.D. as an identification tech."

Stretching, Maris glanced out the glass door. It looked like a beautiful day, not a cloud in sight. She thoughtfully sipped her coffee. "You know, I always thought that once a guy started doing these kinds of crimes, he'd never stop unless he was killed or jailed. I'm beginning to think I was wrong. There are too many of these serial rapes and serial murders that go unsolved and yet seem unrepeated. Could this guy just stop?"

"Assuming the crimes are fantasy-driven . . ." A frown creased her forehead. "And he could continue to feed them, satisfy them somehow . . . then, yes, I think he could quit."

"Suppose he had a collection of videotapes and photographs of the rapes. He could relive them over and over." Maris stood to stretch her back. "John Douglas in his book *Obsession* talks about a series of murders in the early seventies, that were committed by a guy who called himself Search and Destroyer. He supposedly took crime-scene-quality photos and made detailed sketches. And apparently just stopped. Years later, after another series of crimes that were similar in nature, the media speculated that Search and Destroyer was active again. He sent them letters saying, 'It's not me.' If it's authentic, he did apparently just stop." Maris turned to see Lauren staring at her wide-eyed.

"Omigod," Lauren said. " 'It wasn't me.' "

"The card with the flowers." Maris felt a twinge of concern for Shannon's lover. "We've got to call Robin's friend in Denver. And we've got to bring Fort Worth P.D. in on this."

Lauren typed rapidly on the computer. "With Shannon's help, I found Gwen's number this morning."

Maris grabbed a nearby phone and unplugged Lauren's modem. She stretched the cord over to the table. Depending on what information, if any, they got from Robin's ex in Denver, they'd have to decide how much to tell Shannon. That damned Robin. If she was in danger or had been contacted by the rapist, why didn't she go to the police or come to her and Lauren? This wasn't helping her complete

118

the lab work on the Bass Cove murders. And now she was also committed to helping Shannon in delivery. How was she going to find time to fulfill all of her obligations? She waited impatiently as Lauren dialed the number. Gwen's daughter answered and called her mother to the phone. The conversation went downhill from there.

Gwen refused to answer any questions from Lauren or Maris. Lauren identified herself as an FBI agent working to solve a serial rape and looking into Robin's disappearance. Maris pleaded as a friend of Shannon's and tried to play on Gwen's sympathies as a mother and someone who cared about Robin. Gwen confirmed Robin was there but refused to say why. Maris slammed down the receiver in frustration and hurled the phone across the room as Shannon opened the door. She was instantly sorry, for now she had to explain.

"What's wrong?" Shannon dropped her purse on the table, visibly alarmed. The baby-blue maternity dress with white cuffs and collar set off the blue in her eyes.

"You look lovely," Maris said, picking up the phone.

Shannon rubbed the small of her back. "Does she do this to you?" she asked Lauren.

"Change the subject when she doesn't want to tell me something? Yes."

Maris held the chair for Shannon. "What did the doctor say?"

"She said to quit being so impatient." She laughed. "No signs of labor yet. But everything is okay. It was nice of her to meet me so early on a Sunday morning." She reached up and touched Maris's hand. "Tell me what's wrong."

Lauren rose and plugged in her modem.

Maris sighed. "We don't know for sure anything is wrong." She sat next to Shannon and nodded for Lauren to tell her about the attacks.

"I remember those," Shannon said. "I still worked for the P.D. then, doing questioned documents." Concern crossed her face. "What does this have to do with Robin?"

"Maybe nothing." Maris touched her arm. "So don't get alarmed. We're only speculating."

While they talked, Lauren worked on her laptop.

"Shannon," she said, "did Robin keep an apartment in Richland Hills?"

"I'd say no . . ." She sighed. "But I've learned not to be surprised at anything with Robin."

Lauren dug her cell phone out of her purse. She dialed information and jotted down a number. Maris and Shannon listened as Lauren called an apartment manager.

"Wow," she said, cupping the phone. "I caught someone in the office on a Sunday." She talked for a moment and hung up the phone. "She's had an apartment since 'ninety-two." She told them the address.

Shannon threw her head back and closed her eyes. "It's the same one she had when we met. I thought she gave it up when she moved in with me." Her blue eyes moistened.

Lauren tapped her pen on the table. "Gwen said she's still in Denver. Why don't we wait and see what she does? She may come home and explain everything."

"We'll see." Shannon frowned. "I hope she does."

After Sunday brunch at the Chisholm, Maris and Lauren went home.

PART II

Chapter 14

Maris stared at the Internet Web page for *Pregnancy Today*. One more first-birth story like that, and she'd be ready for a shot of Black Jack instead of the ice water she was drinking. And they wanted first-time mothers to read this shit? No wonder women sometimes stole the little things from the hospital. It was damned sure easier than having one. The site should be forced reading for every twelve-year-old girl, Maris thought. They wouldn't uncross their legs until they turned thirty. She particularly liked the story titled "Thirty-six hour labor, birth and heavy bleeding" by "Cindy." What a sweet story about forceps, suction, pulling the baby's head and the mother's almost bleeding to death. The topper was when the woman said she was already five months pregnant with the next one. No doubt about it, she was sneaking a whiskey flask into that delivery room.

Glancing at the clock, she saw it was almost seven-thirty. What a way to spend Sunday evening — reading about babies. After returning from Fort Worth, Lauren left for Bass Cove to attend the funeral for Jennifer and Jill Kerr. She had dreaded it. Afterward she and Sally had planned to run down a few loose ends and talk to some of the kids who knew both Kyle and the girls. Lynette Donley had been buried on Saturday amidst a media circus, according to Sally, who attended it with Chief Kenedy. The murders still dominated the front page of the *Fort Worth Star Telegram* and the *Dallas Morning News*. The local television stations mentioned it on every news broadcast, and the Texas Cable News channel carried it off and on all day. Even Maris received her fair share of reporter phone calls, although she refused to answer questions and referred them to Sally, Kenedy or Lauren. Kyle's family had been nothing short of hounded until Bass Cove P.D. and the S.O. were forced to take turns supplying officers to guard the Parmers and their home. The victims' parents had been treated just slightly better. Of all those touched by the tragedy, only Patrick Starr sought out interviews and media attention. Lauren speculated that it was his way of mourning and assuaging the responsibility he felt as the girls' employer. Maris thought it was a generous assessment but that, in reality, Starr was a publicity hound and an asshole.

Stiff from her recent workout, Maris stood and stretched. Manipulating the mouse from an awkward angle, she debated which article on the *Pregnancy Today* Web site she should read first, the one about birth-partner duties or the stages of labor.

She chose the latter but decided to check her PCR-DNA samples before reading the article. The first ones should be coming off her Perkin-Elmer ABI Prism 310 Genetic Analyzer by now. Buying the new system, even though it meant borrowing about seventy thousand dollars, had been one of her smarter decisions. She'd added another room to the lab just for it, although building it had cost her about a third of her driveway on the lab side of the duplex. This type of automated DNA analysis was fast becoming the industry standard for forensic laboratories. Having it allowed her to participate in the Combined DNA Index System, known as CODIS, a database of DNA profiles consisting of convicted offenders and samples from unsolved crimes. CODIS allowed forensic laboratories to exchange and compare DNA profiles electronically, linking semen or blood from an unknown suspect to convicted offenders. Already suspects had been identified in numerous cases that might have otherwise been overlooked.

In October of 1998, the Austin DPS lab, the first one in the state on the CODIS system, had its initial hit with a previously unknown assailant when they matched biological evidence from the unsolved 1993 sexual assaults of two young sisters in Granbury, Texas. The girls had been playing in a dry creek bed and culvert when they were brutally attacked. CODIS identified Lester Don Parks, a prisoner serving time in Abilene on an indecency-with-a-child conviction filed in Coleman County in 1995. It marked the first time in Texas history that a totally unknown individual had been identified as a criminal suspect solely on the basis of DNA evidence. With the CODIS information, police were able to obtain a search warrant to collect additional blood from Parks. It was tested by the Fort Worth Police Department Crime Lab, since they'd analyzed the original evidence in '93, and again the samples matched.

Maris could hardly wait for her first "hit" and was in a friendly competition with the DPS lab in Garland, her former employer, to see who got the first one. Both labs bought the new equipment at about the same time and had been learning to use it and running the hundreds of samples required for validation of the procedure and instrumentation. After many late nights and long weekends in the lab, she started case work on the 310 Genetic Analyzer the first week in November.

Already she had come to think of the analyzer, which

was about the size of a thirty-inch-screen television with a Macintosh computer attached, as a little workhorse and referred to it affectionately as Jenny. She was doing it before she realized it and couldn't say for sure where the name came from. She assumed it was a subconscious take on *genetics* or *genetic* analyzer. At an evidentiary court hearing on a rape case, she'd slipped and called it Jenny while on the stand, causing a ripple of laughter from the prosecutor, defense attorney, judge and even the defendant. But the defense had quit asking her questions afterward. She guessed they figured a system worthy of a name had to be reliable.

Maris punched the keyboard on the Mac and brought the screen alive. Red, blue, green and yellow peaks of varying heights filled the screen. Her new automated STR-DNA-typing system combined the advantages of the PCR-based testing and fluorescent detection procedures that she was already using with the highly discriminating AmpFLSTR Profiler Plus STR-PCR amplification kit that was designed for human identification. Each kit contained all of the reagents necessary for the amplification of the samples as well as the material needed for genetic typing.

The automated genetic analyzer allowed her to look simultaneously at thirteen core STR loci as well as the Amelogenin locus used to determine if the sample was male or female in origin. Using this system, the probability of obtaining the same genetic type from two individuals increased from approximately one in five thousand, when using her old method of PCR-DNA typing, to an average of one in eighty-two billion. Yet she made it a policy, as did other labs, not to report frequencies greater than the approximate world's population of about 5.7 billion.

Maris clicked the mouse a few times to check the data that Jenny had collected. Satisfied that everything was in order, she was about to return to the on-line article about the stages of labor when she heard someone open the sliding door.

"Oh, she's back here somewhere, or the door wouldn't

be open," Lauren said. "Set that stuff on the cabinet and come see her new pride and joy."

"In here," Maris said. She positioned the pointer, hit enter to return to the original screen and rose to greet her green-eyed lover.

Sally followed Lauren into the DNA room. "I knew all you did was play computer games."

"My secret is out." Maris kissed Lauren lightly.

"I brought you a sample of what we think is blood from the back of a brick building in the alley, between the salon and Kyle's apartment." Sally leaned on the back of the chair and peered at the computer screen. "So this is the miracle machine."

Quickly Maris explained how it worked. "I started for DPS in the summer of 'eighty-five, right at the brink of the forensic DNA era. Our first system, in Austin, used the RFLP-typing procedure and required a dime-size sample of blood. With this, all I need is a speck, and I recently obtained useful data from a sample consisting of only thirty sperm heads."

"Incredible." Sally straightened and shook her head.

"Reed Wilson's samples are running now. Tomorrow I'll start with Kyle's and those from the pet salon." Maris led them into the lab and picked up the submission form Sally brought with the blood sample. "Anything new in the murder investigation?"

Sally leaned on the workbench. "We found another girl who used to work for Patrick Starr. She quit when he came to work late one afternoon after he'd been drinking heavily. She was there alone. She claims he trapped her in his office, exposed himself and wouldn't let her leave until she jacked him off. She quit the next day. We're trying to get her to press charges."

"I'll bet there are others who can back up her story with tales of their own," Maris said.

"I'd imagine. The allegations made me suspicious enough to go back and double-check his alibi. Can't shake it. He picked up his coach buddy like he said, and they

127

were in the bowling-alley bar by five-fifteen. Numerous witnesses and the tab he ran on his MasterCard confirm it."

Busy with the paperwork to officially transfer the evidence from Sally's custody to hers, Maris didn't notice Lauren at her computer until it was too late.

"You've been studying." Lauren dropped into the chair and scrolled down the screen. "You read this yet about birth partners?"

Maris felt the color creep into her cheeks. "Not yet."

"Mind if I print a couple of these articles?"

"Go right ahead." Surprised at the annoyance carried in her voice, Maris grabbed the envelope and hurried to her evidence vault. She spun the combination dial and became more irritated when she screwed it up the first time and had to repeat the numbers. When the lock finally opened, she placed the new sample inside and spun the dial.

Lauren had abandoned the computer and waited near Sally. She looked at Maris quizzically.

"That it?" Sally asked.

"That's it. I'll start tomorrow on the rest of the evidence as soon as I finish the reports on the samples that are running now."

"Great." Sally shifted her feet. "Lauren and I had talked about all of us going out to eat tonight. Interested?"

"Where to?" Maris asked.

After a brief discussion, they made arrangements to meet Sally and her girlfriend at a steakhouse on lower Greenville and talked about going dancing afterward. After Sally left, Lauren went to start the shower while Maris shut down the lab. As she crossed the living room to join her, Irene stopped her.

"I'm sorry. About Friday." Irene's hands shook as she held a Diet Coke. Raising her hand, she flipped her bangs from her eyes.

"That's okay." Maris noticed the bruises around her wrists and upper arm. She pointed. "Did I do those?"

"What's a few bruises?" Irene pulled her hand away.

"I never meant to hurt you. I only wanted to keep you

from driving or hurting Lauren or yourself." Maris saw resignation in her eyes. "Why were you so afraid of me?"

"I don't know what you're talking about." She gave a wry grin.

"When I came in from the lab," Maris prodded, "I yelled at you about smoking in the house, and you spilled your drink. I ran to get a towel, and you acted like I'd gone for a club."

"Let's just say you wouldn't be the first one to beat me in anger." Irene crossed her arms.

"I wasn't going to do that," Maris said. "I'm sorry I hurt you."

Irene fidgeted with her cigarette case and lighter. "Lauren's a lucky woman," she said. "I've never had anyone look at me the way you look at her."

"You deserve someone to treat you right. I hope you find that someone." She rushed to join Lauren.

She found Lauren bent under the water to rinse the suds from her shoulder-length red hair. Maris quickly undressed and stepped into the shower. She wrapped her arms around her and kissed her on a damp shoulder. She traced a pattern of freckles with her finger while Lauren squirmed in her arms and twisted around to face her.

"That tickles." She laughed, locking her hands behind Maris's neck.

Maris blinked as water splashed in her eyes. She pressed her lips against Lauren's, parting her lips. She felt hands on her chest pushing her away.

"We don't have time for this," Lauren said.

Maris licked the water from the base of her neck. "Later then."

"It's a date, Blue Eyes." She slipped from Maris's embrace. "I didn't mean to upset you."

"Next time we'll plan an earlier start." Maris laughed.

"No. About upsetting you in the lab."

"You didn't do anything." Maris picked up the bottle of shampoo.

"Then what was that about?"

Maris stopped lathering her hair and thought for a moment. "I honestly don't know."

Lauren cocked her head and studied her. Then she kissed her lightly. "Hurry up. I'm hungry."

Maris chuckled. "Who's telling who to hurry?" She knew she'd be fully dressed and pacing the floor with her second beer before Lauren decided what to wear.

Chapter 15

Maris disentangled herself from the sheets and reached across Lauren to slap the alarm. No one should have to get up at five o'clock, especially on a Monday, she thought as she picked her way through scattered clothing. Earnhardt barked and she silenced him. He nosed her calves, hurrying her to let him out. Her stiff back and sore legs, the product of almost two hours of continuous dancing, kept her from moving as fast as she or he would've liked. She smiled as she unlocked the door. Last night was special. She shivered as the border collie rushed past her, barking. The more time she spent with Sally and her new girlfriend, the more she enjoyed it. Where Sally was shy, almost taciturn at times,

Carla was affable and saucy. She and Lauren should have called it a night after dinner, but they were having fun and seldom went dancing. Then they made love when they got home, and she wondered if she'd slept for more than three hours. But who's complaining? She grinned. You can rest when you're dead.

She showered, dressed and started the coffee. She noticed the living room was cleaner, neater than usual after Irene had stayed up late watching movies. At least Lauren hadn't cared last night that her sister was home and still awake. They were already undressing each other when they stumbled past her.

After letting Earnhardt in and warning him not to wake Lauren, she flipped on the lights to the lab and started the computers. In a bluesy, country mood, she slapped a Lucinda Williams CD in the player and checked Jenny. She spent the next hour and a half, stopping once to get another cup of coffee, going over the data on the samples from Lynette's boyfriend, Reed Wilson, his clothing and vehicle, and the semen sample on Jennifer Kerr's panties. All the blood was his, but the semen came from someone else. She completed the documentation in the case folder, wrote a report and faxed the results to the Bass County Sheriff's Office, attention Sally Trent.

That done, she poured another cup of coffee, grabbed a bowl of cereal and carried them to the lab. She brought up the Internet, checked her e-mail and returned to the *Pregnancy Today* Web site. She read the article about child-birth partners and gained no more confidence in her ability to help Shannon. Most of the suggestions had to do with making the mother more comfortable during labor, taking her for short walks, rubbing her down and seeing that she drank plenty of fluids and maintained a positive attitude. She particularly liked the one advising her to bring her swimsuit so that if the mother couldn't take a warm bath to relieve contractions, the birth partner could assist her in the shower. Somehow, when she fantasized about showering with Shannon, that wasn't what she had in mind. God, she wished Robin would come to her senses. What, besides guilt, made fathers go through this when most hospitals had perfectly fine waiting rooms?

She decided to check on Shannon and rang her office. Shannon answered cheerfully on the third ring. "You sound good this morning," Maris said.

"I feel better today, and I've got a good case, a rush examination on a will. Wealthy woman disinherited her children and left all her money to some group called Children of the New Millennium. Her own kids are protesting, but it appears authentic."

"Have you heard from Robin?" Maris stretched out her legs.

Shannon sighed and Maris heard her chair creak. "She called and asked about the baby. She apologized for being gone. Then she said it might be a while before she could move back home. No excuses, no explanation." She laughed and Maris caught the bitterness in her tone. "I told her I knew about the apartment and her trip to Denver."

"What'd she say?" Maris drank the last of her coffee.

"The predictable 'It's not what you think.' When I asked what it was, she said she didn't know. I told her not to come home or call me until she had an answer."

"I'm sorry this is happening."

"It's that damned apartment. Of all the things that she's done, I feel more insulted, humiliated to learn she's kept it all this time. To me, it means she never expected us to make it."

"Did you ask her if any of this is related to the 'ninety-one rapes?"

"No. It's her place to tell me if she has a problem." She took a deep breath. "I knew when we decided to have this baby that I might have to go it alone. And it's okay."

"You won't be alone. It may not be the same, but Lauren and I will be there for you. And Timothy, when he returns from his trip."

"Don't worry about me. I'll be fine."

"I know you will." When Shannon hung up, Maris stared at the phone and vowed to track Robin down for a little talk.

* * * * *

The next three days passed quickly as Maris pushed to
complete as much of the analysis on the Starr's Pet Salon
evidence as possible. On Thursday, December 18, she
compiled her bloodstain-pattern interpretations with the
results of laboratory tests, including STR-PCR-DNA typing,
the autopsy report from the medical examiner's office and
Shirley Grimes's fingerprint examinations so she could
document the sequence of events in the pet salon and reconstruct the crime as it occurred. She based her conclusions on scientific fact and expert observation, but
admittedly, some of the conclusions were subjective.

So far, she'd established that the blood from all three
girls was on Kyle Parmer's shoes and the lower cuffs of his
jeans. His shirt had Jennifer's blood on the front. The tear
in the knee of his jeans matched the bloody impression near
her body. From the location of the stains and the impression
of the tear, she had no doubt that he'd tried unsuccessfully
to mount the dead teen and had masturbated on the panties
in frustration. His fingerprints were on the clippers used to
shave Jennifer and scattered throughout the pet salon,
including the counter and the cash register. The analytical
results, her observations and the fingerprints pointed to
Kyle's guilt. Or so she thought until her theory fell apart.

The semen detected on Jennifer Kerr's panties did not
come from Kyle Parmer. She double-checked her technique
and Jenny's results. She compared the DNA on the panties
in this test with the DNA type obtained when she ran the
sample against Reed Wilson's blood. Her results were
consistent and reliable. She started over on the reconstruction, reevaluating every piece of information, including
the lack of cast-off blood spatters on Kyle's clothing and the
possible inconsistencies in the handwriting on the wall. She
concluded someone else murdered the three girls. Kyle came
in later and shaved Jennifer Kerr and possibly tried to have
intercourse. If so, he was unable to penetrate and unable to
complete the act by masturbation or other means. Maybe he
tried sex first and then shaved her in an attempt to make
her less intimidating, more childlike. Before he left, he

robbed the cash register, took the broken shears, possibly as a souvenir and, using the Taco Bell cup to dip the blood, wrote the second line with *Satan* misspelled on the wall. All after the young women were already dead. He may have even witnessed the attacks.

Lynette Donley died first. Maris surmised the stainless-steel shears were on the counter and conveniently within the perpetrator's reach. In the brutal and swift assault, the murderer, wearing leather gloves, stabbed her at least fifteen times as determined by the autopsy and cast-off bloodstain pattern on the ceiling and walls.

Jennifer, grooming the cocker spaniel, heard the commotion and came forward to see what was happening, to assist Lynette or perhaps go for help. He tackled her on the lobby side of the counter, striking the Christmas tree and knocking it to the floor. Stabbed twice while near the tree, she managed to fight him off. He struck her two more times as they struggled near the bulletin board, but she broke away when her little sister came to her aid, as indicated by the mingled blood from both girls. Jennifer rushed to escape, grasped the doorknob and left her blood as proof of her efforts. The killer dragged Jennifer back to the middle of the lobby floor where his hand with the broken shears rose and fell nine more times, casting blood in a high, wide arc.

At some point Jill, also injured, retreated to the bathroom with the portable phone, leaving the blood trail, but he smashed the base, rendering it useless. Trapped in the tiny bathroom with a dead phone, Jill tried to escape through the window. He broke through the hollow door and killed her. Dropping the bloody shears on the towel by the sink, he ripped Jill's jeans down to her ankles, grabbed the nearest object, a hairbrush, and in a state of rage sodomized her.

Maybe he wanted to flee the terrible din inside the kennel. Maybe the cocker spaniel abandoned on the grooming table barked and whined incessantly. At any rate, he picked up the shears and tore out the dog's throat.

Highly agitated, he returned to Lynette Donley, who, judging from the bloody crawl marks, still clung to life. In a frenzy, he mutilated her face and plunged the shears into her until she stopped moving. Aroused by his power and control, he slashed her blouse and peeled off her khaki cargo pants. Then, either from the lack of an erection, the desire to further humiliate her or his remaining anger, he grabbed a nearby broom and thrust it deep inside her.

She pictured him, physically spent, his fury waning, as he lingered near her to catch his breath. The pool of blood caught his attention and, almost giddy with power, he plunged his finger into the sticky liquid to write on the wall.

Calmer, he went to Jennifer and took his time undressing her. He didn't or couldn't rape her, and instead masturbated on her panties. Then he vanished. It was impossible to know if Kyle watched the entire attack from a hiding place or if he arrived later, but she doubted the killer ever knew of his presence. She bet Kyle's arrest shocked him.

The reconstruction completed, she stood and paced the lab. Alarm suddenly overtook her, making her jaw tighten. She knew her interpretation of the events was accurate. Sure, some details, such as when he smashed the phone, when he killed the dog, might be second-guessed, but overall it was correct — and certain to be unwelcome and controversial.

Condemned and crucified by television and newspapers, Kyle Parmer's guilt drew few doubters. Praise for fast police work flooded the police department and sheriff's office, and the parents expressed their gratitude for a fast resolution. None of the investigators, including her lover and Sally, would be pleased with her report. She dreaded telling them.

She racked her brain for any other possible explanation for the semen on Jennifer's panties and the lack of the expected blood spatters on Kyle's clothing. She supposed it was possible that Jill had sex before going to work and failed to clean up or change clothes. But Maris didn't believe it. It didn't fit Jennifer's reputation, and the autopsy showed no signs of recent sexual activity or the presence of semen. And she didn't believe Kyle wore an overcoat or changed clothes between killing the women and turning his attention on Jennifer.

About three, Maris grabbed the phone to page Lauren but stopped when she remembered that she had appointment with Irene's counselor. She wondered what kind of disaster that would be. Irene had gone by herself on Tuesday and came home depressed and teary-eyed. She left Lauren a voice mail and called Sally. She heard the excitement and enthusiasm drain from Sally as she realized the results cast doubt on Kyle as the murderer, although no doubt he was guilty of robbery, among other things. She promised to fax copies of the lab results and her crime reconstruction to Sally, Chief Kenedy and the D.A.'s office. Then she sat back to wait for the storm.

At almost five, as she struggled with her bench press, Lauren rapped on the door. Wiping her face with a towel, Maris let her in. "Hope you don't mind if I finish," she said.

Straddling the bench, she picked up a thirty-pound barbell with each hand and alternated biceps curls. She concentrated on the weights until she had the rhythm and glanced up to see Lauren leaning against the wall, her arms folded across her waist with a hand cupping each elbow. Maris froze with both weights dangling at her side. "What's wrong?"

Lauren shook her head.

Dropping the weights, she went to her. Lauren continued to hug herself until Maris worked her hands free and pulled her close. "My lab results upset you that bad?" She reached back for the towel hanging on the handlebars of the stationary bike.

"No." Lauren waved her hand. "I . . . the therapy session with Irene." Her chin quivered. "I don't know if I can talk about it."

"Where is she?" Maris draped the towel around her neck.

"In her room." Lauren fingered the silver bullet around Maris's neck. "I found out what she meant . . . about things were always better for me." She sighed. "Now it all makes sense."

Maris used the corner of the towel to blot the tears from Lauren's cheek.

"When I was born, an aunt, my father's sister, and an uncle lived next door to us. They had a son about thirteen. Irene was eight —"

Maris grimaced. She knew where this story was going.

Lauren rested her head against Maris's chest. "He abused her sexually for the next four years. Then he dumped her for another little girl. She never told anyone, but something happened. Maybe he got caught or another child told on him, but his father jerked him out of high school halfway through his senior year and made him join the Army. He was killed in a single-car drunk-driving accident a couple of years later."

"Sometimes there is justice." Maris stroked her hair.

"I remember a horrendous argument between Irene and my mother when she refused to go to the funeral." She sniffed. "I'm glad she told me. It explains so much. Her resentment toward me, even what happened with Karin." She smiled. "I'm okay, really."

"Then let's go inside for something to drink. I need a glass of ice water." Maris took her hand and led her inside.

"I need an aspirin." Lauren rubbed her temples. "Fix me some water too, please."

"So what did you think about the results on the panties?"

Lauren searched the cabinet until she found the aspirin. "I was on a conference call with Sally and Kenedy most of the way home. I finally pulled into a Wal-Mart parking lot before I had an accident."

"And?" She let Earnhardt inside and ruffled the hair on his head and back. He barked and charged into the kitchen to greet Lauren. Maris sank into the corner of the sofa. Lauren joined her, snuggling close.

"Kenedy wants to have everything reanalyzed."

"Let me guess," Maris said. "DPS won't take it because I've already worked most of it, and it's against their policy to waste tax dollars analyzing cases that have already been done." She didn't bother to add that she used the same procedures and quality control safeguards that DPS did, and the results would be the same anyway. "And SWIFS," she said, referring to the county lab, "charges for it. Paying twice could get expensive."

"Not only that, but it'd take three or four months to get the results back," Lauren said.

"Look." Maris took her hand. "I have no objections to a second opinion. To keep expenses down, you could have only the panties and samples from Jennifer Kerr and Kyle Parmer analyzed. And if you want another bloodstain-pattern expert to review the case, I'll gladly make the photos and my notes available — if he'll come to my lab and examine them here. Just let me know so we can work around my court schedule."

"Are they going to disagree?" Lauren asked.

"With some minor details, sequencing of events in the reconstruction and so forth — possibly. Nothing major. And the DNA results will be the same, if a legitimate lab does it."

Lauren sipped her water. "The signs were there from the beginning that we had two perps. Both of us noticed the inconsistencies. It bothered me that someone could calmly shave a woman immediately after such a frenzied attack."

"And in addition to Kyle's fingerprints, we had the ones from the leather gloves." Maris rubbed the back of Lauren's neck. "Do you realize, if the murderer hadn't jacked off on her panties, we'd never have proof that Kyle didn't do everything? What do the others say?"

"We all agree that we have to investigate the possibility that Jennifer had consensual sex before going to work and didn't clean up."

"But the autopsy results were negative — no sperm, no signs of recent intercourse."

"I know, and it doesn't fit what we know about Jennifer." Lauren put a hand on Maris's thigh. "Kenedy noticed in the crime scene photos that a smock is missing on one of the hangers in the grooming room. The girls wore them when bathing the dogs. Starr confirmed it."

"So he thinks Kyle had the presence of mind to put it on before engaging in a mad stabbing spree." Maris snorted. "So what now?"

"Start at the beginning and reinterview everyone. Do the things we were already planning to do but haven't had time. Check Kyle's acquaintances and track the county sex offenders."

"What about the weirdos in brown from the church up the street?"

"The Trinity Outreach Church of Redemption." She laughed. "Actually, the pastor has a good reputation for helping troubled kids. All of his counselors are degreed professionals. The night of the murders, the residents were at dinner and in Bible study from four-thirty that afternoon until about ten. He released them to pray at the scene after they heard about it. He swears all his employees and kids were there the whole time."

"Lynette and Kyle had drugs in their possession. Anyone looked into a link there?"

Lauren said, "Shirley found Reed Wilson's prints on the Baggie from Lynette's purse. We think he gave her the drugs." She reached for the remote control. "Mind if we watch the six o'clock news?"

"No," Maris said, noting it was ten minutes before it started.

"I feel like I should be drinking something stronger than water." Lauren laid her head on Maris's shoulder. "I interviewed Al Anderson this morning."

"Who?"

"The former TCU student suspected in the 'ninety-one rapes. His mother worked for the P.D."

Lauren fingered a tear in Maris's sweats. "He was pleasant, good-looking and helpful. He answered all my questions willingly and earnestly. And I felt like I needed a shower afterward." She slid to the edge of the sofa. "He's an I.D. tech for the P.D. Works crime scenes, takes photos and is sort of their unofficial camera and video expert."

"And he has a spotless record," Maris said. "You ever notice how many of these rape suspects are camera, gun or computer nuts?"

"I think *nut* is the operative word." Lauren slipped off her shoes and flexed her toes. "I also talked to the man sent up for the burglary and attempted rape shortly after the assaults stopped. He's been out for a year and a half. Has a job as a brake mechanic. He's recently married, and his wife is expecting. He says he had a drug habit and burglarized about three hundred houses and apartments but swears he's straight now. He says the attempted rape was a misunderstanding. The girl thought he was trying to rape her, but he only wanted to quiet her and convince her not to report him. They struggled, and she assumed rape. May or may not be true, but it's clear he's not the serial rapist." She turned up the volume as the news started. "I'm going to keep looking into those cases."

After a story about a house fire that claimed the life of a toddler while her mother went to the store for cigarettes, Walker Edward, assistant district attorney, strolled out of the courthouse and gave the thumbs-up. Known as an aggressive attorney, sometimes overly so, Walker was rumored to be on his way to the U.S. Attorney's office. Maris wasn't surprised that he'd taken on this case. A small man, only about five-five, he was smooth-shaven with carefully trimmed brown hair. "Today," he said, "the grand jury indicted Kyle Parmer, and, if he's found guilty, we intend to seek the death penalty." Straightening the diamond cuffs on his shirt, he beamed at the cameras. "I'll tell you the parents are relieved to have that monster off the streets. We're very proud of the law enforcement effort that brought such a quick resolution to this case."

"That's it." Maris threw up her hands. "It's over."

Lauren looked stunned. "How can he do that? I didn't think the grand jury was convening until after the first of the year." She reached for the phone, but Maris stopped her.

"Don't waste your breath, honey. The only way to derail this runaway train is to hand them another suspect."

"But how could Sally —"

"She's got to be careful. This is a good job for her, and

141

if she holds on a few years she'll have a shot at making sheriff. No, the best thing for her is what's best for all of us. Keep working until we finish the puzzle." She squeezed Lauren's knee. "But quietly, or we'll all get pulled off the investigation."

"I don't understand how he thinks he can hide the DNA on the panties."

Maris shrugged. "Simple. Walker won't introduce them into evidence, and when I testify he won't ask any questions that will allow me to work it in. Unless the defense is smart enough to figure it out from the material they get in discovery, it'll never come out in court." Merry fucking Christmas, Kyle, she thought.

Chapter 16

After a light lunch on Friday, Maris dumped the contents of a Miller Genuine Draft beer box on the counter in the lab. Plastic bags with tablets, capsules and pharmaceutical vials of liquid spilled in a kaleidoscope of colors. Maris groaned and began sorting the items by exhibit number. As she worked, the murders stayed on her mind. The indictment upset her. Not that Kyle wasn't guilty. He did commit the robbery, among other things. The problem was that the circumstantial case against Kyle was damned near perfect, except for the panties and blood-spatter evidence. The real question, as she saw it, was who else other than Kyle had a connection to the girls? Or maybe a connection to the girls and to Kyle?

Maris mentally ran through a checklist of the evidence that still needed analysis. Hours of hair, fiber and other trace evidence examinations stretched before her, and she had yet to identify the drugs from Lynette's purse and Kyle's mattress. She found it curious that the capsules from Lynette's purse and Kyle's apartment were packaged the same way. The clear capsules, stuffed with sticky, brown Mexican heroin, usually came loose or in tiny resealable bags, not wrapped in aluminum foil. Although years ago heroin powder came in foil packs, she hadn't seen it like that in ages. Normally only methamphetamine, or crank, came in foil. And it was packaged that way for convenience of use as an easy way to share. Hold a candle or cigarette lighter under the unfolded wrapper and anyone standing nearby could inhale the fumes.

Some unknown chain of events set Lynette Donley, Jennifer and Jill Kerr on a collision course with Kyle and the unidentified third party, the killer. He directed his most intense anger at Lynette, indicating that she was the one who drew him there. Not that Maris meant to blame her. Lynette might have caught his attention by something as innocent as a misinterpreted smile or wave of the hand. A shrug of the shoulder, a casual comment, even a mild rebuke could have been magnified in his disturbed mind until it drove him to murder. If Lynette and Kyle crossed paths with the same dealer, could he be the link that led to the tragedy in Starr's Pet Salon? If only there'd been more time with Kyle, before his attorney stopped him from talking, they might have coaxed the kid into telling what he did and saw the night of the murders.

She assumed, based on a visual inspection, that all the capsules contained heroin. If the ones from Lynette and the ones from Kyle didn't contain the same ingredients, she could throw her theory out the window. Maris drummed her fingers on the counter. The inner surface of the foil might have the dealer's fingerprints. Forgetting the pharmaceuticals, she pulled Lynette's and Kyle's drugs from the vault. As she poured Lynette's marijuana into a plastic weigh boat, her pager went off. She recognized the number for Lauren's cell phone and called her.

Lauren answered on the first ring. "Hi," she said. "Just a minute."

A blinker chimed in the background amid the muffled traffic sounds. Maris held the receiver against her shoulder and fished out the foil wrapper as she waited.

"Is there any road in Dallas with no construction?" Lauren groaned. "I can't get anywhere. Don't forget we have a date. My Christmas party."

"Only the devil or the law could keep me away." She peeled back the corner of the packet, marked it and set it aside. "Does this little soiree call for five-hundred-dollar ostrich boots or the ninety-dollar cowhide?"

"Dress nice." Lauren laughed. "'Cause Mama has a new dress and new shoes."

"Then the high-dollar boots it is. Be careful, baby." She hung up the phone, grateful for whatever triggered her girlfriend's sudden desire for them to appear as a couple at an FBI function. Whether it was a good career decision for Lauren remained to be seen.

Whistling, she weighed the capsule, wrote the weight on a worksheet and, after presumptive color tests, screened Lynette's samples on the ultraviolet spectrophotometer, an instrument that measured the molecule's absorption of UV light, and recorded the results on a graph. Next she extracted some of the sticky brown substance for analysis on the automated Hewlett-Packard gas chromatograph/mass spectrometer and repeated the entire process with Kyle's dope, after marking and setting aside the foil wrapper from his case. Even without the results for the mass spec, she'd already discovered something unusual about each capsule. Caffeine was present. Not unusual for amphetamine and methamphetamine cases, it was rare in heroin, at least in north Texas, where it usually came with diphenhydramine, Benadryl. She supposed the capsules could be a poor boy's speedball with caffeine substituted for the cocaine.

While the mass spec did its thing, she turned her attention to the foil wrappers. Fingerprints seemed the best way to determine if the same dealer prepared both samples. She grabbed the phone and flipped through her Rolodex for Shirley Grimes's number at the S.O.

After two transfers and a long hold, Shirley answered.

Maris identified herself and asked, "Can you get fingerprints off foil paper?"

"Sure, honey," Shirley said in her slow east Texas drawl. "Super Glue."

"If I ran a couple of pieces up there, could you do them for me?"

"Not today," she said. "I've got court."

"Damn." Maris dropped to a stool and frowned. She didn't want to wait until Monday.

"Something important?" An oldies but goldies sixties station played in the background.

"I won't know until the prints are developed and compared."

"Don't you have some fingerprint equipment?" Shirley asked. "I thought you told me you bought a latent-print kit to use when no one else with fingerprint expertise was at the scene."

"I did, but I hardly qualify as an expert." The kit contained a thorough instruction manual. Maybe she could do it. "What the hell? Can't dance, might as well develop latents."

"If any come up, lift them with clear tape and slap 'em on an index card. Get them here as quickly as possible, and I'll check them if I get a break in court."

When the phone clicked, Maris snatched her keys from her desk and retrieved the leather case with the latent-print kit from the camper on the Ford pickup. Excited by the challenge of trying something new, she scanned the instruction booklet and bustled about the lab gathering scientific equipment. She hooked up a vacuum chamber in her ventilation hood and, using tweezers, situated the aluminum wrappers inside. She squeezed the glue, a cyanoacrylate ester, from a tube onto a tiny disposable dish and put it between the two pieces of foil. Turning on the vacuum pump, she briefly evacuated the chamber and cut the switch. She set a timer for twenty minutes and resumed taking inventory of the tablets and capsules until it beeped.

Holding her breath, she released the vacuum on the chamber and used tweezers to lift out the foil. Relief flooded through her. Prints exposed to Super Glue formed white ridges. On each piece of foil, she saw clearly a partial thumbprint among a smattering of other smears and indistinct ridges. After taking photographs, she further enhanced each print by dusting with fingerprint powder and used clear lifting tape to transfer them to white index cards. Taking an Ultraloupe magnifier, she studied each thumbprint. To her, they looked the same.

She called a courier service and, after preparing the prints for the trip, turned her attention to the mass spec data. The capsules in Lynette's and Kyle's possession contained heroin and caffeine, in keeping with her suspicions that they came from the same source.

So what, she thought. No proof existed that the dealer was in any way associated with the murders, and if he was, the prints couldn't prove it. The other party at the scene wore gloves. Maris tapped her pen on the desk. Shit, for all she knew the prints might be Reed Wilson's. His were on the Baggie from Lynette's purse that had held her drugs. She threw down her pen in frustration and glanced at the clock. Four-fifteen. She had to talk to Reed, find out if he sold the drugs to Lynette and Kyle. She tried to recall the name of the bar he frequented. Charlie's Sports Bar and Grill in Denton, she remembered. She dialed operator assistance for the Denton area and asked for the phone number. A quick call to the bar gave her the address. As she hung up the phone, the lab doorbell chimed. After peeking through the security window, she gave the waiting messenger the envelope with the prints for delivery to the S.O. With them safely en route, she shut down the lab and hurried to clean up and change clothes.

Maris's red 1970 Oldsmobile 442 convertible, despite the bulk of a Clydesdale, sliced through traffic with the agility of a cutting horse. At five o'clock straight up, she slid to a halt next to a muddy Chevy four-by-four parked near the crimson door of a piss-yellow brick structure not much larger than a 7-Eleven convenience store. *Charlie's Sports Bar and Grill,* in cursive, twelve-inch-high neon letters bolted to the brick, identified the establishment. The exterior reminded her of a gay bar in Waco where she had spent a lost weekend over a decade ago, and she expected a class-A dive, worthy of a women's back-street bar. She was wrong. A rich mahogany bar ran the full length of the wall to her right, backed by a spotless mirror framed with gold and silver inlay. Sliding up on a padded leather stool, Maris propped her boot on a brass foot rail. A sign boasted of twenty-seven beers on tap, and four rows of expensive name-brand liquors and a full wine rack attested to something for everyone. From the kitchen, off the end of the bar, the aroma of hamburgers, fajitas and Mexican spices made her mouth water.

The bartender, a good-looking brunette in a well-filled-out Charlie's Sports Bar and Grill T-shirt loitered near the cash register and dried glasses as she chatted with a handsome, dark-headed cowboy. She reached for a cigarette burning in a Coors' ashtray and smiled. "What'll it be?" she said with a Boston accent.

"Miller Lite." Maris glanced around. A young couple, possibly North Texas University students, played pool on one of two tables along the back wall. He playfully accused her of cheating and made a shot. Another man, in a business suit, talked quietly on the pay phone as he sipped a dark beer in a frosty mug. Six muted televisions suspended about the bar broadcast sporting events, while "My Maria" by Brooks and Dunn played on the jukebox.

The bartender tossed a Winston Cup coaster on the bar and set an ice-coated mug of beer in front of her. Asking her to run a tab, Maris took a sip. Tiny slivers of ice tickled her throat. She licked the foam off her upper lip and grinned. This place was perfect. If it had been a lesbian bar with a dance floor, she'd never go home. A beer-bellied male, about forty-five with a black T-shirt that said *Charlie,* sauntered out of the kitchen and handed the cowboy a two-inch-thick chili cheeseburger with steak-cut fries, a bottle of ketchup and silverware. With a nod and a grin, he returned to the kitchen and came back with a platter of nachos for the pool players. Her nose twitched at the aroma. To pass the time, she struck up a conversation with the brunette behind the bar.

By six, Maris knew that Trisha, the bartender, was from the Boston area but had moved down with her parents when she was in the eighth grade. She loved Texas and was working on a degree in physical therapy from North Texas. As Maris started her second beer, several men and women, some college age, filtered into the bar and another waitress, a blonde, rushed in breathlessly and began waiting tables. Maris reluctantly broke off her conversation with Trisha when Reed Wilson slid his tall, angular body onto the stool recently vacated by the cowboy. He flexed the black dragon on his biceps for Trisha and ordered a Budweiser. Maris saw her roll her eyes. The stitches on his hand were uncovered and healing nicely. Either he wasn't working or he'd gone home to clean up before coming to the bar.

"Put that on my tab," Maris said.

Reed rubbed his dirty-blond goatee and eyed her curiously. "Do I know you?" he asked.

"We met briefly." She waited for Trisha to pour his beer and then said, "Mind if we move to a booth where we can talk?"

Winking at Trisha, he grabbed his beer and followed her. "So where did we meet?" he asked. "Was it here or at a party somewhere?"

"How about in front of Starr's Pet Salon the night of the murders?"

His beer mug crashed to the table, sloshing Budweiser

all over his hand. He dried it on his black jeans and narrowed his eyes. "Thanks but no thanks for the beer." He started to rise.

"I'm not a cop. In fact, you ought to be buying me a beer. If it weren't for me, you'd be sitting in jail instead of Kyle Parmer." She leaned back and casually sipped her drink. "I did the DNA analysis that gave you your alibi."

"Yeah. Set me up on the fucking burglary."

She shrugged. "B.F.D. You did it."

He frowned but relaxed in the booth. "Maybe I'll finish my Bud." He fished a pack of Kools out of the front pocket of his jeans and lit a smoke using a match from a book advertising *Charlie's Sports Bar and Grill*.

Holding her mug between both hands, Maris lowered her voice. "Losing Lynette must have been terrible for you. And then being accused of killing her yourself..."

"Yeah." He blew a smoke ring. "Everyone, including her bitch mother, forgets that I loved her."

"Too bad."

"She wouldn't let me sit with the family at the funeral. And Lynette's fucking doctor father tried to have me removed. So I told them to go fuck themselves and split." His gaze followed the pool players. "The asshole cops never even apologized after they arrested the real murderer either." He drained his glass.

Maris waved at the waitress to order him another.

"Pitchers are happy-hour price until eight."

"Okay. Make it a pitcher," she said.

"Budweiser," he added as the waitress turned to go.

Drawing circles in the moisture on the table, Maris said, "I know you want to see whoever killed Lynette and the other girls punished."

"You're fucking right." He grabbed the pitcher almost before the slender waitress put it down, then refilled his glass.

"Although Kyle's involved, I don't think he killed the girls."

He ground out the cigarette. "What're you saying?"

"The bastard who stabbed them to death and mutilated the bodies is still out there." She leaned over the table. "I need to know where Lynette and Kyle got their drugs — the marijuana and heroin capsules."

He started to reply, and she could tell by his eyes that he was going to lie. But he paused. "Don't misunderstand me. I ain't no saint. But I didn't want her doing heroin." He shook his head. "Give me a little crank so I can party all evening, fuck all night and work all day. A little weed for kicking back." He arched an eyebrow and leered. "And a little Liquid X for serious fucking." Stroking his beard, he asked, "You ever try it? It makes for an awesome good time."

Reaching for the pitcher, she filled her mug. "Any better might kill me."

He laughed and watched something on the TV behind her. "The dude is weird, man. Like seriously warped. Wears this black leather overcoat all the time ... like he's some fucking gunslinger or something. Mouths off Bible verses." He shook his head. "He showed me this scar on his arm." Reed held up his hands to form a circle about four inches in diameter. "About this big. Said an angel told him to get rid of his tattoo. Called it an 'affront to the Almighty.' He used an electric sander to remove it. Then cauterized it with a hot iron. Fucking crazy."

She said nothing as he poured another beer.

"Bastard hasn't been around here very long. Couple of months maybe." He reached for another Kool. "Lynette was a little afraid of him."

He inhaled deeply on his cigarette. Refilling his mug, he topped off Maris's with the last of the pitcher. He waved to the waitress for another. "The weird fucker hung out at the station with Kyle when his old man wasn't around. That's where Lynette met him."

"He and Kyle friends?"

"Oh, hell, no. He made fun of Kyle all the time. Behind his back. Motherfucker only used him. See, Kyle had a truck and could drive."

Maris took a sip. She'd had about enough to drink on an empty stomach. "What's this bastard's name?"

"Who the fuck knows?" Reed blew smoke, smiling as the waitress brought a new pitcher.

151

Maris handed her a credit card to close out the tab. "Any nicknames?"

Reed wiggled in the booth, obviously bored now that Maris was closing out the tab. "Started with a *B*. Blake, Bryce . . . one of those kind of names. Kyle and some of the girls called him Satan."

She clenched the handle of her mug. "Do you know where he lives?"

"Within walking distance of the gas station. He also hangs around that old church."

"Close to Starr's Pet Salon."

"Yeah."

The waitress returned with the receipt and her card. She signed the receipt and put her ard away. Sliding to the end of the booth, she asked, "Why in the hell didn't you tell this to one of the investigators?"

"I was mad at the bastards." He shrugged. "That dyke deputy accused me of selling drugs. Said they found one of my prints on the Baggie of pot in Lynette's purse." He flashed a grin as he lifted his mug. "Probably true. I stole some of her dope to roll a couple of joints."

"But this dealer may have killed the woman you say you loved."

"I did love her. That moron, Kyle, killed her. He's always been weird. Lynette said he used to sneak in the back door to play with the dogs. She didn't like the way he looked at her, but Jennifer was nice to him. She let him help clean the cages." Reed scowled. "Now that you reminded me, I might be able to use the info later if —" He caught himself and waved his cigarette. "You know what I mean . . . the next time I'm busted."

She stood. "Then why tell me?"

"You ain't a cop, and you bought me beer." He smirked. "Anything I tell you is my word against yours —"

"You'll lose that one, bud," she said. Maris finished her beer and wiped her mouth on her sleeve. Leaning palms-down on the table inches from his face, she said, "You're one sorry son-of-a-bitch."

"Hey, goddamn it." He started to rise, and she pushed him down.

"Thanks for the info." Without looking back, she strode toward the door.

Chapter 17

Beer and frustration churned in her empty stomach until she pulled into a McDonald's and slammed down a Quarter Pounder in self-defense. That son-of-a-bitch Reed Wilson acted like he could care less some monster mutilated and destroyed his girlfriend. Where was his outrage?

The 455 Olds big-block hauled her through challenging curves with enough g's to ratchet tight the seat belt and press her against the car door. At the Bass Cove city limits, she slammed on the brakes and downshifted to thirty-five. She rounded the corner at Parmer's Automotive Service and approached Starr's Pet Salon. A solitary street lamp illuminated a sidewalk crowded with wind-blown wreathes, limp cards and wilting flowers. She stopped and stared at the dark building. The barking of big and little dogs blended with the forlorn bay of a hound.

Shifting into first, she bumped across the railroad tracks and rolled past Lucky's Stop and Go. A white clapboard sanctuary with a sharp steeple faced south on a small hilltop two blocks north of the store. Two white-painted brick wings that appeared to be dormitories extended across the back, forming a T-shaped compound. A rusting yellow school bus on a flat tire and three older-model cars decorated the east lot. Permanent no-trespassing signs glowed on sturdy metal posts on each side of the church underneath bright security lamps. A simple black sign with large white letters declared the name, Trinity Outreach Church of Redemption, and the pastor, Maurice Oldham. Someone had wrapped the sign posts in red and green garland and draped a Merry-Christmas banner on one side of the church, and Maris could barely see the unlit plastic nativity scene in the shadows cast by the building and the streetlights.

A cluster of young women trickled out of the side door laughing and clutching Bibles. Dressed in brown, ankle-length dresses with white stockings and black low-heeled shoes, they scattered across a covered porch and loitered on the steps and wooden benches. Lighters flashed, and they drew on fresh cigarettes, forming halos of smoke.

Afraid to circle again in the eye-catching convertible with the loud tailpipes, Maris returned to the store, parked and hiked back to the church. None of the women remained in the yard, but cigarette smoke tickled her nose as Maris slipped inside the church. Voices echoed down a stark, carpetless hallway. Pictures of Jesus lined the walls. A strong male voice rose and fell in cadence as he chanted Scripture and cajoled the sinners to repent and change their wicked ways. Unsure what she'd say if challenged, she pressed her back against the wall and listened. The preacher's low-pitched voice rang out hypnotically, but the sermon he exhorted, sprinkled with street language, wasn't like the lectures she had endured as a child at the First

155

Baptist Church in Sweetwater. Holding her breath, Maris peered around the corner into a fellowship hall furnished in ordinary, brown folding chairs, scarred card tables and a battered podium.

A fleshy male, about fifty to fifty-five, in a sweat-stained, rumpled white shirt lifted his arms to God. Transfixed by the power of his words, the brown-clad women followed his every move as he paced before them, his belly spilling over the waistband of his wrinkled gray trousers. Pausing to grab a drink of water, he ran a meaty hand through his thinning, silver hair, and Maris assumed that she'd found the esteemed Reverend Maurice Oldham.

"This is a private meeting," a voice behind her growled.

She turned. Before her, clad in a dark, short-sleeved T-shirt over black jeans, stood Brian Blake. Recognition and hate blazed in his dark eyes. He drew himself to his full height and towered over her. Gone were the pimples, the pierced earrings and nose ring. He tossed his stringy, jet-black hair away from his forehead and said, "I ought to —"

"Brian Blake, you bastard." She stared at the ruddy four-inch scar on his forearm. Gone was the inverted cross and an upside-down pentagram tattoo he once had. It confirmed what she knew in her heart the moment she recognized him. Brian was the dealer who sold heroin to both Kyle and Lynette. And he was entirely capable of murder. "I should have killed you when I had the chance," she added.

A door slammed, and she heard heavy footsteps on the linoleum. "Stay right there," barked a uniformed Bass Cove police officer.

"Fuck!" she muttered under her breath.

The sermonizer jerked his head toward the commotion and clapped his hands. "Dismissed." The young women scrambled to their feet and, murmuring, left the fellowship hall.

"A trespasser," Brian said to the preacher.

The police officer, one she didn't know, shoved her against the wall and frisked her. She never broke her glare at Brian. The mere presence of the depraved bastard who'd corrupted Lauren's niece, Karin, and drew her into Satanism, drugs and group sex infuriated Maris.

Brian threw back his head and laughed.

She narrowed her eyes. "You know, when the light hits your hair just right, I can see a little dent."

His face clouded with rage. "Get her out of here," he said, through clenched teeth.

She smelled his stale, smoker's breath. If only she'd hit him a little harder with that ax handle. Her stomach churned.

"How'd you get here so fast?" Maris asked as she handed the officer her driver's license. Her pager went off and she quickly silenced it.

"Saw you park at the Stop and Go and walk to the church." He squinted at her license and then at her. "Thought it odd."

She nodded. Obviously they were watching the area around the salon for unusual activity.

"Why are you here, young lady?" Reverend Oldham asked.

Maris heard a door slam, and Little Ricky raced around the corner into the hallway. "Maris?" he said, somewhat out of breath. He pulled the other Bass Cove officer aside. After conferring for a moment, he told his buddy, "I'll take it from here."

"Fine. I don't need the paperwork." The officer flipped his notebook closed and handed Maris her driver's license. He nodded to Brian and the Reverend and left.

"You want to press charges?" Rick asked.

"She hasn't said why she was here." Brian glared at Maris.

"Curiosity, I guess." Maris shrugged.

"I can vouch for her," Little Ricky said.

"We can't be too careful . . . with all these young people

around. Sometimes we have to protect them from their past." Reverend Oldham hesitated. "But no, we won't press charges."

Brian protested, but Little Ricky took her arm and led her out of the church.

"It's a long story," she replied to Little Ricky's questions as she leaned against his patrol car.

"Well, it's lucky for you I'm the one who answered the call for backup. Otherwise you might be facing a trespassing charge."

She ignored his comment and asked, "What do you know about this place?"

"Not much." He shrugged. "It's a religious drug rehab center for teens. From what I understand it's all privately funded through donations and by charging the parents who can afford it. Some of these kids were literally living on the streets and working as prostitutes when the reverend took them in."

"It's weird. The brown dresses the girls wear." Maris crossed her arms against the chill in the night air.

"Yeah, and the silly brown tunics that the boys wear. Supposedly the attire is part of their discipline and is based on a strongly conservative, fundamentalist ministry." He stepped away from the car and pointed to the T-shaped wings. "That's the boys' dorm, and this is the girls'. They say the sexes are kept separate most of the time. And they attend school here, not in town. Most people seem to think the program is a good thing." He shrugged. "I don't know. But we don't have any trouble with them." He looked around uneasily. "Except for a suicide a year ago and an OD the day before the murders. Guess some of that's to be expected with their background."

"Male or female, the OD?" Maris asked.

"Female." Pausing on the winter lawn, he asked, "Why are you here?"

"I was drawn to the word of God."

"Uh-huh." He frowned. "Well, at least I don't have to book you for trespassing."

She knew he was unsatisfied, but she didn't want word filtering back to Chief Kenedy about Brian Blake before she told Lauren and Sally. Her pager screamed, and she flinched when she saw the number for Lauren's cellular phone. She remembered the Christmas party and checked the number for the page she received inside the church. It was from her home number. Probably Lauren's first attempt to reach her. With a wave, she thanked Rick and ran to the Stop and Go where her red convertible was parked.

Maris noted it was a quarter to nine as she dialed Lauren's number while backing out of the parking place. They were supposed to have been there by seven-thirty. Lauren would be furious. The phone rang once and switched to Lauren's voice mail. Maris left an apology and killed the connection. She called home, and Irene confirmed that Lauren had left for the party.

Feeling guilty and depressed, not wanting to go home and put up with Irene, Maris called her friend, Kathy, and invited herself over. She'd known Kathy since she'd first moved to Dallas to start her job in the DPS crime lab. Kathy and her ex-lover, Lynn, often spent time with Maris and Mary Ann, and she didn't know what she'd have done without them when Mary Ann died. She knew Kathy would give her a good place to hang out for a couple of hours.

The garage door lowered with a whine, and Maris killed the engine on the Olds, draining the last of the tallboy Miller Lite that she'd bought to sip on the way home from Kathy's. To Maris's relief, Lauren was already home, although it was only eleven-thirty.

"You're in deep shit," Irene said, sprawled in Maris's recliner. She pointed to the patio when Maris glared at her. "She's outside."

Maris paused with her hand on the latch to the storm door. In the glow from the backyard mercury-vapor light, she saw Lauren clearly. In a stunning black party dress and three-inch, come-fuck-me heels, she stood with her back to the house. She inhaled deeply on a cigarette and, with her feet slightly ajar, crossed one arm over her stomach to prop her other elbow. Her red hair flashed as she tossed her head and angrily blew smoke into the cool night air. Earnhardt, his head on his paws, lay a few feet away, his eyes following Lauren's every move.

At the click of the latch, Lauren blew smoke but said nothing.

Maris's chest ached with regret and longing. She stopped behind Lauren, wanting to embrace her. "Baby," she said. "I'm sorry. I completely forgot your Christmas party."

Lauren put the cigarette to her lips and inhaled deeply.

Maris realized that she'd never seen her smoke. She touched her arm, and Lauren shrugged her hand away.

"Why didn't you call?" Lauren asked. With her little finger, she wiped a tear away. The end of the cigarette burned red as she drew on it again.

"I called as soon as I could . . . once I remembered." She caressed her upper arms and nuzzled the back of her hair, taking in her perfume.

Lauren jerked away and turned. Her eyes glistened. "You smell like a bar."

Maris eased the cigarette from her hand, took a hit and tossed it away. "Honey, I was working, not playing" She lifted her chin. "God, you're beautiful. That dress takes my breath away." She kissed her and considered it a partial victory that she didn't pull away. Lauren sighed and rested her head on Maris's shoulder. Maris drew her close. "You're cold." She rubbed Lauren's arms. "Did you go without me?" She felt a prick of jealousy at the thought of Lauren looking like this — at a party without her.

"Yes." She pressed a fist against Maris's chest. "Damn it. I was counting on you." She twisted away and walked to the edge of the patio, her heels tapping the concrete.

Maris cocked her head. Something had been funny about this party from the beginning. She'd assumed it was Lauren's apprehension about making an appearance as a couple. "There's more to this than what you've told me."

Lauren looked at the sky briefly before facing her. With a hand on her hip, she said, "Not really. I'm tired of the innuendos. And one of the new agents keeps asking me out." She rolled her eyes. "I told him I'm a lesbian, but he thinks I'm joking."

Maris watched a shimmer of light bring out the red in her hair and waited.

"He's nothing I can't handle." Lauren pressed her hands together and touched her lips with her fingertips. "But I thought if he saw us together —"

"I'd scare the hell out of him." Maris grinned.

"Something like that." She shrugged.

Maris went to her. "Let's go inside where it's warmer."

"No —" She nodded toward the house. "Irene."

Maris slipped out of her jacket and wrapped it around Lauren's shoulders. Taking her hand, she led her to a bench against the house. "I'm going to fix us a drink. I'll be right back."

"Everything's fine, for now," Maris said in response to Irene's questions. Quickly she poured Bushmills over ice for Lauren and added a splash of water. For herself, she chose a generous amount of Jack Daniel's over ice, no water. Returning to the patio, she handed Lauren her drink and sat next to her. She threw an arm around her and pulled her close. Earnhardt trotted over and nudged Maris's knee. "I guess I'm forgiven." She fingered Lauren's hair. "At least by him. I think he's taking your side."

Lauren laughed softly. "He knew I was upset."

Maris sipped her drink and took a deep breath. "Remember I told you that only the devil or the law could keep me from attending your party? Well, I met the devil and was escorted away by the law."

Lauren laughed until she saw that Maris was serious. "I guess you better tell me about it." She sipped her drink and rubbed her forehead as if warding off a headache.

Maris began with the significance of the drug evidence from Lynette's purse and Kyle's apartment, explaining the fingerprints on the foil paper and the presence of caffeine in the heroin. Pausing only to sip her whiskey, she repeated the conversation with Reed Wilson.

"You took a risk going alone." Lauren shifted under

161

Maris's arm. "You should have let Sally and me talk to him."

"No one showed any interest in pursuing the drug evidence." She straightened her jacket on Lauren's shoulders. "There's more."

Lauren took her hand. "Please tell me you didn't do anything illegal."

Maris laughed. "Only misdemeanor trespassing. But they didn't press charges." She described the church and the preacher. "And I saw Brian Blake."

Her eyes widened. "Are you sure?"

"He's changed. Filled out in the last . . . what? Almost a year and a half." Maris absently rubbed the scar on her cheek. "His complexion has cleared. But his eyes . . . his eyes are the same."

Lauren rose and walked to the edge of the patio. "You shouldn't have gone there."

"How was I to know the drug dealer was going to be Brian?"

"It doesn't matter. What if he runs, or destroys evidence?" She stopped in front of Maris and held out her arms. "Couldn't you have told me first and trusted me to handle this?"

Maris heard the catch in her voice and said nothing.

Lauren gripped the jacket and pulled it tight around her shoulders. "We weren't ignoring the drugs. We thought Reed Wilson provided them to Lynette. But I have it on my list to look into and find out where Kyle got his. I simply haven't had time."

Maris jumped to her feet. "Reed Wilson wouldn't have told you or Sally anything. And this couldn't wait until you finally got around to it."

"You make it sound like we're framing an innocent man." Lauren's voice rose. "Kyle's not innocent."

"I know."

"So tell me. What am I supposed to do now?" Lauren put her hands on her hips. "All you've got is evidence to justify a drug investigation, and that's flimsy, based on Reed Wilson's story. Unless the prints from the foil are Brian's, you have nothing."

"The fact that he was within a few blocks of Starr's Pet Salon is enough to question him." Maris clenched her teeth. "Damn it, why hasn't someone already uncovered Brian's background and hauled his ass in for a little talk?"

"You don't know everything that's gone on in this investigation." She shook her head and threw up her hands. "You'll be lucky if Kenedy doesn't charge you with interfering in an official investigation." She started for the door.

"Where the hell are you going?" Maris asked.

"To make some damage-control calls."

"What the fuck is wrong with you?" She grabbed Lauren's elbow. "You act like you don't remember Mr. Blake. Let me remind you, he's capable of anything. Think what he did —"

"Don't worry. I remember." She jerked her arm away. "And I know he's capable of killing those girls. But damn it, there's a systematic way to handle these things. This is not the Old West and Hell's Half Acre. You can't strap on a six-shooter and challenge him to a gunfight. God, I need another one of Irene's cigarettes." Lauren slammed the door behind her.

Maris stalked the porch, sipping her whiskey. Liquid fire burned her throat and warmed her chest. After a while, her anger subsided. No matter what Lauren said, Troy Dan Kenedy and the assistant D.A., Walker Edward, ran the investigation. If her actions, right or wrong, forced them to look at other possibilities, then she'd accomplished her goal, and she'd gladly suffer the consequences.

Chapter 18

Still dressed to go out, Lauren rested against the headboard and talked earnestly on the phone. Without disturbing her, Maris showered and threw on a threadbare gray T-shirt and shabby pair of sweats. She returned and caught Lauren in front of the dresser removing her earrings and pearl necklace. Closing the door, she leaned against it.

"You're so beautiful," Maris said.

"Thank you." Lauren smiled tiredly. "Come unzip me."

Maris stroked her hair, and Lauren drew it aside for her to unzip the dress. "For the rest of my life, I'll regret that I didn't go with you tonight."

"You didn't miss anything." Lauren dropped her earrings and necklace on the dresser. "For standing me up, I think you should take me to dinner sometime soon." She faced her and draped her arms around Maris's neck. "Somewhere fancy and expensive. Very expensive."

"Ouch." Maris kissed her. "Does this mean I'm forgiven?"

Lauren caressed her hair, drawing tiny circles. "I can't stay angry with you." She released her and moved to the side of the bed to take off her heels.

Maris intervened, slipped off first one, then the other, dropping them to the carpet. She caught Lauren's hand and kissed her palm.

"Lord, what that does to me." Lauren shivered. She rose and peeled off her dress. Taking a hanger from the closet, she said, "You take too many chances, honey."

"Calculated risks." Maris grinned. She stripped off her T-shirt and sweats and slipped between the sheets. Propped on one elbow, she watched Lauren.

"Don't make light of this." Lauren took off her slip and wiggled out of her pantyhose. "What were you thinking? 'No man in the wrong can stand up against a fellow' — or woman — 'that's in the right and keeps on acoming.'"

Maris chuckled. "You're quoting the Texas Ranger creed to me?"

"It seemed appropriate."

Off came the panties and bra and Maris felt her pulse quicken.

"I'm standing by you on this." Opening the middle dresser drawer, Lauren selected a teal nightshirt. "I'm getting up early and driving to Pierce to get Brian Blake's fingerprint card from the S.O. I talked to Shirley tonight . . . and Sally. Shirley will come in early tomorrow morning to compare the prints." She shrugged and pulled the nightshirt over her head. "We go from there."

Maris, disappointed, interpreted the nightshirt as a sign for no sex. Lauren clicked off the light and crawled into bed. Her perfume floated around her, and Maris breathed deeply.

Lauren kissed her. Brushing back her bangs, she traced the muscles of her neck and shoulders with a long fingernail. "I love you," she said.

"I want to make love to you," Maris whispered, drawing her into a deep kiss.

"I'm too tired." She nestled against Maris. "Sorry."

"It's okay." Maris brushed her hair with the back of her hand.

"It was a rough afternoon." She added, "There was another rape in Fort Worth, about three this morning."

Maris frowned, puzzled. "I don't know which —"

"The 'Pussy Barber,' as one officer said." She groaned. "I pinned his ears back when I heard him say it. If he could have seen the victim . . ."

"I'd have decked him."

"I wanted to. He was young, a rookie, and he apologized."

Maris felt her shrug. "Maybe he learned something."

"Is it a copycat?" Maris stroked her hair.

"I don't think so. The things he said to her, did to her, were the same, and those details were never released to the public. The P.D. brought in a retired detective, and he verified the similarities. Said it made him physically ill to think the bastard was back." Lauren sighed. "I interviewed the victim at the hospital. She's an eighteen-year-old college freshman, a virgin. She shared an apartment with an older cousin."

"What a shame." She kissed Lauren's forehead. "I have a friend who used to say the first time for everyone should be in the back seat of a Chevrolet with someone you think you love."

"It should never be like this. He really hurt her." Lauren sighed again. "She was curled up in a fetal position when I saw her this afternoon. The doctors had already put in stitches. Her face was battered and swollen. Bruises on her arms and legs. Her parents were out of state on a business trip and hadn't arrived yet. I felt awful having to interview her."

"You think the publicity of the pet salon murders set him off?"

"The police are hoping he's been recently released from prison. The girl fought like a tiger and scratched him. They have a good blood and tissue sample taken from under one of her fingernails. As in the previous rapes, he wore a condom and made her shower afterward." Admiration rang in Lauren's voice as she said, "When she realized he was going to make her shower, she managed to bite off her fingernail and hide it in a piece of tissue paper."

"Brave. Maybe she's tough enough to get through this okay." Maris held her hand, interlacing her fingers with Lauren's. "If he's a documented sex offender recently released from the pen, you might get a CODIS hit on his DNA."

"It'd be nice, but I think hearing about the murders and Jennifer Kerr's pubic area being shaved was too much for him. His fantasies weren't enough anymore. And I think there's a possibility that Al Anderson is the rapist. He's the former TCU student who now works for Fort Worth P.D. This could be a reaction to my interview with the press. Looking at that girl, curled up in that hospital bed, I kept thinking, God, don't let me be responsible for this."

"He's the only one responsible for his actions." Maris pressed her lips against Lauren's hand. "I think it's fortunate that he didn't take the next step and kill this girl."

"I'm afraid the next one might not be so lucky." Lauren kissed Maris's cheek. "Since I have to get up at four-thirty, I better try to sleep."

Maris lay awake for some time. Lauren's breathing fell into the rhythm of sleep, but she tossed and turned, mumbling in her dreams.

Anyone up at four-thirty on Saturday morning should just be getting home, Maris decided as she killed the alarm and rolled out of bed. Throwing on jeans and a NASCAR T-shirt, she started the coffee and threw together a quick breakfast, surprising Lauren with a bacon and cheese omelet when she emerged from the bedroom, showered and dressed for the day. By six, Maris was in the lab, cranking out the drug cases. She worked steadily until lunchtime. Putting away her evidence, she prepared to stop for lunch just as the phone rang. She grabbed it.

"The prints didn't match," Lauren said in an even voice. "They were the same on both pieces of foil, but they're not from Brian Blake."

"Son-of-a-bitch," Maris said. She dropped to a stool. "Whose are they?"

"Shirley ran them through AFIS. No hits."

"Damn," Maris said. AFIS was the automated fingerprint system that searched through a local and national database.

Lauren said, "Sally and Kenedy are going to talk to Brian and Reverend Oldham. I though it best that I didn't go, because of Karin and Irene. The P.D. checked out the employees at the church right after the murders. Brian's name never came up."

"Maybe he didn't use his real one."

"Possibly. Or he doesn't work there. Maybe he's a volunteer or a churchgoer. Whatever. I've got to go."

Maris hung up the phone. During the investigation of the disappearance of Lauren's niece, Karin, they had discovered that Brian sold drugs, mostly marijuana and hallucinogens, not heroin. So maybe he didn't sell the capsules to Lynette and Kyle. Or maybe someone else prepared them for him. She threw up her hands in disgust and rose from the stool.

The night she went to the church, Little Ricky told her that one of the women in the reverend's drug rehab program had overdosed the day before the murders. Could she have obtained the drugs from Brian? If so, she might know if he'd sold any to Lynette or Kyle. It was worth a try.

Maris called Bass Cove P.D., but Rick didn't come on duty until four. She searched her mind for other ways to find the girl's identity. The local news media had actively reported heroin overdoses since the nationally publicized deaths of several affluent students in Plano. She hurried to her computer and clicked on the Internet connection. Once she had the home page for the *Dallas Morning News*, she searched the archives from September to the present. But she needn't have gone back that far. She found no specific stories about the Bass Cove overdose, but she stumbled on an article that she'd missed from last Sunday about heroin abuse in north Texas. She entered a credit card number to purchase a copy of the story and downloaded it to her printer.

Starving, she made a sandwich and read the article as she ate. The last portion addressed the personal price of heroin addiction with comments from several parents and their kids. The last parent interviewed, H. A. Taylor of Plano, told of the struggle to get his daughter off the drug. After trying numerous rehab programs, a friend had recommended Reverend Maurice Oldham at the Trinity Outreach Church of Redemption, and he had sent her there. A mistake, he acknowledged and advised parents to stick to the professionals. His daughter, Tamara, had almost died of an overdose in the good Reverend's care.

She paged Lauren, and, while she waited for her to call, she used a search program to find Taylor's phone number and address in Plano. She knew she'd go whether Lauren went or not.

Maris slammed the door on Lauren's Ford Taurus and leaned across the console to kiss her lover. "I missed you, babe," she said. "Thanks for indulging me — about Tamara Taylor."

"I promised I'd stand by you on this drug evidence." Lauren put the Taurus in gear. She wore a loose-fitting green blouse with beige, pleated trousers and a black vest that Maris had never seen before. "Besides, that was clever investigative work," she said.

"Did you call ahead?" Maris asked. She dusted dog hair from her faded jeans.

"Her mother refused to let us see her at first." Lauren smiled. "I convinced her."

Maris loosened the collar on her blue oxford shirt. It and her charcoal blazer felt tight across her shoulders and upper arms. The results, she hoped, of her stepped-up work-outs.

"I did some checking this morning," Lauren said. "Brian went to live with his sister in Denton. She's a cook at Luby's Cafeteria on Interstate Thirty-five, and she got him a job washing dishes. He lasted two weeks before they fired him. She told me over the phone that he scared her with his mood swings and tantrums. She tossed him out after catching him in her daughter's room late one night."

"Turn here," Maris said as they approached the Parker exit off Interstate 75. "How did he hook up with the church?"

"He took to hanging out at some kind of halfway house for troubled teens. Reverend Oldham works with the group twice a week. He took an interest in Brian and offered him a janitorial job." She curled her lip in disgust. Turning on Tamara's street, Lauren slowed to read the addresses. "The night of the murder, Brian was supposedly cleaning the women's dorm while the residents ate and attended Bible study. And get this, Brian supplied the good Reverend with a phony last name and social security number. That's how we missed him on the initial sweep."

They found the Taylor home easily and parked on the rose-colored stone drive behind a Lexus. Tall ivory columns guarded the entrance to the front door, which was recessed between two white lanterns bolted to the red brick facade. Maris pressed the doorbell, and Mrs. Taylor frostily greeted them and demanded to see Lauren's badge. Then, with a nod, she led them into a sunken den in the middle of the spacious house. Tamara waited on a white leather sofa. A matching love seat and chair, arranged around an elegant Persian rug, formed the conversation area.

Lauren introduced herself and Maris and sat on the sofa next to the dark-haired young woman. As Maris shook her hand, Tamara surprised her by pressing a scrap of paper into her palm. She closed her fist around it and settled on the love seat. While Lauren explained why they wanted to talk to Tamara, Maris glanced at the note. She read, "I can't talk in front of my mother. Get me out of here."

Maris studied Tamara and guessed her age at about

seventeen. She looked clean, her eyes normal. Dark, stringy hair hung limply about melancholy features and an oversize T-shirt and baggy jeans made her diminutive size seem even smaller. In a bored monotone, she answered Lauren's questions, adverting her eyes.

"Who gave you the heroin?" Lauren asked.

"Drugs were impossible to get," Tamara said, "until Reverend Oldham hired Brian." Prompted to describe him, she expressed a perfect image of Brian Blake as he looked when Maris saw him. Tamara didn't know where Brian obtained the heroin, but she often helped him cut it and load it in clear capsules. She remembered cutting the sticky substance with a white powder but didn't know it was caffeine. And he always made her wrap the capsules in foil paper, usually two per pack. Tamara glanced at Maris and asked her mother for something to drink. At the mother's absence, Maris handed the note to Lauren.

Lauren read it, nodded and stuck it in her pocket. After a few more questions, she suggested that Tamara accompany her to the Plano police department so they could fingerprint her. She agreed and her mother objected. Lauren insisted.

As soon as the house was out of sight, Tamara's demeanor transformed completely. "God, that ol' bitch smothers me," she said, drawing a warning glance from Maris. She cracked her window and produced a pack of Camels.

"Not in the car," Maris said.

"Fucking hell," she said and tossed the pack back in her purse.

"And that'll be enough of that kind of language."

"I thought this would be fun, or I wouldn't have come."

Lauren whirled into the parking lot of an Albertson's grocery store and slammed the car into park. Ripping off her seat belt, she jumped out of the car and jerked open Tamara's door. She snapped her fingers and ordered her out.

Suppressing a laugh, Maris casually stepped out of the car and sauntered around to stand on the other side of the girl.

171

Lauren shook a finger about an inch from the teen's nose. "This is not for fun. I'm trying to find out who brutally massacred three young women, about your age, with a hell of a lot more promising futures. As for your agreeing to come, honey, you had no choice. Either you voluntarily help me, or I call DEA and have your ass hauled in on federal drug-trafficking and conspiracy charges. Got it?"

Tamara wiped all expression from her face and shrugged. "Whatever."

Lauren dropped her hand to her side and stepped away. "You wrote the note asking us to get you out of the house. So what did you have to tell us?"

"Can I smoke?" she asked sullenly.

Lauren nodded.

That was the real reason she wanted out, Maris figured, noticing a slight tremor in the teen's hands as she plucked a cigarette out of the pack and flicked her lighter.

Tamara inhaled deeply and released a puff of smoke. After a moment, she said, "I overdosed on purpose ... to get out of there." She took another drag on the cigarette and stared across the parking lot. "That Brian guy is one weird motherfucker."

"Does Reverend Oldham know he deals drugs?" Maris asked.

"No. The Reverend is on the level. He really helps a lot of kids. Brian has him fooled." She squinted in the bright sunlight.

"What's it like there?" Maris leaned against the car and crossed her arms.

"Boring, but ... you know ... safe. He keeps the guys completely separate from us, except for mealtime and occasionally at Bible study."

"Did Brian live in the dorm?" Lauren asked.

"No. He has his own apartment at the Englenook complex just a few blocks away from the church. But he hangs out in the church attic a lot." She dropped the butt to the ground and immediately lit another Camel. "Only two male and two female counselors live there. And Oldham."

172

Lauren shaded her eyes with her hand. "Tell us about Brian?"

"He's fucking strange." She rolled her eyes. "Quotes Bible verses all the time about redemption and Satan. Always wears black." She scratched her cheek with the hand that held her smoke. "He has this heavy overcoat, solid black, that he wore all the time. Looked like a goddamn vampire. He talked tough like he was a real stud. Only he couldn't get it up about half the time."

"If the Reverend kept such a close watch, how did you and Brian get to spend time together?" Lauren asked.

"I'd sneak out. One of the counselors caught us fucking in the dorm one night while the others were eating, but Brian made sure she didn't tell."

"How?" Maris asked.

"I didn't want to know." Tamara tossed her smoke away and glanced from Maris to Lauren. "I knew those girls in the pet salon. Not well, but in passing around town. Lynette was a bitch, but the other two were all right. Brian was the first one I thought of when I heard about what happened. I was shocked when Kyle was arrested. I mean, you know, the dude was not the brightest, but he wasn't mean. I was never afraid of Kyle."

"And you are of Brian?" Lauren opened the car door for her.

"Terrified. That's why I overdosed. To get the hell out of there."

Maris climbed into the front passenger seat. "Why didn't you call your parents?"

"I did, but I was afraid to tell them why I wanted to leave. The Reverend convinced them I was trying to get out of drug treatment." She shrugged.

Lauren and Maris drove her to Plano P.D., where the identification tech rolled Tamara's hands with ink and made fingerprint cards. With the help of Plano police personnel, she gave an official statement, describing how she helped Brian prepare and distribute the heroin. After Tamara signed the typed statement, Maris and Lauren took her home.

Maris wanted to go with Lauren to take Tamara's prints

to Shirley Grimes, who would compare them with the prints from the foil paper. Instead, she let Lauren drop her off at the house so she could work a few more drug cases and possibly squeeze in a workout. "You know," Maris said before Lauren drove away. "Tamara's intentional overdose, resulting in her abrupt departure, might be a triggering factor for Brian's behavior."

Maris wiped the sweat from her face and tossed the towel over the handlebars of her exercise bicycle next to her leather weight belt. Before leaving the lab, she checked her voice mail and paused at the GC/MS to make sure her overnight samples were running without problems. Satisfied, she closed and locked the sliding glass door.

"No Lauren?" Maris asked, noting it was almost seven-thirty. She glanced at Irene once, then back again for a double take. "Damn, you look nice tonight." Her brunette hair, recently styled and trimmed, appeared lighter with more streaks of red, and she wore a tight-fitting pair of red Wranglers with a white Western-style shirt and a black vest embroidered with red roses. "And you have new boots."

"Yes, and like a fool I'm going dancing in them the first night." She straightened the vest. "I borrowed this from Lauren."

"Saturday night date?" Maris went into the kitchen and poured a glass of ice water.

"Of sorts. An old friend called, a man who used to drive trucks for Bobby. He's a partner in a transport company in Irving. He invited me to their Christmas party." She picked up the remote control and clicked to the country music video station. "Quick, before I have to go. Help me practice. I haven't danced in years."

"I'm too sweaty. You'll get dirty." Maris laughed. "If you're like your sister, you have nothing to worry about."

Irene grabbed her hand and led her onto the kitchen linoleum. "Oh, this is a fast one," she said, as a Shania Twain song started.

Setting down her ice water, Maris counted out the beat

for a fast double-two-step. They stumbled once, mainly due to the small kitchen and Maris's rubber-soled athletic shoes. "Promise me. If I tear out a knee, you'll go along with whatever story I make up. I'm not telling anyone I was dancing in the kitchen in my Reeboks."

Irene insisted they dance the next two songs, Terri Clark's "Better Things to Do" and Lone Star's "Tequila Talkin'." The phone rang and Maris snatched it up, laughing as Irene tried to get her to do a George Strait waltz.

"What's going on there?" Lauren asked.

"I'm dancing in the kitchen with your sister."

"As long as you've got clothes on," she said.

"We will by the time you get home," Maris teased. "Actually she's going to a Christmas party and wanted to practice."

Irene grabbed her purse off the counter. "Thanks," she whispered and pecked Maris on the cheek. "Don't wait up."

"Sounds like you two are getting along better."

Maris heard Sally's voice in the background and a male she didn't recognize. "You still at the S.O.?"

"Yes. I hope you have enough energy after dancing with my sister to go to work tonight." She lowered her voice. "Tamara's prints matched those on the foil paper. Sally just got back from bringing Brian in for questioning. Naturally he's already hollering for a lawyer."

"What do you need me for?"

"Well . . ." She paused and said something to someone in the background. "Hal Childress, Kyle's attorney, has decided that it's in the best interest of his client to talk to us again."

"I guess so," Maris said, "since it could save him from the death penalty if he'll tell us what really happened."

"If he puts Brian in the pet salon, we're going after a search warrant."

"I am at your service, madam. Want me to wait here or there? It could be hours before you get the warrant." Maris reached for her ice water.

Lauren laughed. "I didn't call about that, but bring your equipment so you'll be ready."

Puzzled, she asked, "Then why do you want me? Lonesome?"

"Always, but someone else is asking for you. Kyle Parmer. He's convinced you saved his life the other day in the interview room when you kept the nurse from taking his blood. He refuses to talk to anyone else."

"I haven't had any training at this."

"It doesn't matter," Lauren said. "I'll be in the interview room with you. Hal's tried to change his mind and so have I. He closes his eyes and pretends he can't hear us."

"Okay. Let me grab a shower and change clothes."

"Kyle says bring Tootsie Roll Pops. Good-bye, lover."

Maris heard the exhaustion in her voice. They'd been up since four-thirty, and it looked like a long night ahead. Were they really getting close to finding all the answers?

Chapter 19

About two hours later, Maris dumped a bag of Tootsie
Roll Pops on the table and tossed Kyle Parmer a grape one.
"Sorry, man, had to cut the sticks short before you could
have them." She set a list of handwritten questions from
Lauren in front of her.

"That's okay." He held it in his cuffed hands.

Maris shook hands with his attorney, Hal Childress,
admiring his Texas-shaped gold nugget ring. She settled into
the chair directly across from Kyle.

Childress ran a veined hand through his silver hair. "I'll
just sit here quietly unless Kyle needs me," he said.

Maris nodded and faced Kyle. "They told me you

wouldn't talk to anyone but me, so let's get started. I've been up since four this morning, and I'm tired."

As previously planned, Lauren came in and sat at Maris's right. She started the tape recorder and quietly noted the names of those present, the time and place. Kyle watched her silently, his cheek swollen from the Tootsie Roll Pop.

"Kyle, do you know a man named Brian?"

"Yes." He squinted his eyes.

"He a friend of yours?"

He nodded. "I guess."

"What do you do together?" Maris asked.

For the next ten minutes she painstakingly drew details of the relationship from Kyle. Brian, who Kyle sometimes called Satan, hung out at the gas station when Kyle's father wasn't around. Only after careful prodding did Kyle admit Brian sold drugs and had given him the ones they found in his room in exchange for rides to different places.

"Why didn't Brian drive?" Maris asked.

Kyle scratched his nose with the back of his hand. "He didn't have money to buy a car. And my dad told me not to let nobody drive my truck but me."

"You remember the day the girls, Jennifer, Jill and Lynette, were killed?"

He shifted his second sucker in his mouth. "Yes."

"You work that day?" Maris fingered the edge of the paper with Lauren's questions.

"Yes."

"Tell me what happened. Did you see Jill Kerr that day?" She knew he had from the receipt found in her purse.

He looked at her and at Lauren and bit into the sucker with a crunch. "Don't know."

Maris's stomach dropped. They were fucked on getting a search warrant for Brian's apartment if Kyle wouldn't talk.

Hal leaned over and took a Tootsie Roll Pop from the table. "Now Kyle, we talked about this. You have to tell them what happened that evening."

Kyle hung his head as if chastised. "I sold her some gas and a Dr Pepper."

He asked for another Tootsie Roll Pop, a chocolate one,

and Maris handed it to him. Slowly, question by question, his story emerged. Brian was acting strange that day, maybe fucked up on drugs, and he stole a quart-size bottle of Miller beer from the gas station. Kyle got mad over that, but Brian laughed. Brian started talking about wanting to fuck Lynette and maybe Jill and Jennifer too. He was upset because his girlfriend took too much dope and got sick. He didn't think she'd come back to the church. When he got off work, Kyle was lonesome, so he decided to go down to the kennel, pet the dogs. Sometimes he helped clean out the pens if the girls weren't finished. He wished he could quit the gas station and go to work somewhere else, taking care of dogs. Starting his fourth sucker, Kyle told them that he knew something was wrong when he went to the kennel that day. The dogs barked like crazy and wouldn't settle down. The back door was unlocked, and he went inside. He saw Jill in the bathroom. He was really scared. He snuck into the grooming room. The door leading from it to the front counter was open, and he saw Brian do a bad thing on Jennifer's underwear. He hid in a supply cabinet until Brian left.

"Did Brian kill Lynette, Jill and Jennifer?" Maris selected a red Tootsie Roll Pop.

"Yes," Kyle said. His chin touched his chest, and he hunched his muscular shoulders.

"What did you do after Brian left?"

"Nothing," Kyle said. "I don't want to talk anymore."

"May I confer with my client a moment, ladies?" Childress stood as they rose to leave. Lauren clicked off the tape recorder.

On the way out, Maris unwrapped her Tootsie Roll Pop. "I've been wanting one of these since I sat down in there. And I need a drink, beer preferably, but I'll settle for water."

"You didn't grab me a sucker?" Lauren held the door to the observation room.

"Just for you." Maris whipped a purple one out of her pocket. "Tell me, do we have enough for the warrant?"

Sally, in starched blue jeans and a light blue shirt, stood at the window near Walker Edward, the assistant district attorney. He looked like they'd caught him at the gym in his bright red windbreaker and Nike athletic shoes. "Good job," he said. For once his short brown hair was rumpled.

"Where's mine?" Sally pointed to the suckers.

"And mine?" Walker said.

Taking two out of her pocket, Maris pitched an orange one to Walker and a chocolate to Sally.

"What are you doing? Hoarding those things?" Lauren leaned on the windowsill. "We've lost him now. He'll never admit what he did to Jennifer Kerr." She tiredly rubbed her neck. "I'd say we have enough for a search warrant on Brian's apartment."

"We do," Walker said. "I've been helping Kenedy write it."

Lauren nodded. "Where is he?"

"Using the computer in my office," Sally said. "He can't stand these little rooms." She grinned almost wickedly. "Now we know how to get rid of him when we're tired of him snapping and unsnapping that damned safety catch."

Maris dropped onto the ugly lime-green, plastic-covered sofa on the back wall. Every muscle in her body felt stiff from her workout on top of the long day. She bit into her Tootsie Roll Pop and smiled as Lauren sat next to her.

"You bit yours," Lauren said. She twirled hers using the short stick remaining. "I still have mine." To Walker, she said, "Are they still talking?"

"Yeah," the prosecutor said. "If he can get Kyle to agree to tell us everything, he'll approach with a plea offer."

"He'll never admit touching Jennifer Kerr, much less trying to have intercourse with her and shaving her pubic hair." Lauren's voice sounded muffled from the Tootsie Roll Pop.

"You going to reduce the charges against him?" Maris asked.

He shook his head and pulled the sucker out of his mouth, using the tiny stick that remained. "Not yet. And I won't deal either. Not until we get some corroborating evidence. Then, if you're right and Brian killed them, we'll reduce. Kyle's still looking at a long sentence."

"Childress is calling you." Sally said.

Maris pushed herself off the couch. "Damn, my legs are killing me." She followed Walker and Lauren to the interrogation room.

"Too much dancing naked in the kitchen?" Lauren whispered.

"Ask me when we get home, and I'll show you." Maris walked into the room ahead of her. "Hey, Kyle," she said. "We going to talk some more?"

"No." He bowed his head, slumping in the chair. "Can I keep the Tootsie Roll Pops?"

"Sure," Maris said. Only three orange ones remained.

After the deputy led Kyle away, Sally called Chief Kenedy out of her office, and they all adjourned to the coffee shop. Exhausted, everyone agreed the search warrant could wait until morning. Rather than rousting a judge out of bed at midnight, Kenedy and Walker would catch him before church, the next morning. Maris didn't want Lauren driving alone as tired as she was, so Sally found a safe place at the S.O. for Maris to leave her truck. She'd have to return with Lauren the next morning. Lauren fell asleep before they reached the highway.

Sunday morning the skies swirled in ever-darkening gray clouds. Maris, wearing faded jeans and a navy blue Middleton Forensic Services T-shirt, sat on the tailgate of her pickup and faced number 1C, Brian Blake's residence, in the Englenook apartment complex, a twenty-unit, twenty-year-old building in east Bass Cove. She scanned the sky absently, munching on a chocolate-covered doughnut and sipping a large black coffee. Fetid odors from a nearby Dumpster wafted over her, mixing with the aromas of detergent, bleach and drying clothes from the laundry room. Bits and pieces of conversation, mostly rapid Spanish, filtered to her from the second floor. A little girl, about three or four, gripped the rusty metal railing and watched her shyly from above. Maris waved, wishing she had an extra doughnut to give the kid. She swallowed her last bite and licked the chocolate from her fingers. The air, humid and warm for December, hung around her like an invisible, weighty curtain, and the ankle she broke less than a year ago throbbed against the side of her Justin work boots. A weather change was coming.

She glanced at her watch, ten-thirty, time for something to happen. Hopping off the tailgate, she kicked aside an empty bottle of power-steering fluid and strayed down the sidewalk. Bending to stretch her back and hamstrings, she heard tires crunching on gravel as two Bass Cove patrol cars, Lauren's Ford Taurus and Sally's Chevy Caprice rolled into the parking lot. Maris went to meet them.

Climbing out of her car, Lauren smiled, looking rested and relaxed in her black, five-pocket tactical pants and a black T-shirt with *FBI* emblazoned on the front and *Federal Agent* on the back. "You ready?"

"I was born ready." Maris crushed her coffee cup and tossed it on the tailgate of the pickup. Lowering her voice, she said, "Anybody ever tell you how good-looking you are in your field outfit?"

"You're the only one that counts." Lauren leaned against her affectionately and brushed her hand. Her smile faded. "What's the chance of finding anything in Brian's apartment?"

"Good," Maris said. "If he came here immediately afterward. And I think he did, given the bloodstain they found on the back of the abandoned building." Starr's Pet Salon stood directly in the path between Brian Blake's apartment and the Trinity Outreach Church of Redemption. Maris estimated his travel time, from home to the church, at a leisurely fifteen-minute walk. "Who's got Brian's key?" she asked.

"Kenedy." Sally gestured with her thumb over her shoulder. "Brain wasn't any too happy when we served him and his attorney with the search warrant. He was smoldering in the holding cell. How are we going to do this?"

Kenedy approached with his usual saunter, thumbs hooked in his gun belt, and propped his foot on the curb. He held up the key. "Let's get on with it."

Maris caught Sally's eye and suppressed a grin. "I

suggest that two people handle the inside while the other two search the parking lot and the alley from here back to where the blood was found on the back of the building."

"I'll handle that . . . Rick can help me." Sally nodded toward the young officer who loitered near his patrol car, waiting for orders.

"Then, when we get inside, I'll search for bloodstains, starting at the front door. While I do that, Lauren and Kenedy can look for any stained clothing or shoes."

They approached the apartment. Lauren knocked on the door and listened, although they expected it to be empty. "Police. Federal Agent," she called out.

When there was no answer, Chief Kenedy inserted the key and turned the handle. Maris followed him and Lauren inside. He flicked on the light, and Maris scanned the sparsely furnished interior with one used recliner, a card table with two chairs, and an old nineteen-inch color television resting on soiled beige carpet. An ancient refrigerator with a bad bearing rumbled from the kitchen. A back door opened to a small, oil-stained patio.

Skirting scattered newspapers and empty Taco Bell and McDonald's wrappers, Maris crossed to the opening between the kitchen and living room that led to the only bedroom and bathroom. Overall, Brian kept a cleaner apartment than Kyle. And to her disappointment, she detected nothing out of the ordinary. After photographing the exterior and interior of the dwelling, she turned her attention to the front door. With a magnifying glass, she studied the doorknob, the edge and the doorjamb. She tested some brownish-red stains on the metal weather stripping with TMB, a presumptive test for blood, but they proved to be only rust.

She assumed his first impulse would be to wash his hands. She checked the knobs on the kitchen sink and the porcelain, moved to the bathroom and did the same with the sink and bathtub. Again nothing. Around her, Lauren and Kenedy pawed through clothing, towels and bed sheets. Frustration sounded in their voices. Using a flashlight, Maris went over the walls, especially near entrances, looking for stains. All she observed was dirt and grease.

She stood in the living room with her hands on her hips and a sinking heart. "Let's Luminol," Maris said. "Then we'll continue to look for hairs, fibers and other trace." With the kitchen window painted black and heavy curtains on the living room and bedroom windows, plus the cloudy weather, she'd have no trouble making the apartment dark enough to see the luminescence produced from the reaction of Luminol with blood.

Maris prepared the reagent in a plastic aerosol bottle and stuck a flashlight and piece of chalk in her pocket. Starting with the bedroom, she squeezed the pump. Lauren and Kenedy stood nearby. Lauren's presence in the dark, was marked by the agreeable fragrance of her perfume, his by the endless snapping and unsnapping of the safety strap. Three sets of eyes spotted none of the bluish luminescence indicating blood. Next came the bathroom. Unfortunately the porcelain had been recently bleached, and all of it glowed eerily.

"False positive," she said and moved to the kitchen and living room after replenishing her squirt bottle.

Although four stains produced a luminescence with the Luminol, all subsequently were negative with the TMB presumptive test for blood. When she finished, they had nothing.

Distant thunder rumbled when Maris stepped outside for fresh air. Lauren and Kenedy followed. Sally and Rick leaned on her tailgate.

"I can't believe I missed the start of the Cowboy game for this fucking wild-goose chase." Kenedy threw up his hands. "Not even any fucking drugs." He cocked his fists on his hips and glared at Maris. "I told you Kyle Parmer acted alone."

"No. Someone else was there." Maris stared back at him, her jaw tightening.

"Maybe he didn't come here afterward," Lauren said. "Maybe he went to the church."

"I don't think so," Sally said. "The bloodstain in the alley indicates the killer came this direction."

"Oh, yeah," Kenedy said. "The stains leading in the

direction of Kyle's apartment." His words dripped with sarcasm. "Anything else you want to do before we lock up and return to important things, like looking for whatever Kyle wore over his clothes and finding out who Jennifer Kerr was fucking?"

"Watch it, Troy Dan." Maris took a step forward.

"Spoken like a true gentleman and professional." Lauren stepped between them and tossed her red hair angrily. "Remember, you're talking about a murdered eighteen-year-old."

"Show a little respect, Kenedy," Sally said.

Lauren said, "I want to go through the trash and papers he has strewn about. After that I'll lock up. I won't need the key."

"Fine." He rubbed his jaw. "I'll give it to Brian when I have him released from jail."

Maris watched him go. "I'll stay and wipe up some of the Luminol," she said. "Or I'll be hearing from Brian's lawyer." She scrounged in the back of her truck for some heavy towels.

"I'll help," Sally said. "I don't want to see the bastard's smirking face when he's released."

In less than thirty minutes, Maris and Sally had dried most of the apartment, except for the carpet and linoleum. When Sally left, Maris found Lauren at the kitchen cabinet, sorting through the trash and scattered papers from the living room.

"Look at these receipts." Lauren pointed to a stack of register receipts, mostly from convenience stores and fast food restaurants. "Notice anything?"

Maris thumbed through them. Startled by a crack of thunder, she and Lauren both jumped. "Shit," Maris said. She ran outside to close up the back of her pickup. The sky had split, and rain fell in solid sheets. A tiny hailstone skittered across the asphalt.

Her hair and T-shirt soaked, she returned to the kitchen. Throwing an arm around Lauren, she picked up a couple of receipts. "What about these?"

"The dates."

Maris flipped through them. The receipts and newspapers were dated after December 13, three days after the murders. "There's nothing here dating before the murders."

Lauren searched the kitchen drawers. "Look for some mail. His bills or something."

"He can't have many bills. He doesn't even have cable or a telephone. I'll bet utilities are paid through the rent." Maris opened and closed drawers. "Kenedy went through these earlier."

"Yeah. But he wasn't looking for what I am." Lauren knelt and pried open a sticking lower drawer. "How can anyone not have mail? Help me get this drawer out."

Maris bent and jerked the drawer out with a grunt. She set it on the countertop.

"Bingo," Lauren said. "A letter from the Social Security Administration and a doctor's bill." She pointed to the address.

Maris squinted to read it. "Englenook Apartments, two C." She grinned at Lauren. "The bastard moved after the murders. From upstairs to here. We searched the wrong fucking place." She laughed with relief. They still had a shot at him.

Chapter 20

Wind whipped down the collar of Maris's windbreaker. She shivered and rubbed her hands together as she waited outside of Bass Cove P.D. for Texas Ranger Wayne Coffey. Water dripped from the trees, cars and roof, and she noticed downed limbs scattered along the street. She'd spent most of Sunday afternoon in the P.D., chatting with the radio dispatcher as communities around Lake Lewisville and throughout most of north Texas reported high winds, hail and flash flooding. She'd even gone herself to help an elderly woman remove a large branch from her living-room window and put up a temporary repair. It had been worth her second soaking of the day for the hot apple pie and rich hazelnut coffee the woman gave her.

Finally, at about four, Lauren called. A real estate company in Lewisville managed the Englenook Apartments, and their records verified that Brian Blake had moved from an efficiency apartment on the top floor to the one-bedroom just below on December 13, three days after the murders. The efficiency on the top floor was now rented to a Hispanic male, supposedly the only tenant, but Maris knew from observations made that morning that at least one woman, a child and maybe a baby lived there and likely spoke little or no English. At her suggestion, Lauren pressured Kenedy into requesting assistance from Wayne, who spoke Spanish well. She also told Lauren to authorize the family a hotel room until a cleaning service could properly remove the Luminol residue after they finished the search. There was little or no documentation on the long-term effects of Luminol in adults, much less short-term in children, and she didn't want the responsibility of letting an innocent family return to a possible health hazard.

Wayne pulled into the parking lot in a shiny black new Ford Crown Victoria. Maris slid into the passenger seat. "Very nice," she said, admiring the interior.

"I don't know what we'll do when they quit making these big, rear-wheel drive cars. Anything smaller I'll have to cut a hole in the roof." He smiled. At six-five and two hundred and thirty pounds or so, he looked cramped in the Vic. He rubbed his chin. "So we cross paths with that bastard Brian Blake again. Well, we predicted that."

"Don't remind me. I feel like three young women would be alive today if I'd swung that ax handle a little harder." She sighed and frowned. "Or hit him one more time."

He squeezed her shoulder. "How's that dickhead Kenedy treating you?"

Maris spent the next thirty minutes catching him up on the investigation and evidence against Kyle Parmer and Brian Blake. She told him about the morning search of Brian's apartment and how they discovered that he had moved after the murders. She finished as Lauren rolled into the parking place beside them and urged them to follow her.

Maris dodged a broken beer bottle as she backed her pickup into a spot near the stairs leading to the second floor of the Englenook Apartments. At six-thirty, night had fallen but streetlights illuminated the parking lot and the front of the apartments. She lowered the tailgate and loaded her camera with film. After a brief discussion, Wayne, favoring his right knee, lumbered up the stairs with Lauren and Kenedy following. The rusty rail swayed, threatening to give way.

She and Sally waited below, watching. Little Ricky was stationed nearby in his cruiser. Wayne removed his charcoal cowboy hat and knocked on the door. A yellow porch light came, on and a muscular young Hispanic male dressed in a sleeveless T-shirt and baggy jeans, opened the door. Even from the parking lot, Maris saw the panther tattoo on his upper arm. Wayne spoke to him quietly in Spanish. The young man nervously stroked his goatee, and a woman carrying a baby peered over his shoulder.

"When are you going to believe my innocence?" Brian suddenly appeared on the edge of the parking lot. Clad in his ever-present black shirt and trousers, arms crossed, he stared at Maris and Sally. A young woman with heavy black eyeliner and short, straight hair clung to his elbow. Her plain brown dress marked her as a parishioner of Oldham's church. Maris knew at a glance she was stoned on heroin.

Sally approached the girl. "How old are you?"

"Eighteen," Brian said.

"You ever get headaches, Brian?" Maris asked. "You know, I still have that ax handle. Right behind the seat."

Color flared in his cheeks. "My lawyer says if the harassment continues —"

"How about some ID?" Sally asked the girl. She pulled her away from Brian when she couldn't produce any.

Maris lowered her voice. "We'll get you, Brian. Sooner or later."

The girl leaned petulantly against Sally's Caprice and chomped on a piece of gum.

Wayne trudged down the concrete stairs. "They want thirty minutes to pack, and then one of us will take them to a hotel." He spotted Brian and pointed to Rick's Bass Cove police car parked perpendicular to Maris's truck. "Over there."

"Is she under arrest?" Brian asked.

Wayne looked questioningly at Sally.

"No ID," Sally said. "She might be underage and a runaway."

He glared at Brian. "Then you're detained until we find out what the deal is with this girl." He took his arm and propelled him into Little Ricky's custody. "Watch him until we're finished."

In a few minutes, the family from the efficiency unit descended the stairs. The dad carried a small suitcase and diaper bag while Mom held a baby and helped the little girl. She smiled shyly, and Maris winked back as Chief Kenedy led them to his patrol car.

Wayne grinned. "They're excited about going to a hotel."

Maris hauled a heavy-duty spotlight and gas-powered generator from the back of her truck. After several tries, she got the generator running and plugged the extension cord from the spotlight into it. On hands and knees, she crawled up the damp stairs, examining the rusty rail, once painted dark brown. Using the TMB reagent, she tested several suspicious spots for blood, but with no luck.

With the magnifying glass, she studied the doorknob. "Look." Lauren's hair tickled her cheek as she leaned over her shoulder to view the neck of the knob. Maris pointed. "Blood."

"The man who lives here is a construction worker. It could be his, from a cut," Lauren said. "Or from a minor injury to the child."

"Have faith." Maris smiled. "And hand me my squeeze bottle with water and one of those red-topped plastic tubes with the cotton swab inside." After taking photographs, she took a sample of the blood.

Moving inside, she discovered a cramped but clean apartment with only two rooms, counting the bathroom. A tiny stove stood in the corner next to a refrigerator even older than the one in Brian's apartment downstairs. She stepped over toys and crowded between a lace-doily-covered sleeper-sofa, a chair and the baby bed. With help, she moved the furniture and items aside and Luminoled only the carpet and walls. A tiny smudge, as if from a bloody finger, glowed on the edge of the bathroom door. The area tested positive for blood with the TMB but was not enough for further testing. A few more spots showed on the dingy, gray carpet — with similar results. She checked the kitchen sink and sprayed the cabinets, discovering nothing.

Maris flipped on the light in the bathroom. Although chipped and permanently stained from cigarette burns, the bathroom sink appeared freshly scrubbed. Maris carefully examined the faucet, the hot and cold water controls and around the drain. She didn't spray with Luminol since she expected it to react falsely with the bathroom cleaners. Turning her attention to the bathtub, she repeated her visual inspection.

"The woman who lives here is too good of a house-keeper," Maris said. "Turn off the lights, and we'll check the tile with the Luminol."

Wayne's huge frame loomed in the doorway, and he shook his head. "She told me this place was filthy when they moved in, but she and her husband scrubbed it from top to bottom."

Blind in the complete darkness, Maris bumped her shin on the commode as she pointed the plastic spray bottle in the direction of the tile. She pumped until she was sure she had covered the entire shower enclosure. Nothing glowed. "Turn on the lights. There's nothing here."

"We're doomed," Sally said. "Might as well get it over with and tell Kenedy and Brian."

"Jesus." Maris slammed the plastic bottle against her side. "There has to be more."

Lauren touched her arm. "You have the stain from the door. It might match one of the girls' DNA."

She shook her head. "On the *outside* of the door. We'll never prove it wasn't a plant."

Maris twisted the handle for the cold-water tap and lifted the control for the shower. Reaching behind the spray to direct the showerhead, she sprayed cold water on the tile and rinsed away the Luminol. Water, slow to drain, pooled in the tub. She cut the water and waited. Then turned it back on and rinsed the tile again.

Lauren waited for her in the living room. "I think I'll set up a meeting with DEA and DPS. Let them investigate the heroin distribution. It's the only way we're going to get him."

Kenedy stood in the doorway. "And in the meantime, we've built a great defense for Kyle Parmer. Fucking good job." He went to the rail and called to Rick. "Let him go."

Maris and Lauren plodded down the steps to the parking lot.

Sally said, "I'm taking the girl to the P.D. to call her parents. I'm not releasing her until I know she's of age or is here with parental consent."

"Good idea," Lauren said. "While you're at it, you might enlighten them on Mr. Blake's background."

Maris thrust her investigation kit into the back of the pickup. To Lauren she said, "I'm stunned there wasn't more inside the apartment. I honestly expected to find faint bloodstains and maybe some dog hair from the cocker spaniel on the door, the floor coverings, around the kitchen and bathroom cabinets . . ." She paused and looked at Lauren in amazement. "The bathtub drain."

"What?" she asked.

"The bathtub drain — it was partially stopped up. I need a coat hanger." Maris unlocked the cab of the truck and reached behind the seat. An extra set of jeans and a shirt hung on hangers from the hook in the corner of the cab. She cast the clothes aside and began unraveling the coat hanger. "A long shot, so keep your fingers crossed."

"If this doesn't work, we'll call a plumber to bring a snake," Lauren said.

Maris straightened the hanger and, with a pair of pliers from her toolbox, fashioned a slightly curved hook on the end. "Get some paper towels out of the truck and a package of plastic petri dishes." She pointed Lauren to the correct box. As she bounded up the steps, she noticed Brian Blake watching from across the street, the smirk gone from his face. He left in the direction of Starr's Pet Salon and the Trinity Outreach Church of Redemption.

Maris stepped into the tub and sat down cross-legged. Her jeans soaked up the residual moisture, chilling her skin as she fed the coat hanger down the drain. She hit an obstruction, possibly an elbow in the drain, and forced the wire passed it. She attempted to twist and twirl the wire without success and slowly withdrew it. A mass of fibers, hair, grim and greasy, soapy sludge came with it.

"God, what is that?" Lauren held out a petri dish.

"Our case, I hope." Maris wiped the mass from the end of the stiff wire.

She bent the wire into a sharper hook and ran it through the drain once more. "I can feel it scrapping the sides," she said. "And it feels like it's going around an elbow in the pipe." She twisted the wire. "But then it's like I hit something semi-solid. Ahh, I felt it move." Deliberately slowly, she pulled the wire from the drain. Something black, covered in slime, came into view, trapped by the steel crossbars on the drain. Maris held the wire stationary and slipped a set of tweezers from her back pocket. "Hand me another petri dish," she said. Smiling, she added, "Please, honey."

Biting the tip of her tongue in concentration, she worked the black, pliable material through the drain catch and dropped it in the dish. "Looks like black leather." She passed the dish to Lauren. "Leave them open around the cabinet, and we'll photograph them when I get through."

Lauren squinted at the black leather. "Looks like about a dime-size piece of black leather. Think it's from the leather coat everyone says Brian used to wear?"

"Maybe he washed it in the shower to get rid of the blood." Maris dumped more hair and slime into a petri dish and stood up. "God, my ass is wet."

"We need to find that coat. It wasn't in his apartment." Lauren frowned. "I hope he hasn't destroyed it."

Lauren went to fetch the camera, and Maris gently separated some of the hair from the sludge. Relief and excitement swept through her. A long reddish-brown hair, which could very well have been from one of the Kerr girls, coiled around gobs of blonde, wavy dog hair. The black leather had a dark stain on the inner, less slick side. She hoped it was blood, although the likelihood of it responding to DNA-typing was slim.

"Do we really have anything?" Lauren asked.

"I can't say for sure until I get to the lab, clean these samples and examine them microscopically. I'll need hair samples from the family that lives here."

Lauren nodded. "I'll handle that. Maybe another night in the hotel will help."

"Yes. That and knowing that they'll help nail a man who killed three women."

"But aren't hair comparisons shaky?" Lauren said.

"I can't positively say that a single hair came from a certain person on just microscopic comparisons. Unfortunately, even if there's a root on any of these, I think the conditions in the drain and the exposure to soap and cleaners will render it useless for DNA. But —" She grinned and held up a finger. "There's always mitochondrial DNA. Great for hairs."

"Can you do that?"

"No, baby. But the FBI can. And it just so happens I have a girlfriend with connections." More seriously, she added, "Let me secure this evidence and pack my equipment. Then let's meet at the P. D. with all the investigators. I'll explain everything then."

"I'd better call Walker Edward and get him down here." She pressed her index finger to her lips. "Then I'll get Wayne to go with me and explain to the Garzas why we need the hair samples."

As Lauren hurried away, Maris pulled at the seat of her wet jeans. The first thing she planned to do at the P.D. was change clothes.

More comfortable in dry jeans, Maris surveyed the Bass Cove Police Department conference room. Wayne stood in the corner, arms crossed, as far from Chief Kenedy as possible. The chief took the chair at the head of the scarred wooden table, directly across from Maris. Lauren, Sally and Rick crowded around in the metal-folding chairs remaining.

"So what do we have on Brian Blake?" Chief Kenedy asked with an air of bored impatience. "Now that we've managed to miss all of today's football games."

Walker Edward swept in, wearing a London Fog trench coat, black wool trousers and a gray turtleneck. "I hope this isn't a waste of time." He hung his coat on the rusted rack in the corner and took the chair at Kenedy's right elbow.

Maris described the hair and the piece of leather that she'd dug out of the bathtub drain. "I can't tell you anything definite until I complete my examinations. But if some of the hair is consistent with the known hair from the victims or the deceased cocker spaniel —"

"Hair comparisons aren't going to get anyone convicted in a triple homicide." Walker folded his hands on the table.

"Not microscopic identification," Maris said. "The STR-DNA typing that I do can only be done on cells with intact nuclei — hair with a root sheath attached. And even though STR allows us to do more degraded and smaller samples than before, the questioned DNA still has to be in pretty good shape." She watched Walker and Kenedy shift in their chairs restlessly. "But if I examine these samples and find hair that could have come from one of the victims, or dog hair similar to the ones I have from the cocker spaniel, then we can seek mitochondrial-DNA testing. The difference is, mitochondrial DNA is located outside the cell nucleus and is much more plentiful in the cell. It's present in hair, bone and teeth."

"So it could strengthen the evidence," Lauren said.

"Yeah, but there's a catch. Mitochondrial DNA is inherited only from the mother, not half from the mother and half from the father like nuclear DNA. In other words, a person's mitochondrial DNA type is shared by his siblings, mother and all of her maternal relatives for generations. In the case of a woman, her children would have the same type. In our case, with mitochondrial DNA, we can't distinguish Jill Kerr's hair from Jennifer's. Not that it'll make that much difference." She shrugged. "Also, instead of a likelihood that two people, other than identical twins, could have the same DNA in the ratio of one to billions, you're looking at maybe one to a thousand or less for mitochondrial DNA."

Walker rubbed his closely shaved chin. "Still it's better than microscopic alone."

"Yes. And it can be done on the dog hair also."

"Who can do it, and how much does it cost?" Chief Kenedy asked.

"The FBI lab can do the human hair," Maris said. "But I don't know who in the U.S. can do the dog hair, maybe Texas A and M. I've heard that the Royal Institute of Technology in Stockholm is using the procedure on dog hair in forensic casework." She frowned. "I expect that the FBI lab can help us find someone to do the dog hair, if they can't."

"Let's pursue it," Walker said.

"What about Brian Blake?" Sally said.

Walker Edward brushed the side of his sharply trimmed hair. "What about blood? Any in the apartment?"

"Yes," Maris said. "If it's human, I found enough on the doorknob for DNA."

"Too bad it wasn't on the inside," Walker said. "But that's the defense's problem. You get a match on the blood with one of the victims, and if the microscopic hair exams are positive, we'll get a warrant for Brian Blake's blood so you can compare it to the semen on Jennifer's panties. And we'll send the hair for mito . . . whatever it is."

Maris nodded, pleased to have one more shot at Mr. Blake.

PART III

Chapter 21

Shannon's voice betrayed no emotion when she phoned at one-thirty, Tuesday morning, two days before Christmas, a week before she was due. Apologizing for waking her up, she assured Maris that the baby was okay, and it wasn't time to go the hospital.

Lauren stirred in the bed beside Maris, and she urged her to go back to sleep.

"It's Robin. She called me a few minutes ago," Shannon said. "I swear her behavior gets more and more bizarre, even for her. I didn't know she was back from Denver until I saw her on the Channel Five news at ten. She gave an interview about the 'ninety-one rapes. Talked about her part in the original investigations." Maris heard disgust in her voice as she added, "She's been in Fort Worth since Sunday evening, and she didn't bother to call me until now."

"Is she okay?" Maris asked, sitting up in bed.

"I don't know. She's drunk and talking nonsense. She's upset that I'm here at the ranch and wants me to stay with my brother or at the hotel. When I told her I wanted to be home for Christmas, she begged me not to stay here by myself. Yet she refused to say why and became morose when I pushed her. I'm concerned for her."

"You don't think she'd do anything to hurt herself, do you?" Maris asked.

"No. Well, I don't know. When I tried to call her back after she hung up on me, no one answered." She sighed.

As they talked Maris realized Shannon wanted to check on Robin, but was afraid to go by herself. She asked Maris to take her to Robin's, but she talked her into staying home and trying to rest. Lauren offered to go, but Maris didn't see the need. While she dressed, Lauren found the address to Robin's apartment and looked it up on the map, jotting the directions on a piece of scratch paper. Maris kissed her, stuck her .38 Smith and Wesson in her waistband and hurried to the Olds convertible.

Exhausted, she lowered the car window and took in the cool air as she drove south on Highway 75. With her adrenaline rush from Shannon's call rapidly dissipating, she struggled to stay awake. Sleep had been a hard horse to catch since they'd run the search warrants on Sunday.

Three days, she'd promised Walker Edward, Kenedy and the other investigators, three days to complete the DNA typing on the blood obtained in the search warrant Sunday and to determine if they had a case on Brian Blake. She rubbed her bleary eyes. She'd worked practically around the clock trying to shave time from the normal DNA-analytical procedure. What a fucked-up week it had been. A repairman came to update the software on her GC/MS and fried the controller board on the autosampler. She couldn't batch samples and run them overnight until it was replaced. Then, since Monday was only two days before Christmas Eve, her mother and her sister called demanding to know her plans. She'd been putting them off for days, using the

Bass Cove case as an excuse. In reality, she was hoping Lauren would change her holiday plans.

Maris slowed and downshifted to switch lanes toward the southbound bin on the Dallas North Tollway. Lauren wanted to accompany Irene to Federicksburg for Christmas. Her parents refused to acknowledge Maris's existence, and they damned sure wouldn't let her in the house for Christmas dinner. Lauren said it was a chance for her family to heal. Maris thought it sucked that Lauren would think about going somewhere on Christmas where she wasn't welcome. She felt almost betrayed. It made it difficult for her to get excited about the holiday season and meeting her own family at her sister's home in Austin. Plus, she hadn't bought a single Christmas present, not even for Lauren, and had only managed to send out Christmas cards to her clients because Irene did them for her. But she promised her mother that she'd do her best to be there Christmas Day.

At least at two a.m. the traffic was light and she made good time. Taking Interstate 30 west to the 820 loop and then north to Richland Hills, a suburb northeast of Fort Worth, she located Robin's apartment easier than she expected. At two-forty, she pounded on number 135 and waited. After a moment, she banged a second time. Placing her ear against the door, she heard only silence. It figured, she thought, that Robin would be asleep or passed out by the time she got there. She wondered how she could assure Shannon that Robin was fine if she couldn't get her to open the door. More out of habit than anything, she tried the knob. Apprehension settled over her when it turned in her hand. She pushed open the door and peered inside. Seeing nothing, she crept inside, closing the door behind her. Cupping the small penlight on her keychain to keep from alerting anyone to her presence, she used it to study her surroundings. The foyer opened into the living room where soft light filtered through the sliding glass door at the back. A series of photographs on the wall to her right caught her attention, and she studied them with the small penlight. In all of them, a younger Robin grinned back at her with a stunning, dark-headed woman and a little brown-haired girl.

Love shone in the eyes of the women as they held hands. Gwen, she assumed. So this is the one who got under your skin, Maris thought, clicking off the light as she stepped into the larger room.

Bright blinding light suddenly hit her full in the face from an armchair in the corner of the room. She threw up an arm to block the light and heard a blurry voice say, "What are you doing here?"

Barely recognizing the husky voice as Robin's, Maris looked at her and froze. Robin jacked the pump on an automatic shotgun, and Maris's stomach tumbled. "Goddamn it, Robin." She took a couple of steps sideways. "It's Maris," she added to avoid any possible confusion.

The flashlight clicked off, and Robin flicked on the pole lamp near the chair. The room was illuminated. Maris blinked away spots, stunned at what she saw. The twelve-gauge pump shotgun rested across Robin's lap. With bloodshot eyes and a shaking hand, she picked up a fifth of Chivas Regal and slugged down a healthy dose. Wearing a navy blue shirt and faded jeans, she ran a hand through her disheveled brunette hair and said, "Why the fuck did you come?"

Angry, Maris closed the distance between them and ripped the shotgun off her lap. Pointing it to the ceiling, she ejected the shells, letting them drop to the blue-gray carpet. Setting it on the glass dining table between the kitchen and living area, she asked, "What the hell are you doing? Working up the courage to blow your fucking head off?"

"As if you'd give a goddamn." Robin rose shakily to her feet. She waved the bottle at Maris and took another gulp.

Maris ground her teeth and jerked the bottle from Robin's hand. She shoved her in the chest, knocking her into the chair. "Actually, I do care." She paced a few feet away, trying to control her temper. "This is a new low, even for you."

Pain crossed Robin's face before she drunkenly pulled herself upright. She half bowed. "I thank you for having such a high opinion of me. Now can I have my bottle back, or should I open another?" She pointed to a second fifth by her chair.

"Anything else in here?"

"Just expensive scotch."

Disgusted but resigned, Maris took a swig and handed her the bottle. Smaller and leaner than Maris, with well-defined muscles and classic features, Robin flashed her a crooked grin and tossed her light brown hair off her forehead. A lady-killer, Maris grudgingly admitted, even fucked up and needing a shower. No wonder her women always took her back.

"There's a beer in the fridge, if you want," Robin said.

Maris strode into the kitchen and grabbed a Bud Lite from the fridge. Twisting off the top, she asked, "Why, Robin?"

Her bronze eyes fell to the floor. "I think the real question is, 'Why not?' "

Maris pulled over a tall-backed rocking chair. "You haven't even asked how she is."

"How is she?" Robin asked in a voice so low she could barely hear it.

"Okay, I guess. She's had a lot of pain from what they call Braxton-Hicks contractions." Maris sipped her beer. "I think her emotional state is making it worse."

Robin's jaw tightened. "I know you don't believe it, but I'm not doing this to hurt her." Her voice cracked. She shook her head and swallowed more scotch. "Tell her I love her."

"I'll fucking burn in hell before I'll tell her that lie." Maris rose to leave. "You ain't no good to her like this."

"I figured you, of all people, would understand."

"I don't." Maris faced her. "So why don't you explain it to me?"

Robin waved her hand around the apartment. "It's why I kept this place . . . all these years."

"She has a pretty good idea why you have this place." Maris sipped her beer, trying to wash the bitter taste from her mouth.

Without a word, Robin stood, somewhat unsteadily, and

slammed a videotape into the VCR. "Fucking watch this." Using two remote controls, she clicked on the television and started the tape. "I can't watch this shit. Call me when it's over — or you can't stomach anymore." Weaving, she carried her Chivas to the balcony.

Maris gritted her teeth when she heard a woman plead, "Don't hurt my little girl. I'll do whatever you say." She fell into Robin's chair.

A guttural voice sneered, "You'll do that anyway."

The unfocused picture rocked dizzily as he set the video camera on a tripod. Soon the picture focused on a naked woman with her arms tied to the headboard. She averted her face and cried. Blood trickled from a cut on her lip, and Maris saw choke marks on her neck. A man, average in build and height, appeared on screen wearing dark jeans, a black T-shirt and a ski cap. Startled when he applied shaving cream to her pubic area, the woman turned her head. With a sick feeling, Maris recognized Gwen, Robin's ex, the woman in photographs. She agonizingly watched him shave Gwen, tempted to fast-forward the tape, but he talked continually, and Maris wanted to hear his words, to learn more about him. He berated her with degrading and frightening language. Often he threatened her daughter. He asked about Robin, what they did in bed together. Unable to sit, Maris stalked around the room, listening but not watching.

When he'd finished shaving her, he stripped and, wearing only the black ski mask and a condom, systematically beat her, his erection growing as he punched her. Maris muted the television to silence the screams. She stopped the player and fast-forwarded for long stretches. Every time she restarted it, the assault continued in a different way. The attack lasted for hours. At last the scene switched to the bathroom, where, already dressed, he held the camera somewhat unsteadily and filmed as she showered. Maris turned up the volume and wondered how Gwen stayed on her feet. He talked little, except to give instructions, and she followed them wordlessly. The tape went black, and Maris almost punched the stop button.

Then a head shot of a man in a green ski mask appeared on the screen.

"Remember this? Our covenant?" He curled his lips, held up an audio-cassette recorder and pushed play. The same voice, that of the rapist, ranted at Robin, calling her by name. He threatened to rape the daughter, to come back for the woman again. Then he made a bargain. "I won't rape anymore, if you back off. Cross me and I'll find her and the girl, wherever they are. None of your whores will ever be safe." The man in the green ski mask cut the recording and laughed. "The covenant is broken. All bets are off." He shrugged. "Hope you enjoyed the movie. Many others have. See ya."

Her feet frozen to the carpet, Maris stood in silence for a several seconds before rewinding the tape and calling Robin inside. When she came in, Maris noticed a large portion of the scotch was gone. Slipping the bottle from Robin's hand, she took a stiff drink. The scotch burned her throat and warmed her chest. "The daughter?" she asked.

"He shoved her unharmed into a closet and blocked the door with a heavy dresser. She was only four." Robin collapsed in her chair. "She heard her mother's screams."

"I'm sorry," Maris said. "When did you get the video?"

"Today." Bitterness burned in her laughter. "Some Christmas present. Help yourself to another beer, more scotch. You probably need it." Robin rubbed her chin. "I can't get enough."

Maris handed her the scotch, went to the kitchen and returned with another Bud Lite.

Robin wiped a trickle of scotch from her chin. "After the rape, she called me. I don't remember the drive home. She wanted to call the police. I talked her out of it." She sighed, shaking her head. "Some officer of the court I am. The doctor, a trusted friend, agreed to treat her without reporting it. Then a couple of days later, I got an audiotape in the mail with the 'covenant,' as he called it. He'd stop hurting women if I dropped out of the case." She looked directly at Maris, her hazel eyes burning with intensity. "Then I wanted to report the rape, but she refused."

"Then you quit the D.A.'s office and went into private practice with Starla."

Robin nodded.

"How are they?" Maris ran her fingers through her hair. "Gwen and the girl."

"Now? They're mostly okay. But back then it was rough. We couldn't hold it together. The pain, the guilt was too much. It happened in January of 'ninety-two. We broke up four months later, and she took a job in Denver with the same company. I moved into this apartment, listed the phone and put my full name on the mailbox." The corner of her lip twitched. "You know, all the things you're not supposed to do. I wanted him to know where I lived. So he'd come here first, no matter what happened. Gwen went back to her maiden name and legally changed the girl's."

"Good idea." Maris leaned back in the rocker.

"No matter who I was with, including Shannon, I kept getting my mail here. I pray to God he doesn't know about her."

"Why send the video to you? I don't understand." Maris said. "Why now?"

Robin cleared her throat. In a low voice, only slightly slurred, she said, "I've thought about that. At first, I thought it was because I gave an interview to the *Fort Worth Star Telegram* and Channel Five news yesterday. I talked about the original investigation, the task force, although I didn't mention Gwen's assault." She shook her head. "But it was more than a warning. It's a message. He's telling me he's starting back." She took a small sip of Chivas and coughed. "He sent me a message, the Friday after the murders. 'It wasn't me,' it said. I went to see Gwen to ask her to let me hand over the audiotape, tell about her assault. She's too afraid, especially for her daughter. And goddamn it, we did nothing, and he's raped again. He sent the tape because he thinks I'll do nothing again." Clutching the neck of the bottle, she gulped the brown liquor. "I was so fucking sure of myself, so goddamned cocky then. Until Gwen called me that afternoon." Tears ran down her cheek. "I'm a fucking failure, a goddamned coward. Then and now. I don't have enough guts to blow my head off. Not for the latest victim. Not for Shannon's or the baby's safety." She angrily flicked away the teardrops. "Go ahead. Tell me what you'd have done."

"It doesn't matter."

Robin flung her head. "I know anyway. You'd hunt down the bastard and kill him. I couldn't do that. I didn't know for sure it was Anderson. I was too afraid to take a chance on getting the wrong guy. Too afraid to risk prison. Too afraid . . . of everything."

"One of us needs to call Shannon."

"I'm too afraid of that too."

Maris nodded. "Now what?"

Robin shrugged. "Life goes on."

"Cut the fucking bullshit," Maris said. She felt her face redden as her temper flared. "Think like the goddamned lawyer you're supposed to be." She returned to the rocker and picked up her beer. "I've been thinking about what he said — 'Many have seen it.' What's he mean?"

"I don't want to think about it," Robin said.

"Maybe he's selling the tape." Maris frowned as Robin shakily raised the bottle again. Maris was amazed that she remained conscious. "A Dallas police officer was arrested recently for selling rape videos over the Net, although he claimed the women were actresses and the assaults were staged." She tiredly rubbed her neck. Lauren wasn't the case agent, but she'd seen parts of the tapes and told Maris about them. One involved a baseball bat, a lot of blood and real, not faked, screams of pain and terror. There'd been a brief investigative report on one of the local television stations, but she'd seen nothing about the tapes or the officer's arrest in the newspaper. She'd found the lack of media and public outrage disturbing. Maris added, "We need to show the tape to Lauren, bring in the FBI. Let's see if he's distributing it some way. Maybe they can identify Anderson as the man on the tape. Compare the voices, moles, freckles, wrinkles — something."

"No." Robin lurched to her feet. "No! Gwen doesn't know he sent me the tape."

Maris threw back the rest of the beer and rose. "Then tell her and get her to agree to bring in the feds. They got a tissue sample in the last assault. If this tape somehow leads to probable cause for a search warrant, they can get blood and do DNA. And I'll bet they'll find tapes of the other women. For once, do the right goddamned thing."

"I have to tell her." Robin laughed harshly and capped the Chivas. "And I need to tell Shannon, but I can't. You tell her what happened."

Maris's jaw tightened. "It's not my place."

"Since when does that make any difference?" Hands on her hips, she rocked unsteadily.

"Since right now." Maris stood and stuck the phone in Robin's gut. Taking another beer, she stepped out on the balcony to wait and watch the city come to life. By the time the sliding door opened behind her, she was cold, tired and hungry. She faced Robin.

"She told me not to call or come home until I've taken care of my unfinished business."

Maris sighed. "Go get yourself cleaned up and pack a bag. We'll grab some breakfast, and I'll take you to the airport."

Robin nodded. "Maybe I can catch a seat on the early flight to Denver, even if it is one of the busiest travel days of the year. If not, I'll just wait until I get one."

Chapter 22

Maris arrived home at nine-thirty, Tuesday morning. She'd have been home sooner, but after taking Robin to the airport, she decided to swing by Fort Worth to see Shannon and leave her the .38 Smith and Wesson. She protested, but at Maris's insistence she put it in her purse. Glad to catch Lauren still at home, she gratefully accepted the cup of coffee and asked for a glass of milk. Sitting at the kitchen bar, she gulped the milk to soothe her irritated stomach and told Lauren everything about her early morning with Robin.

"I didn't realize how hot a commodity rape videos are on the Internet until that Dallas officer was arrested," Lauren said. "We have a special unit looking into it now."

She kissed Maris on the forehead. "Let me see what I can find out."

Maris debated whether to go to bed or to check last night's DNA run on Jenny, but the physical and emotional exertion combined with the lack of sleep were exacting a price. Her entire body hurt, and she couldn't risk making a mistake while tired.

Lauren hugged her. "Go to bed, honey." She led her to the bedroom. "Don't worry about Brian. He's being kept under constant surveillance. The test results can wait."

Her head hit the pillow and she snuggled under the covers. The last thing she remembered was Earnhardt jumping on the bed.

At four-thirty, Lauren shook her awake. She rose on one elbow and groaned. "Oh, God, don't tell me Shannon's in real labor."

"Is that all you worry about?" Lauren patted her rear.

"No, baby. I worry about making a living and whether we'll ever have time for sex again."

Lauren bent over her and whispered, "You don't have to worry about the latter."

"Good," Maris said, reaching for her.

She laughed and slipped away. "But it won't be now."

"At least my luck is consistent." Maris crawled out of bed and threw on a navy FBI Academy T-shirt, a ragged pair of faded blue jeans and sneakers. "Consistently bad."

Lauren's eyes sparkled with excitement. "I've got to go to Plano to help with a robbery at the drive-in teller window. The Wells Fargo on Interstate Seventy-five in Plano. But I wanted you to know that you may be on to something about the rape video. I talked to the agent in charge of the Internet pornography unit. He hasn't run across any videos like that, but he's put out some feelers. They are so unique, with the perp shaving the victims, that he's confident he can find the tapes if they are in Internet circulation. Photographs from Fort Worth P.D. of all the victims are on their way to the porno unit as we speak, so they'll have them if they run across a rape video. Of course, they won't have Gwen's photo, but if her video is in circulation, I bet some of the others are also." She kissed Maris. "Have to run. Love you."

"Be careful," Maris said to her back. Feeling semi-rested, she rushed to the lab. Loading the CD player with Brooks and Dunn, Wynonna and Dwight Yoakam, all fast-paced, she cranked up the volume and went to check her results. Within an hour, she lifted the DNA printouts from the laser printer. The relief flooded through her, and the tension in her neck and shoulders evaporated. The blood on the doorknob to Brian Blake's first apartment came from Lynette Donley. In retrospect, it made sense. Her blood probably saturated his gloves when he dipped his fingers in it to print the crude message on the wall. Maris spent another hour preparing the official report. When finished, she punched in the first two numbers of Lauren's pager but stopped when she heard two sharp raps on the sliding glass door. Lauren stepped into her arms as she opened the door.

"Missed you," she said.

"Any luck with the bank robber?" Maris asked, content to hold her for a moment.

"The fool wrote the note on the back of one of his checks." She laughed. "Complete with his name, address and driver's license number. So we went straight to his apartment and caught him in the shower trying to remove the exploding dye from the bank bag with paint thinner. He has a nasty rash. Said he wanted a little money to buy Christmas presents."

"I got a little money, just no time. Come here." Maris took her hand and led her to the closest counter. "Here're the DNA results."

"I've finished my shopping, and you'd better get busy. Tomorrow is Christmas Eve." She took the results from Maris. "You know I can't read . . ." She squinted and studied the table. "Lynette Donley's type."

"Yes. I was going to page you. I haven't had time to notify Kenedy and Sally yet."

Lauren pursed her lips. "The surveillance team reports

213

that Brian's behavior is more and more bizarre. He's taken to ranting and raving Bible verses at them. Those from the book of Revelation."

"Just as he did, with a little improvisation, shortly before he escaped from the hospital and attacked Irene." Maris glanced at her lover in amazement. "God, has it really been only a year and four months ago? It seems like forever."

"Forever? Only a year and a half?" Lauren put her hand on her hip and cocked an eyebrow. "What happened to 'It seems like only yesterday . . .'?" She sighed. "I guess the honeymoon is over."

Maris grabbed her around the waist and pulled her close. "When the sun comes up in the west and the clock runs backward." She kissed her and released her. "I'll call Sally and Kenedy and fax copies of the report. Woman, go get me the blood of Brian Blake." She rubbed her hands together like a figure in a black-and-white horror movie.

"It is done." Lauren bowed. "By the way, Irene and I are planning to leave for home about eight tomorrow morning." She left to arrange the warrant.

After two and a half hours of fighting the last-minute shopping crowd at Collin Creek Mall in Plano, Maris reclaimed her recliner, chatted with Irene and pitched the tennis ball for Earnhardt while they watched *Operation Petticoat*, a Navy comedy, featuring Cary Grant, Tony Curtis and a World War II pink submarine pressed into service during refit to rescue a crew of nurses. It felt good to have her Christmas shopping finished, even if everything wasn't wrapped yet. Snacking on microwave popcorn, shared with Earnhardt, she caught herself enjoying Irene's company and wondered if it might not be nice, for her and Lauren, to have someone else around.

At a quarter to ten, the phone rang and Maris grabbed it, expecting to hear Lauren's voice. Instead she heard a woman sobbing. It took two tries for her to understand that the caller wanted to talk to Lauren.

214

"She's not here," Maris said. "Is this an emergency? Could I page her for you?" Thinking the young woman might be an informant of Lauren's, Maris wanted to handle her cautiously.

"Are you the one that was with her ... the other day?" the caller asked, her voice clearer.

"The other day?" Maris hesitated.

"At my house —"

"Tamara," Maris said.

Irene muted the television and watched her intently.

"The FBI lady gave me her card. Said to call if I thought of anything ..."

"Where are you?" Maris heard a car horn in the background. "And are you okay?"

"I know about some evidence. It'll be worth a lot to her ..." Her words became muffled.

Was she fucked up or really upset and crying? Maris couldn't tell. "Let me call the po —"

"No!" she said. In a calmer tone, she added, "No police. Only her."

"Or your parents."

"Screw my parents. I'm never going home again."

"If all you're wanting is drug money, I don't think Lauren will be too interested." She rolled her eyes at Irene.

"I don't want money."

Maris heard anger in her voice but was unsure if it was directed at her or something else. She waited.

"Brian ... hurt me. Said I was a fucking traitor for talking to you." She coughed. "He shouldn't have done that. I know where he hid his precious leather slicker."

"I'll be there as soon as I can." She jotted down directions to a gas station at Knox and Central in Dallas. Not the worst place in town for a young woman alone, but not the best either. "I'll be there in forty-five minutes," Maris said.

Hanging up the phone, she paged Lauren. While she waited for her to call, she explained the situation to Irene. "I don't trust the little whore. She's the type to get me down there and try to blackmail me with claims of inappropriate behavior."

215

"Want me to go with you?" Irene balanced on the edge of the sofa.

Maris glanced at her watch. Ten minutes and no call from Lauren. "If you don't mind," she said. The irony of taking Irene to vouch for her behavior struck her as she changed into jeans. She laughed aloud with Earnhardt eyeing her quizzically, head cocked, one ear up.

Traffic on Central Expressway was heavy yet flowed well despite the never-ending construction to dig tunnels for the DART train lines to downtown Dallas. Using Maris's cell phone, Irene tried to page Lauren a second time. They still had not heard from her when Maris turned the pickup onto Knox and cut sharply into the gas station. Tamara sat on the cold concrete with her back to the wall, her dark head bent and arms wrapped tightly around her tucked knees. Wearing hip-hugger flared jeans and a rose-printed knit cardigan with a matching top, she visibly shivered as Maris approached.

"Tamara," she said.

The girl raised her head, and the sight of her battered face stopped Maris dead in her tracks. A crooked split cut diagonally across her swollen upper lip. A deep purple bruise colored her cheek below a black eye. Another cut marred her forehead just above the puffed-up eye.

Maris helped her to her feet. "You need a doctor."

She shook her head violently.

"Brian did this to you?"

"Most of it." Tamara dried her eyes and defiantly squared her shoulders. "It's nothing."

Her slurred voice and dilated pupils gave her away, and Maris knew she was fucked up. She noticed the black and blue marks around her neck and frowned. "Who did the rest?"

Tamara jerked her arm from Maris's grasp and stumbled. "None of your business."

Maris ignored her comment and offered to buy her something to eat and drink. She chose coffee and a bran muffin. Maris also bought coffee for her and Irene. She led her to the pickup and introduced her to Irene, who'd watched and listened from the truck. With Tamara in the middle, they rode in silence north on Central until they were almost to Plano. Lauren still hadn't called, and Maris was unsure what to do with Tamara.

Tamara ate her muffin, pinching off tiny pieces because of her injured lip, then crumpled up the napkin and said, with no feeling, no inflection, "The man who gave me a ride to Dallas did the rest."

Maris narrowed her eyes and glanced at her. "Be more specific."

"Specifically, he made me suck his cock."

Irene took her hand, but Tamara jerked away and held her coffee cup tightly. "It's nothing. I don't want to go to the cops or anything. Shit like that just happens. It means nothing."

"Oh, honey," Irene said.

"It damn sure means something to me." Maris slapped the steering wheel with the palm of her hand. "You're a minor. I don't know if I can legally not call the police. And I still think you need to see a doctor."

"No. Not until you take me to the church and let me talk to the pastor."

Fucking hell, Maris thought, why didn't Lauren call? They were only a quarter-mile away from the exit to the nearest hospital. And only blocks from Tamara's parents.

As if reading her mind, Tamara lightly touched her knee. "Don't. Let me show you where Brian's overcoat is and talk to the pastor." Maris saw a real tear in her eye. "He's the only one who's always been good to me. He honestly thought he could help." Incredulously, Maris read pity in her expression. Tamara lowered her head and gripped her coffee cup until the sides caved. In a low voice, she added. "I had sex with another man since then. To get the drugs."

"We'll go to the church on one condition." Maris held up her finger. "You let me call your mother and tell her where you are and what's happened. It's almost Christmas Eve."

Tamara started to protest and stopped. Her shoulders sagged. "If that's what it takes."

Irene wrapped an arm around her and held her the rest of the way.

Every light in the sanctuary and fellowship hall blazed, although it was almost eleven-fifteen. The dormitories, except for an occasional dim nightlight, were quiet and still. The side entrance stood open, and she could see into the hallway. Maris listened and heard only silence.

"The kids have to be in bed by ten, but most have gone home for the holidays. Only those who have no place to go, or who haven't been in drug rehab long enough to earn family leave will be here." Tamara squinted at the church. "But the church lights aren't usually on this late."

"Could it be something special for Christmas?" Irene asked. "A special service?"

"Not likely," the teen said. "That's tomorrow night."

"I don't like this." Maris stopped Tamara from sliding across the seat. She looked past her to Irene. "And I don't like it that Lauren hasn't returned our pages."

"Do you have a gun?" Irene asked.

"No. Believe it or not." She felt naked. "I gave it to Shannon this morning." She had three more at home but, uncharacteristically, didn't think to grab one. "All I have is the ax handle behind the seat. Where's Reverend Oldham's quarters?"

"Behind the fellowship hall between the boys' and girls' dorms."

"Okay. Let's see if he's there." Maris helped her out of the truck and took the ax handle from behind the seat. Carrying it like a staff, she went ahead. Irene followed close to Tamara, clutching Maris's phone.

Their feet rang out in the deserted church as they followed the linoleum-floored hallway and crossed the fellowship hall, threading between folding chairs and card tables. A silver-flocked spruce loaded with Christmas decorations and multicolored lights was centered in front of the east window, to the right. About a dozen presents were scattered under its branches. Maris peeked into the pastor's office. It was empty. She scanned the room, noting the simple decor with shelves of books on spirituality and Biblical history. Leaving the office via the back door, they cut across a stark hallway connecting the two dorms, and she knocked on the door Tamara pointed out. After no one answered, she turned the handle. A military cot, one folding chair and a small throw rug almost filled the tiny room.

"What now?" she asked Tamara. "Does Oldham have a pager or cell phone?"

"No." Tamara wrapped her arms across her chest. "This is his day to preach to the halfway houses, but he's rarely out this late. Most of the time he's in his office or room."

"I thought he preached at night." Maris frowned.

"Sometimes he teaches the nightly Bible hour and sometimes a counselor does."

"I think it's time to call the police," Maris said. "This doesn't feel right to me."

"I'm worried about Lauren," Irene said. "She always answers her pages immediately."

"Maybe the system is down," Maris said, not believing it.

"Let me show you Brian's leather coat first." Tamara turned toward the fellowship hall.

Maris followed, carrying the ax handle. "How do you know where it is?" An ugly suspicion began to form in the back of her mind, until she recalled that Tamara had overdosed the day before the murders.

In the fellowship hall, Tamara pointed out a closet in the northwest corner. She flipped a switch on the back wall. A few plastic foam cups and paper plates littered the dusty shelves. A ceiling panel with a built in stairway to the attic had been pulled down. A dim light was visible through the opening.

"I saw it up there this morning." She crossed her arms tightly in the draft from the opening. "This is Brian's hideaway." She rolled her eyes. "It's where he keeps the drugs. Where I shot up. Where he has his strange rituals."

"Wait here." Maris handed the ax handle to Irene and climbed the stairs. With her head just above floor level, she stopped and scanned the room. Amidst boxes of old hymnals, additional Christmas and Easter decorations and props from past pageants, Reverend Maurice Oldham sat hunched on a three-legged wooden stool, holding a leather-bound book. A black silk cloth covered a makeshift altar against the far corner. Satanic symbols had been spray-painted on the walls. A razor-sharp machete rested in the center between a black and red candle. A black full-length overcoat hung on a wooden frame. Darker stains shone on the smooth side of the leather, and Maris felt the weight of three deaths on her shoulders. She took the last few steps into the attic and felt the cold breeze that whistled through the vents against her cheek.

Looking up, tears in his eyes, Reverend Oldham said, "A satanic bible. In my church." He cleared his throat and rose. "I recognize you from the other night —"

"Yes." She told him her name. "I'm assisting the police in the murder investigation."

"They tried to tell me. The police and the FBI agent. I refused to believe Brian could be guilty, even after they told me he'd lied about his last name and given me a fake social security number. I thought he was the son I'd never had. I hoped to make him my assistant someday." He closed the book and set it on the stool. "They wanted to search the attic this evening, and I refused. 'Not in God's house,' I said." He sighed. "Guess I'd better call Chief Kenedy."

Maris called down the stairs. "Reverend Oldham is up here, and we're coming down."

"What brings you here?" the Reverend said, stopping her with a hand on her shoulder.

In a low voice, she explained about Tamara. He rushed down the stairs and embraced the teen. After a brief discussion, Tamara agreed to let him take her home. Maris and Irene would stay at the church and call the police to report the discovery of Brian's blood-stained leather coat. Feeling responsible for Tamara's well-being since she'd picked her up in Dallas, Maris called Tamara's parents to see if it was okay for the reverend to bring their daughter home. Relief flooded her voice as the teen's mother gave her permission.

"Call nine-one-one, Irene," Maris said as she waited with Tamara for Oldham to retrieve his jacket and keys.

When he returned, she asked, "What made you change your mind and look in the attic?"

He smiled. "The word of God." Tamara waved good-bye from the hallway.

"The police haven't even answered yet," Irene said.

"Hang up and call again," Maris said. A sick feeling clutched her stomach.

Irene dialed again. "It's busy this time."

Distant sirens broke the silence of the night and grew louder. Grabbing Irene's arm, Maris ushered her into Oldham's office. "Get on the floor behind the desk and stay there until someone comes for you."

"What are you going to do?" Irene asked.

"I don't know." Maris took the ax handle from her.

"What do you think is going on?"

"God, I hope I'm wrong, but my gut tells me Brian Blake has escaped and is en route here, to his lair." She tried to convince herself that Lauren was in pursuit, too busy to return pages, but the icy fingers of fear constricted her throat.

As the wail of the sirens grew louder, Maris hunted for a strategic hiding place. The speaker's podium caught her eye. Made of yellow pine, it faced the entrance to the fellowship hall and stood parallel and about three yards from the closet. Anyone going to the closet or to Oldham's office had to pass nearby. Squatting, she examined the inner cavity of the stand. If she sat and scrunched her knees, she might just fit.

Tires squealed outside and a car door slammed. She heard a male cursing. Hurriedly, she took her place under the podium, the ax handle at her side. Luckily, a circular hole, about an inch and a half in diameter, pierced the front of the pine facade to allow passage of the wire for the slide projector's remote control. By straining her neck and closing one eye, she possessed a clear view of the door.

Engines roared and tires crunched gravel. She heard the unmistakable sound of a collision as more doors banged. Her neck cramped, and she felt her right hamstring tighten. Two shots rang out, and she flinched.

Sally Trent shouted. "Don't fire. Hold your fire."

Maris strained to hear Lauren's voice. The back of Brian's black shirt and trousers came into view as he struggled to drag someone or something around the corner into the hallway. Relief and guilt swept simultaneously over her as she realized he had his arm crooked around a hand-cuffed Chief Kenedy, not Lauren.

Brian waved Kenedy's Colt .45 semiautomatic pistol, pointing first at the chief's temple then around the corner. He fired a shot and laughed. Back-pedaling rapidly, he dragged the red-faced chief toward the closet. A bluish-purple knot trickled blood down Kenedy's temple. Shock and confusion showed in his eyes. Maris smelled male sweat and fear as they moved closer.

Lauren, wearing a blue vest with *FBI* across the front, crouched near the wall and followed Brian. "Stop now, Brian. Put down the gun and you won't get hurt."

Little Ricky, gun drawn, appeared at her elbow followed by the Bass Cove officer, who'd frisked Maris at the church a few nights ago.

"He's the motherfucker that needs to worry about getting hurt." Brian rapped the barrel against Kenedy's cheek.

Sally skittered across the hallway and took up a bent position. As Brian backed within two yards of the podium, Lauren, followed by Sally, raced into the room. Ricky and the other Bass Cove officer took up positions on opposite sides of the doorway. Lauren and Sally flipped over a card table and knelt behind it. Maris cringed. The table couldn't slow a .45 slug.

God, ladies and gentlemen, she thought, please don't shoot me or give me away too soon. A centimeter at a time, Maris unfolded from the podium and rolled to her knees. As Brian and his hostage approached, she rose, cocking the ax handle like a Louisville Slugger. The back of Brian's head loomed before her like an errant split-fingered fastball, running high and outside, tempting her. Instead, as he pointed the gun away from Kenedy, she grunted and unleashed her best home run swing, aiming for Brian's knee. The corner of her eye registered Lauren's and Sally's surprise as they sprang to their feet. Shock waves reverberated up the wooden handle, stinging her hands, and Brian collapsed with a scream, releasing Kenedy, who crumpled to the floor. Brian writhed in pain. Maris converted the handle from a baseball bat to a hockey stick and sent the Colt .45 spinning toward the far wall. Pinning Brian's chest with her foot, she bore down with all her weight and pressed the butt of the handle against his Adam's apple. Through clenched teeth, she said, "If I ever see you again outside of court or death row, I'll kill you on sight."

Lauren clutched her shoulder and pulled her away. Sally cuffed him.

"What are you doing here?" Lauren grabbed her hand.

"Gettin' in a little batting practice." Maris grinned. She pulled a chair closer to the chief. She and Lauren helped him to his feet while Sally fished the handcuff key out of Brian's trousers. Brian groaned in pain and began raving. Spit flew from his mouth as he ranted about hellfire and redemption and something about the true messiah.

Wayne hobbled into the room, favoring his knee. Wadding his handkerchief around his fingers, he stuffed it in Brian's mouth. "You have the right to remain silent..." Clearly relishing the act, he read him his rights.

Maris and Lauren lowered Kenedy to the chair, and Sally used her hand-held to call for an ambulance after removing the cuffs. Kenedy rubbed his wrists before burying his head in his hands. "I can't believe I let him take my gun."

Maris took Lauren's elbow and led her aside. "I was worried when you didn't answer my pages. I thought maybe..." She sighed. "I thought maybe you were hurt or in trouble."

"I'm sorry." Lauren cocked her head and smiled. "I don't think it's working. My low battery warning went off when we were arresting Brian, and I didn't have any new ones."

Maris told her how she came to be in the church. "Irene is in there." She pointed to the office. "Reverend Oldham should be back soon."

The fellowship doors swung open, and three sleepy-eyed

young men, four teenaged women and two adult supervisors filed in, drawn by the commotion. One of the supervisors explained that they'd been asleep in the dorms when the sirens awakened them. Rick and another Bass Cove officer, with help from a deputy, led them to the sanctuary after assuring them everything was under control and Reverend Oldham would be present soon.

"What happened to you?" Maris asked Wayne, pointing to his knee, clearly swollen under his trousers.

"Son-of-a-bitch Kenedy kept snapping and unsnapping that goddamned safety catch. It finally caught up with him. We'd arrested Brian without incident as he walked out of Taco Bell this evening. There wasn't a nurse at the jail tonight, so we took him to the hospital to have blood drawn. Hell, Lauren was in the parking lot, getting ready to go home, when all hell broke loose. Brian grabbed Kenedy's pistol, catching the safety strap off. He busted Kenedy in the head, cuffed him while he was dazed and held him hostage. He fled the hospital, and Sally and I followed on foot. I took a bad spill down some steps." He winced. "Looks like I'll be having surgery sooner than I wanted."

"So will he." Maris grinned as paramedics packed ice around Brian's knee as he mumbled on the stretcher, minus the handkerchief in his mouth. A deputy rode in the ambulance with Brian and Wayne followed in his car, hoping to get medical attention for his own knee while he kept an eye on Brian.

At a quarter to one Christmas Eve morning, Maris gave an official statement describing why she came to the church and what happened afterward. Oldham arrived as Irene gave a brief statement and assured them Tamara was okay. Sally agreed to take her statement at her parent's home the next morning. The reverend led Kenedy, Lauren and Sally to the attic to see the altar and Brian's coat.

While Irene waited with Reverend Oldham in his office, Maris assisted as Sally, Lauren and Kenedy processed the attic as a crime scene and took photographs and helped document the items they recovered. She took custody of the leather coat for serologic testing and helped Sally and

Lauren carry the makeshift altar down the stairs. Finished by five, she sat in the pickup with Irene, waiting for a deputy to bring a sample of Brian's blood from the hospital. On the drive home, Maris and Irene watched the sunrise on Christmas Eve.

Chapter 23

Monday, December twenty-ninth, Maris signed her name with a flourish and dropped the pen. Finished at last, she carried her final report on the evidence in the murders of Lynette Donley, Jennifer and Jill Kerr to the copier. The DNA proved it was Brian Blake's semen on Jennifer's panties. But the real DNA bonanza came from his leather slicker found in the church attic. She identified bloodstains with DNA matching all three girls. She fully expected the FBI to add more nails to his coffin when they concluded the mitochondrial DNA on the human hair samples that she'd discovered in the bathtub drain of his former apartment. It looked like they wouldn't even need DNA on the dog hair to prove the case. Huntsville might as well get a death-row cell ready for Mr. Blake, Maris thought with grim satisfaction.

She photocopied the report, folded the three copies and placed them in envelopes addressed to Sally Trent, Chief Troy Kenedy and Texas Ranger Wayne Coffey. Mailing them was the only other official duty she planned to carry out the remainder of the day — hell, the remainder of the holidays. Christmas had worked out okay. Exhausted from the long night on the twenty-third, they slept most of Christmas Eve. Rising late that afternoon, Maris, Irene and Lauren went out for a dinner. Afterward, they cruised the El Dorado division in McKinney admiring the elaborate Christmas decorations and holiday lights and returned home to exchange Christmas presents. Lauren and Irene left about five Christmas morning for Fredericksburg. Resigned, but still not happy about spending Christmas without Lauren, Maris took off for Austin with Earnhardt about six-thirty that morning. Once there, she enjoyed the time with her family and returned home late Friday afternoon to an empty house. She spent the rest of the weekend in the lab, wrapping up the Bass Cove evidence, so she and Lauren could enjoy their time off the remainder of the holiday season. Lauren and Irene came back late Saturday.

She glanced at the clock. She had promised Lauren she'd wake her up at ten and she was right on time. She clicked off her computer and the lights to the lab. It felt good to be off with nothing pressing to do.

Irene sat cross-legged on the sofa and thumbed through college catalogs from the University of North Texas and the University of Texas at Dallas. Over Christmas, after meeting Tamara, she resolved to return to school and take the courses necessary to get a job helping troubled adolescents. Her redemption, Maris supposed. She'd also taken a part-time job with her friend's trucking firm. Although she didn't need the money, she needed the structure, the responsibility.

Looking up, Irene smiled. "With that grin, I'm afraid to ask what you're up to."

Maris winked. "Later."

Closing the bedroom door, she stripped and slipped under the covers. Planning to gently wake the sleeping redhead, she jumped when Lauren said, "Where've you been?" She locked her arms around Maris's neck. "You're late."

Maris kissed her, tasting the mint flavoring of fresh toothpaste. "You've already been up."

"As I said, you're late." Lauren tousled Maris's hair and brushed a stray strand back from her forehead.

Maris grinned. Her hand roved down her side and under her emerald nightshirt. She unfastened the top button. "Then why didn't you take this off?"

Lauren's green eyes sparkled. "Because I know how much you like to do it."

Another button fell open under Maris's touch, and she reached under the smooth fabric to caress Lauren's breast. The nipple hardened and Maris kissed her.

"Take it off," Lauren whispered.

Maris released the remaining buttons, spread open the nightshirt and kicked the sheet and blanket off the end of the bed. "It's getting warm in here," she said. The sight of Lauren's breasts, the gentle curves, the passion in her eyes sent a surge of desire through Maris. Lauren lifted her shoulders, and Maris helped her out of the nightshirt, dropping it on the floor. Maris's hands roamed over Lauren, trying to touch her everywhere at once. She stroked her stomach, thighs and breasts. Her lover moved with her, her cool fingertips seeking and finding places of heightened sensitivity. Maris urgently parted Lauren's thighs, and her fingers danced as Lauren's grip tightened on her shoulder.

"It's been —" Lauren gasped for breath. "So long."

Maris slid down her stomach, kissing her. The phone rang. "Ignore it," Maris mumbled against her flesh.

"Don't . . . worry." She ran her hand through Maris's hair. She shuddered.

A knock on the door sent them scurrying for the covers.

"Shit!" Lauren said as Maris pulled up the sheet and blanket.

Maris fell to her back beside her. "Cruel and unusual punishment." She groaned.

Lauren rose on one elbow. "Come in."

Irene stuck her head around the door. "Sorry, guys. Your friend Shannon's on the phone. She's in labor."

"Oh, God." Maris grabbed the phone, her heart pounding.

Lauren threw her hair back over her shoulder and sighed. "Thanks, Irene."

Irene laughed and winked. "First-time deliveries usually take a while." She shut the door.

"You sure are breathing hard. You working out?" Shannon asked, her voice calm.

"Sort of," Maris said.

"Sorry." She laughed. "I forgot people still do that. I'll make it quick. Just got back from the doctor. She said I'd started dilating and told me to wait until about two to go to the hospital."

Maris glanced at the clock; it was almost eleven. "Two, huh?" She grinned at Lauren.

"Come get me at the hotel about one-thirty. If I need you sooner, I'll call back." Shannon chuckled. "Go make your lover happy." She hung up.

Maris rolled over, embracing Lauren. "She says to make you happy and then come over."

"Let's not keep the lady waiting." Lauren took her hand and warmed it against her stomach. Guiding it between her legs, she said, "As I remember this was about here."

Maris felt the warmth. "Seems about right," she said as Lauren trembled. "And I was about here —" She kissed her and slid downward.

Lauren wrapped her arms around Maris's neck. "Stay up here, where I can hold you," she whispered and Maris did, for a while.

Lauren insisted on driving to Fort Worth, saying Maris was too excited, but she suspected her red-headed lover wanted an excuse to drive the 442 Olds. Maris let her, since it gave her a chance, after much internal debate, to pull the number for Robin's ex out of her wallet and call Denver.

When a woman answered, she heard laughter in the background. It stopped when she identified herself and asked for Robin. When Robin answered in a guarded tone, Maris told her they were on their way to take Shannon to the hospital. She politely thanked her for calling and made no comment, no commitment, and Maris wondered if she did the right thing by calling.

Shannon teased her about being nervous. Despite frequent and painful contractions, she remained upbeat and calm. Since the hospital expected her arrival, they were ushered into a room without delay. A pretty black nurse, about twenty-five, with slender graceful hands, slipped on a pair of gloves. Chatting amiably, she performed a pelvic while Maris stood at the head of the bed and talked to Shannon. The nurse advised she was only three centimeters dilated, still the early stages of labor. To ease her pain, keep her occupied and perhaps hurry the baby along, Maris and Lauren, one on each side, walked Shannon up and down the hallways. When she became nauseated, the nurse suggested a warm, not hot, shower.

"Damn." Maris winked at Lauren. " I forgot my bathing suit." She explained about the instructions for birth partners that she'd read on the Internet. "Guess we could all get naked. Have a three-way in the shower. What does sex do for contractions?"

"Maris Middleton, you are an evil person." Shannon sucked in her breath as a contraction came and went. "If you knew how horny I've been —"

"I keep telling her pregnancy affects some women that way, but she still says no." Lauren helped Shannon slip from her gown, while Maris adjusted the water until it was comfortably warm. The shower relaxed her. Afterward, she sat in the chair to rest while Maris and Lauren slipped out for a breath of fresh air and a cold drink.

Sipping a Diet Coke, Maris said, "What's taking so long?"

A surprised look swept across Lauren's face before she smiled. Touching Maris's arm, she said, "Honey, I hate to break it to you, but she probably has at least ten or twelve more hours. Maybe more."

Maris groaned and dropped into a chair.

Lauren brushed a curl from Maris's forehead. "Come on. Let's get back."

Shannon wanted to walk. Lauren's pager went off, and she excused herself to make a phone call. Maris took Shannon's arm, and they strolled around the ward. During a particularly strong contraction, she leaned against the wall. Taking Maris's hand, she showed her how to press the small of her back firmly to relieve some of her back pain.

"Timothy called this morning." Shannon smiled. "He'll be back tomorrow to handle the office until I get on my feet. I never thought I'd say this, but I missed him."

Maris laughed. Heavy metal in motion, Shannon once said about him. Hyperactive, impulsive and too good-looking for his own good, Timothy led a life of high highs and low lows. He kept Shannon's office rocking. He'd worked for Shannon since he was eighteen, except for last summer when Rick, a friend of his, filled in for a few weeks. "Face it," Maris said, "After raising Timothy, a baby will be easy."

They walked slowly back to her room with Maris rubbing Shannon's back. Lauren brought her cool compresses for her neck and forehead. They watched television to pass the time between walks. Lauren went out for a hamburgers for the two of them, and they took turns eating in the waiting room.

By seven, Shannon's fatigue began to show, but she perked up when Alice Young, a nurse who used to date a friend of Maris's, came on duty. Between contractions Alice performed another pelvic exam. Shannon had progressed to six centimeters and, to Maris's relief, said she was ready for the epidural to help with pain. While they started the epidural, Alice explained to Maris that active labor occurred when the cervix was between four and six centimeters dilated with what's called the transition stage between seven and ten. At ten, pushing starts.

Lauren left to make another phone call after a second

page. Returning, she went to the side of the bed. "I have some news concerning Robin's problem — if it won't upset you to hear it." When Shannon nodded, Lauren said, "At Maris's suggestion, I talked to the FBI experts in pornography about the rape video. These cases are so unusual, since he shaves the victims, that the boys came up with something quickly. Working with Fort Worth P.D., they located tapes showing two of the victims that are circulating on the Internet."

"Good," Maris said. "They'll be able to nail Al Anderson on federal and state charges." It was time he went down, Maris thought. He started the string of rapes in '91 as a student at TCU. Although he was a suspect, the police investigation eventually went nowhere. Currently an identification tech for Fort Worth P.D., he had the audacity not only to sell the tapes and resume his activities, but also to taunt Robin.

"I hope so," Lauren said. "Assuming they can trace the tapes back to him, and I think they can."

"Have they heard from Robin and Gwen?" Shannon asked.

"No, honey. Not yet." Lauren patted her arm.

Maris saw the disappointment in Shannon's eyes.

"I've been able to keep her name out of it," Lauren said. "Since I don't have the tape and haven't seen it, I told them an informant had described the video to me. It was enough to get them on the right track."

"She'll never get her life in order until she confronts this." Shannon winced and gritted her teeth at a particularly intense contraction. "And neither can Gwen."

"Robin could face some legal and ethical problems over this, if it comes out that she withheld information as a prosecutor," Lauren said. "But it's unlikely anything would happen."

"She won't come forward." Shannon shook her head. "She only told me because Maris shamed her into it."

When Shannon reached eight centimeters, Alice attached the fetal monitor to the baby's scalp. The contractions intensified and became more frequent, and Maris wished she knew more about the proper breathing techniques so she could prompt Shannon. But she seemed to do well on her own. She inhaled quick, shallow breaths at the peak of the contraction and slower, deeper ones in between.

At ten o'clock, Shannon's doctor, a small dark-haired woman about forty-five, arrived and did a pelvic. Pleased to see that Shannon had progressed to about nine and a half, she decided to break the membrane and release the water. While she worked, Shannon introduced Maris and Lauren. The doctor teased Maris about being so pale and made her promise not to faint. Shannon and Lauren both laughed and told the doctor what Maris did for a living. Maris squared her shoulders and assured them all that she'd never fainted in her life.

With Shannon's legs in the stirrups, a nurse bathed her in a yellow antiseptic to guard against infection. Shannon progressed to ten rapidly, taking two shallow, controlled breaths and blowing the air out quickly. Maris washed her face with a wet cloth and tried to talk encouragingly. Alice and another nurse came into the room, and Lauren offered to leave to make more room.

"No need to leave the party," the doctor said. "The guest of honor is about to arrive." To Shannon, she added, "I can see the top of her head." She picked up a scalpel. "I'm going to do the episiotomy now."

Maris's knees weakened as the doctor made the cut to enlarge the birth canal, and she gripped the side of the bed. She tried to smile at Shannon, hoping she didn't look as queasy as she felt. Lauren rubbed her shoulders, hiding her amusement after Maris glared at her. Shannon assured her that she felt no pain, thanks to the epidural, but her disclaimer didn't help Maris's churning stomach.

"Okay," the doctor said. "Push hard and it'll come down farther this time."

Shannon strained while Alice watched the fetal monitor. "The baby's heart rate is dropping," she said.

Fear crossed Shannon's face. Maris took her hand and wiped her face with the damp rag. "It's okay, honey. They'll take care of your baby."

"Push harder," the doctor ordered. "Now a little mini-push. That's right. Feel that? It's the wrinkle on the baby's brow. And here's the nose."

"More decels," Alice said, and Maris thought she caught a hint of concern in her voice.

"Okay. Don't push," the doctor said. "Shannon, whatever you do, don't push."

Shannon's eyes widened. She gripped Maris's arm. "What's wrong? Is something wrong with the baby?"

"Easy now. The cord is wrapped around the baby's neck, at least twice." The doctor nodded to the other nurse, who reached in to help. "I think we can get it off. If not, we'll clamp and cut the cord."

The fatigue and pain were too much, and Shannon began to cry quietly. Maris tried to reassure her. "Tell me what it looks like. What are they doing?" Shannon asked.

Lauren wiped Shannon's forehead with a damp cloth. "It'll be okay," she said. "Try to relax."

With trepidation, Maris peered at the baby. The nurse held the slick, protruding head while the doctor struggled to work the cord loose. The baby's face was dark red, but not blue, and surprisingly animated. Maris felt a tingle of excitement. "The baby looks fine, honey."

The doctor lifted the second loop over the baby's head. "Okay, Shannon. Time to have this baby." She used a suction hose to clear the baby's mouth and nose.

Shannon gripped Maris's forearm and strained mightily.

"Shoulders are out," the doctor said.

Maris peeked over the sheet as the baby started crying. "Her eyes are open," she said.

"It's not a puppy." Lauren laughed.

"You have a little girl." The doctor lifted the baby and watched her for a moment before laying her on Shannon's stomach. "Let's clamp that cord."

"She's beautiful," Shannon said. Her eyes brimmed with tears, and she smiled at Maris.

The doctor clamped off the cord and handed the baby to

Alice, who wiped her face and did the initial Apgar readings to assess her condition. "This baby looks fine," she said. The baby jerked her arms and kicked her legs. Alice wrapped her in a blanket and handed her to Shannon.

She began crying, and Shannon rocked her gently. "Want to hold her before the nurse takes her for a few minutes?" she asked Maris.

"No." Maris shook her head. "I might drop her." She stepped back from the bed.

"Hold her." Lauren touched Maris's shoulder. Wiping tears from her eyes, she said, "She's beautiful."

As Maris took her, she wiggled in the blanket and waved her tiny fists. "Everything is so small, her little fingers, nose. She's so . . . little."

Alice laughed. "Not really, as baby's go. I'd put her at almost nine pounds, just guessing. I can tell you for sure later."

The baby began to cry, and Maris, with Shannon's permission, handed her to Lauren. She quieted almost immediately as Lauren cuddled her and stroked the top of her head. Lauren's green eyes sparkled. "She's wonderful, Shannon." She returned the baby to her mother.

Alice took the baby to clean it up while the doctor delivered the placenta. They gave Lauren pitocin through her IV to make the uterus clamp and to control the bleeding. Maris and Lauren stood out of the way while the doctor sewed up the episiotomy and made sure all of the placenta had delivered. The other nurse cleaned Shannon up and helped her out of the stirrups. She brought her an ice bag and promised to return every fifteen minutes to take her blood pressure and check for excess bleeding.

At eleven-thirty, Alice gave the baby back to Shannon, and she began to breast-feed her. Maris brushed a stray hair away from Shannon's cheek and said, "Have you decided what to name her?"

"Yes." Her blue eyes moistened. "I can't believe I'm holding my baby."

Lauren hooked her arm through Maris's and leaned her head on her shoulder. "So what's her name?"

Shannon smiled. "Sarah Marie Stockwell."

"Pretty name," Maris said. "She's going to have your blonde hair and blue eyes."

Someone rapped sharply on the door and pushed it open when Shannon said, "Come in."

Robin, dressed in a sharp red-and-black striped shirt and black jeans stood hesitantly in the threshold.

Shannon sighed and smiled at her. "Come see Sarah Marie," she said.

Robin took a few steps toward the bed. "I . . . I can't stay."

"I know." The baby lost Shannon's nipple, so she shifted positions and rubbed it gently across the baby's pink mouth until she took it again.

Maris guided Lauren to the door.

"No. Don't go," Robin said. Looking over her shoulder, she waved to a hazel-eyed brunette with a silver-streaked temples. "Come in, Gwen."

Maris recognized her from the photos in Robin's apartment and tried to forget the video.

Gwen nervously touched the sides of her hair. "How are you and the baby doing?"

"We'll be fine," Shannon said.

Robin took Gwen's hand and approached the bed. "She's beautiful," she said with a catch in her voice. She fingered the fine hair on the baby's head. "I'm sorry this has happened now — with the baby coming." She kept her eyes on the baby. "I'll always care for —"

"Don't." Shannon held up her hand. "Take care of your unfinished business, Robin. Or you'll never be happy. I hope things work out for both of you." She blinked back tears. "Give me a few days before you come to get your things. Okay?"

"All right." Robin squeezed Shannon's hand. "You'll make a wonderful mother. Sarah will be better off, if I'm not around." Facing Maris, she added, "Forget about what I showed you. It doesn't exist anymore."

"Can you forget it?" Maris asked.

Lauren cleared her throat. "We want you to know that the FBI pornography unit has already located tapes in distribution on the Internet that we think will be traced back to Anderson. Don't be surprised if one of yours surfaces."

"Oh, God," Gwen said. "I hope not."

Robin nodded. Taking Gwen's hand, she led her away. Over her shoulder, she said, "Good luck, Shannon."

"Damn her," Shannon said when they were gone. "She always finds a soft place to land." She wiped her cheek with the back of her hand. "So that's that."

"Is there anything we can do?" Lauren asked.

Shannon shook her head. "No. I have my baby, and I'll be fine."

"We're going to get some air and let you rest a while." Maris kissed her cheek. "We'll be back shortly."

"You don't have to stay." She lifted the baby to her shoulder.

"We know, but we want to." Maris took Lauren's hand.

They rode the elevator to the first floor and walked into a small garden area. A few late-shift nurses and weary family members loitered on scattered benches and chairs and smoked. Maris drew Lauren into her arms. "That was an incredible experience."

"Yes." Lauren touched Maris's cheek, and they embraced.

"I didn't expect it too be so . . . emotional. I'm drained."

"Think how Shannon must feel." Lauren placed her head on Maris's shoulder. "She's right. Robin's never going to be happy."

"But she'll survive as she always does." Maris ran a hand through Lauren's hair.

After a moment, Lauren asked, "So does this mean you're ready for us to have a baby?"

"Sure, darling." Maris hugged her. "What kind of puppy do you want? Another border collie? Or maybe a feisty terrier?"

"No, thanks. I already have something feisty enough."

Chilled, they returned to Shannon's room. Hoping she was asleep, Maris and Lauren quietly peeked into the room.

Talking in soothing tones, Shannon cuddled Sarah and rocked her gently. Maris and Lauren ducked into the hall before Shannon noticed them, and Maris led Lauren to a corner sofa in the empty waiting room. With Lauren in her arms, they dozed, giving mother and baby a chance to get acquainted.

A few of the publications of
THE NAIAD PRESS, INC.
P.O. Box 10543   Tallahassee, Florida 32302
Phone (850) 539-5965
Toll-Free Order Number: 1-800-533-1973
Web Site: WWW.NAIADPRESS.COM
Mail orders welcome. Please include 15% postage.
Write or call for our free catalog which also features an
incredible selection of lesbian videos.

INTIMATE STRANGER by Laura DeHart Young. 192 pp.
Ignoring Tray's myserious past, could Cole be playing with fire?
ISBN 1-56280-249-6 $11.95

SHATTERED ILLUSIONS by Kaye Davis. 256 pp. 4th
Maris Middleton mystery.   ISBN 1-56280-252-6   11.95

SETUP by Claire McNab. 240 pp. 11th Detective Inspector Carol
Ashton mystery.   ISBN 1-56280-255-0   11.95

THE DAWNING by Laura Adams. 224 pp. What if you had the
power to change the past?   ISBN 1-56280-246-1   11.95

NEVER ENDING by Marianne Martin. 224 pp. Temptation
appears in the form of an old friend and lover. ISBN 1-56280-247-X   11.95

ONE OF OUR OWN by Diane Salvatore. 240 pp. Carly Matson
has a secret. So does Lela Johns.   ISBN 1-56280-243-7   11.95

DOUBLE TAKEOUT by Tracey Richardson. 176 pp. 3rd Stevie
Houston mystery.   ISBN 1-56280-244-5   11.95

CAPTIVE HEART by Frankie J. Jones. 176 pp. Love in the
fast lane or heartside romance?   ISBN 1-56280-258-5   11.95

WICKED GOOD TIME by Diana Tremain Braund. 224 pp. In
charge at work, out of control in her heart.   ISBN 1-56280-241-0   11.95

SNAKE EYES by Pat Welch. 256 pp. 7th Helen Black mystery.
ISBN 1-56280-242-9   11.95

CHANGE OF HEART by Linda Hill. 176 pp. High fashion and
love in a glamorous world.   ISBN 1-56280-238-0   11.95

UNSTRUNG HEART by Robbi Sommers. 176 pp. Putting life
in order again.   ISBN 1-56280-239-9   11.95

BIRDS OF A FEATHER by Jackie Calhoun. 240 pp. Life begins
with love.   ISBN 1-56280-240-2   11.95

THE DRIVE by Trisha Todd. 176 pp. The star of *Claire of the
Moon* tells all!   ISBN 1-56280-237-2   11.95

PRIVATE PASSIONS by Laura DeHart Young. 192 pp. An
unforgettable new portrait of lesbian love ...   ISBN 1-56280-215-1   11.95

BAD MOON RISING by Barbara Johnson. 208 pp. 2nd Colleen
Fitzgerald mystery.   ISBN 1-56280-211-9   11.95

RIVER QUAY by Janet McClellan. 208 pp. 3rd Tru North
mystery.   ISBN 1-56280-212-7   11.95

ENDLESS LOVE by Lisa Shapiro. 272 pp. To believe, once
again, that love can be forever.   ISBN 1-56280-213-5   11.95

FALLEN FROM GRACE by Pat Welch. 256 pp. 6th Helen Black
mystery.   ISBN 1-56280-209-7   11.95

THE NAKED EYE by Catherine Ennis. 208 pp. Her lover in the
camera's eye ...   ISBN 1-56280-210-0   11.95

OVER THE LINE by Tracey Richardson. 176 pp. 2nd Stevie
Houston mystery.   ISBN 1-56280-202-X   11.95

JULIA'S SONG by Ann O'Leary. 208 pp. Strangely
disturbing ... strangely exciting.   ISBN 1-56280-197-X   11.95

LOVE IN THE BALANCE by Marianne K. Martin. 256 pp.
Weighing the costs of love ...   ISBN 1-56280-199-6   11.95

PIECE OF MY HEART by Julia Watts. 208 pp. All the
stuff that dreams are made of —   ISBN 1-56280-206-2   11.95

MAKING UP FOR LOST TIME by Karin Kallmaker. 240 pp.
Nobody does it better ...   ISBN 1-56280-196-1   11.95

GOLD FEVER by Lyn Denison. 224 pp. By author of *Dream
Lover.*   ISBN 1-56280-201-1   11.95

WHEN THE DEAD SPEAK by Therese Szymanski. 224 pp. 2nd
Brett Higgins mystery.   ISBN 1-56280-198-8   11.95

FOURTH DOWN by Kate Calloway. 240 pp. 4th Cassidy James
mystery.   ISBN 1-56280-205-4   11.95

A MOMENT'S INDISCRETION by Peggy J. Herring. 176 pp.
There's a fine line between love and lust ...   ISBN 1-56280-194-5   11.95

CITY LIGHTS/COUNTRY CANDLES by Penny Hayes. 208 pp.
About the women she has known ...   ISBN 1-56280-195-3   11.95

POSSESSIONS by Kaye Davis. 240 pp. 2nd Maris Middleton
mystery.   ISBN 1-56280-192-9   11.95

A QUESTION OF LOVE by Saxon Bennett. 208 pp. Every
woman is granted one great love.   ISBN 1-56280-205-4   11.95

RHYTHM TIDE by Frankie J. Jones. 160 pp. ... to desire
passionately and be passionately desired.   ISBN 1-56280-189-9   11.95

PENN VALLEY PHOENIX by Janet McClellan. 208 pp. 2nd
Tru North Mystery.   ISBN 1-56280-200-3   11.95

BY RESERVATION ONLY by Jackie Calhoun. 240 pp. A
chance for true happiness.   ISBN 1-56280-191-0   11.95

OLD BLACK MAGIC by Jaye Maiman. 272 pp. 9th Robin
Miller mystery.   ISBN 1-56280-175-9   11.95

LEGACY OF LOVE by Marianne K. Martin. 240 pp. Women
will do anything for her . . .   ISBN 1-56280-184-8   11.95

LETTING GO by Ann O'Leary. 160 pp. Laura, at 39, in love
with 23-year-old Kate.   ISBN 1-56280-183-X   11.95

LADY BE GOOD edited by Barbara Grier and Christine Cassidy.
288 pp. Erotic stories by Naiad Press authors.   ISBN 1-56280-180-5   14.95

CHAIN LETTER by Claire McNab. 288 pp. 9th Carol Ashton
mystery.   ISBN 1-56280-181-3   11.95

NIGHT VISION by Laura Adams. 256 pp. Erotic fantasy romance
by "famous" author.   ISBN 1-56280-182-1   11.95

SEA TO SHINING SEA by Lisa Shapiro. 256 pp. Unable to resist
the raging passion . . .   ISBN 1-56280-177-5   11.95

THIRD DEGREE by Kate Calloway. 224 pp. 3rd Cassidy James
mystery.   ISBN 1-56280-185-6   11.95

WHEN THE DANCING STOPS by Therese Szymanski. 272 pp.
1st Brett Higgins mystery.   ISBN 1-56280-186-4   11.95

PHASES OF THE MOON by Julia Watts. 192 pp. . . . . hungry
for everything life has to offer.   ISBN 1-56280-176-7   11.95

BABY IT'S COLD by Jaye Maiman. 256 pp. 5th Robin Miller
mystery.   ISBN 1-56280-156-2   10.95

CLASS REUNION by Linda Hill. 176 pp. The girl from her
past . . .   ISBN 1-56280-178-3   11.95

DREAM LOVER by Lyn Denison. 224 pp. A soft, sensuous,
romantic fantasy.   ISBN 1-56280-173-1   11.95

FORTY LOVE by Diana Simmonds. 288 pp. Joyous, heart-
warming romance.   ISBN 1-56280-171-6   11.95

IN THE MOOD by Robbi Sommers. 160 pp. The queen of
erotic tension!   ISBN 1-56280-172-4   11.95

SWIMMING CAT COVE by Lauren Douglas. 192 pp. 2nd
Allison O'Neil Mystery.   ISBN 1-56280-168-6   11.95

THE LOVING LESBIAN by Claire McNab and Sharon Gedan.
240 pp. Explore the experiences that make lesbian love unique.
                                         ISBN 1-56280-169-4   14.95

COURTED by Celia Cohen. 160 pp. Sparkling romantic
encounter.   ISBN 1-56280-166-X   11.95

SEASONS OF THE HEART by Jackie Calhoun. 240 pp. Romance
through the years.   ISBN 1-56280-167-8   11.95

K. C. BOMBER by Janet McClellan. 208 pp. 1st Tru North
mystery.   ISBN 1-56280-157-0   11.95

LAST RITES by Tracey Richardson. 192 pp. 1st Stevie Houston
mystery.   ISBN 1-56280-164-3   11.95

EMBRACE IN MOTION by Karin Kallmaker. 256 pp. A whirlwind
love affair.   ISBN 1-56280-165-1   11.95

HOT CHECK by Peggy J. Herring. 192 pp. Will workaholic Alice
fall for guitarist Ricky?   ISBN 1-56280-163-5   11.95

OLD TIES by Saxon Bennett. 176 pp. Can Cleo surrender to a
passionate new love?   ISBN 1-56280-159-7   11.95

LOVE ON THE LINE by Laura DeHart Young. 176 pp. Will Stef
win Kay's heart?   ISBN 1-56280-162-7   11.95

DEVIL'S LEG CROSSING by Kaye Davis. 192 pp. 1st Maris
Middleton mystery.   ISBN 1-56280-158-9   11.95

COSTA BRAVA by Marta Balletbo Coll. 144 pp. Read the book,
see the movie!   ISBN 1-56280-153-8   11.95

MEETING MAGDALENE & OTHER STORIES by
Marilyn Freeman. 144 pp. Read the book, see the movie!
                                            ISBN 1-56280-170-8   11.95

SECOND FIDDLE by Kate 208 pp. 2nd P.I. Cassidy James
mystery.   ISBN 1-56280-169-6   11.95

LAUREL by Isabel Miller. 128 pp. By the author of the beloved
Patience and Sarah.   ISBN 1-56280-146-5   10.95

LOVE OR MONEY by Jackie Calhoun. 240 pp. The romance of
real life.   ISBN 1-56280-147-3   10.95

SMOKE AND MIRRORS by Pat Welch. 224 pp. 5th Helen Black
Mystery.   ISBN 1-56280-143-0   10.95

DANCING IN THE DARK edited by Barbara Grier & Christine
Cassidy. 272 pp. Erotic love stories by Naiad Press authors.
                                            ISBN 1-56280-144-9   14.95

TIME AND TIME AGAIN by Catherine Ennis. 176 pp. Passionate
love affair.   ISBN 1-56280-145-7   10.95

PAXTON COURT by Diane Salvatore. 256 pp. Erotic and wickedly
funny contemporary tale about the business of learning to live
together.   ISBN 1-56280-114-7   10.95

INNER CIRCLE by Claire McNab. 208 pp. 8th Carol Ashton
Mystery.   ISBN 1-56280-135-X   11.95

LESBIAN SEX: AN ORAL HISTORY by Susan Johnson.
240 pp. Need we say more?   ISBN 1-56280-142-2   14.95

WILD THINGS by Karin Kallmaker. 240 pp. By the undisputed
mistress of lesbian romance.   ISBN 1-56280-139-2   11.95

THE GIRL NEXT DOOR by Mindy Kaplan. 208 pp. Just what
you d expect.   ISBN 1-56280-140-6   11.95

NOW AND THEN by Penny Hayes. 240 pp. Romance on the
westward journey. ISBN 1-56280-121-X   11.95

HEART ON FIRE by Diana Simmonds. 176 pp. The romantic and
erotic rival of *Curious Wine.* ISBN 1-56280-152-X   11.95

DEATH AT LAVENDER BAY by Lauren Wright Douglas. 208 pp.
1st Allison O'Neil Mystery. ISBN 1-56280-085-X   11.95

YES I SAID YES I WILL by Judith McDaniel. 272 pp. Hot
romance by famous author. ISBN 1-56280-138-4   11.95

FORBIDDEN FIRES by Margaret C. Anderson. Edited by Mathilda
Hills. 176 pp. Famous author's "unpublished" Lesbian romance.
ISBN 1-56280-123-6   21.95

SIDE TRACKS by Teresa Stores. 160 pp. Gender-bending
Lesbians on the road. ISBN 1-56280-122-8   10.95

WILDWOOD FLOWERS by Julia Watts. 208 pp. Hilarious and
heart-warming tale of true love. ISBN 1-56280-127-9   10.95

NEVER SAY NEVER by Linda Hill. 224 pp. Rule #1: Never get
involved with . . . ISBN 1-56280-126-0   11.95

THE WISH LIST by Saxon Bennett. 192 pp. Romance through
the years. ISBN 1-56280-125-2   10.95

OUT OF THE NIGHT by Kris Bruyer. 192 pp. Spine-tingling
thriller. ISBN 1-56280-120-1   10.95

LOVE'S HARVEST by Peggy J. Herring. 176 pp. by the author of
Once More With Feeling. ISBN 1-56280-117-1   10.95

FAMILY SECRETS by Laura DeHart Young. 208 pp. Enthralling
romance and suspense. ISBN 1-56280-119-8   10.95

INLAND PASSAGE by Jane Rule. 288 pp. Tales exploring conven-
tional & unconventional relationships. ISBN 0-930044-56-8   10.95

DOUBLE BLUFF by Claire McNab. 208 pp. 7th Carol Ashton
Mystery. ISBN 1-56280-096-5   10.95

BAR GIRLS by Lauran Hoffman. 176 pp. See the movie, read
the book! ISBN 1-56280-115-5   10.95

THE FIRST TIME EVER edited by Barbara Grier & Christine
Cassidy. 272 pp. Love stories by Naiad Press authors.
ISBN 1-56280-086-8   14.95

MISS PETTIBONE AND MISS McGRAW by Brenda Weathers.
208 pp. A charming ghostly love story. ISBN 1-56280-151-1   10.95

CHANGES by Jackie Calhoun. 208 pp. Involved romance and
relationships. ISBN 1-56280-083-3   10.95

FAIR PLAY by Rose Beecham. 256 pp. An Amanda Valentine
Mystery. ISBN 1-56280-081-7   10.95

PAYBACK by Celia Cohen. 176 pp. A gripping thriller of romance,
revenge and betrayal. ISBN 1-56280-084-1   10.95

LOOKING FOR NAIAD?

Buy our books at
www.naiadpress.com

or call our toll-free number
1-800-533-1973

or by fax (24 hours a day)
1-850-539-9731

THE BEACH AFFAIR by Barbara Johnson. 224 pp. Sizzling
summer romance/mystery/intrigue.   ISBN 1-56280-090-6   10.95

GETTING THERE by Robbi Sommers. 192 pp. Nobody does it
like Robbi!   ISBN 1-56280-099-X   10.95

FINAL CUT by Lisa Haddock. 208 pp. 2nd Carmen Ramirez
Mystery.   ISBN 1-56280-088-4   10.95

FLASHPOINT by Katherine V. Forrest. 256 pp. A Lesbian
blockbuster!   ISBN 1-56280-079-5   10.95

CLAIRE OF THE MOON by Nicole Conn. Audio Book —
Read by Marianne Hyatt.   ISBN 1-56280-113-9   16.95

FOR LOVE AND FOR LIFE: INTIMATE PORTRAITS OF
LESBIAN COUPLES by Susan Johnson. 224 pp.
                                                     ISBN 1-56280-091-4   14.95

DEVOTION by Mindy Kaplan. 192 pp. See the movie — read
the book!   ISBN 1-56280-093-0   10.95

SOMEONE TO WATCH by Jaye Maiman. 272 pp. 4th Robin
Miller Mystery.   ISBN 1-56280-095-7   10.95

GREENER THAN GRASS by Jennifer Fulton. 208 pp. A young
woman — a stranger in her bed.   ISBN 1-56280-092-2   10.95

TRAVELS WITH DIANA HUNTER by Regine Sands. Erotic
lesbian romp. Audio Book (2 cassettes)   ISBN 1-56280-107-4   16.95

CABIN FEVER by Carol Schmidt. 256 pp. Sizzling suspense
and passion.   ISBN 1-56280-089-1   10.95

THERE WILL BE NO GOODBYES by Laura DeHart Young. 192
pp. Romantic love, strength, and friendship.   ISBN 1-56280-103-1   10.95

FAULTLINE by Sheila Ortiz Taylor. 144 pp. Joyous comic
lesbian novel.   ISBN 1-56280-108-2   9.95

OPEN HOUSE by Pat Welch. 176 pp. 4th Helen Black Mystery.
                                                     ISBN 1-56280-102-3   10.95

ONCE MORE WITH FEELING by Peggy J. Herring. 240 pp.
Lighthearted, loving romantic adventure.   ISBN 1-56280-089-2   11.95

WHISPERS by Kris Bruyer. 176 pp. Romantic ghost story.
                                                     ISBN 1-56280-082-5   10.95

NIGHT SONGS by Penny Mickelbury. 224 pp. 2nd Gianna
Maglione Mystery.   ISBN 1-56280-097-3   10.95

These are just a few of the many Naiad Press titles — we are the oldest and
largest lesbian/feminist publishing company in the world. We also offer an
enormous selection of lesbian video products. Please request a complete
catalog. We offer personal service; we encourage and welcome direct mail
orders from individuals who have limited access to bookstores carrying our
publications.